THE SPELTH

Spelthorpe Peace

BOOK THREE

ASHLEY CLARK

The manufacturer's authorised representative in the EU for product safety is
Authorised Rep Compliance Ltd, 71 Lower Baggot Street, Dublin D02 P593
Ireland (www.arccompliance.com)

Troubador Publishing Ltd
Unit E2 Airfield Business Park,
Harrison Road, Market Harborough,
Leicestershire. LE16 7UL
Tel: 0116 2792299
Email: books@troubador.co.uk
Web: www.troubador.co.uk

ISBN 978-1-83628-408-6

British Library Cataloguing in Publication Data.
A catalogue record for this book is available from the British Library.

Printed and bound in Great Britain by 4edge Limited
Typeset in 11pt Minion Pro by Troubador Publishing Ltd, Leicester, UK

This book is dedicated to my wife and best friend, Caroline, and son Michael, who have tolerated my eccentricities over the years and have swum with the merdogs.

Contents

Dramatis Personae 1953

Michael Cromwell DSO and bar, DFC, BEM. b. 1920. (Estate Manager) – (son of Ash and the late Lisette Cromwell).
Victoria Cromwell (née Spelthorpe – Countess of Spelthorpe) b. 1920 – (daughter of Helen Cromwell and the late Earl Simon Spelthorpe).
Lisette Cromwell b. 1940. Simon Cromwell b. 1941.

Sir Ash Cromwell MC, GM, BEM. b.1890 (formerly married to the late Lisette Cromwell).
Helen Cromwell – (Dowager Countess of Spelthorpe) b.1893 (formerly married to the late 12th Earl of Spelthorpe).
Michael Cromwell b. 1920; Lucy Muller (née Cromwell) b 1920; Victoria Cromwell (née Spelthorpe) b. 1920; Professor Edward Spelthorpe b. 1923; Major George Spelthorpe MC. b. 1924

Major George Spelthorpe b. 1924, Emma Spelthorpe b. 1924.
Caroline Spelthorpe b. 1921
Katie Spelthorpe b. 1946; George Spelthorpe b. 1947; Elizabeth Spelthorpe b. 1948; Olivia Spelthorpe b. 1953.

Julian Johnson (Retired Estate Manager) b 1881
Julia Johnson b. 1888
Joanna b. 1914, Jennifer b. 1916

Dr Johann Muller (Doctor at Spelthorpe Medical Practice) b.1917; Lucy Muller GC. b. 1920 (daughter of Ash and Lisette Cromwell) Matilda b. 1944; Leo b. 1948

Professor Edward Spelthorpe b. 1923 (Professor of Mathematics at Cambridge University) Dr Olivia Spelthorpe b.1922 Aldous Spelthorpe b. 1953

William Roy (Estate Chief Engineer) b. 1915 Dr Jennifer Roy b. 1916 (née Johnson) (Doctor at Spelthorpe Medical Practice) Jack Roy b. 1942; Josephine Roy b. 1948

Jeremy de Lisle (Estate Veterinary Surgeon) b.1911 Joanna de Lisle (née Johnson) (Estate Veterinary Surgeon) b.1914 James de Lisle b. 1937; Juliet de Lisle b. 1942

Gabriel Boynton GM, MM, BEM. b. 1890 (Head Keeper) b.1890 Agatha Boynton (School Headmistress) b. 1893 Beverley Boynton b. 1932; Harry Boynton b 1934 (both adopted)

Reverend Paddy Collins MC (Vicar of Spelthorpe) b. 1880 Ruth Collins b. 1882

Amrik Singh (Butler to the Hall Household) b. 1883 Jasmir Singh (Estate Shop Manager) b. 1884

Albert Armstrong (Owner of Armstrong Estates, Nyeri, Kenya.) b.1870 (father of Dowager Helen Cromwell)

See chapter 15 for other family members.

Introduction

This is the third and final book in what has become The Spelthorpe Trilogy. In the first book, "*The Tale of the Merdogs*," we introduced the estate, the characters who made the estate, and created the unique 'Spelthorpe Way' of doing things with imagination and protecting the greater community in which they found themselves. There was an element of mystery as the dogs on the estate, with their supernatural connection, were able to link up with and introduce the previous lives of the key characters and world events that had moulded the area and would continue to influence matters.

The second book brought us through the high and low points of the Second World War and how it involved and changed the lives of those on the estate. It was a tale of sacrifice, huge personal triumph, courage and achievement in helping to bring an end to that war. Despite the difficulties, the determination and loyalty of those involved allowed Spelthorpe to thrive. It also prepared the new generation, through adversity, to better prepare themselves to take over the estate as the war came to an end.

In the third book, we shall see that despite victory in war the challenges that came with the peace were in many ways as great, if not greater, with an economy in ruins and beset with another ten years of rationing and hardship, government meddling with a one-size-fits-all approach, increasing crime, appalling weather, and the huge cost in lives and expense in the dismantling of what had been the world's largest empire. It also deals with how individuals reacted and came to terms with spending time under the fear of death, and the acceptability of having to kill the king's enemies, some of whom were no different from themselves, yet once peace had been established, they found themselves frustrated at their inability within the law to deal with criminality that blighted the lives of good people.

Despite all this, Spelthorpe, with its doctrine of converting problems into solutions will find a unique way of tackling all these issues to come shining through in a further roller coaster ride of imagination, preparedness and human courage whilst at the same time, sharing moments of entertainment to keep the reader amused and guessing.

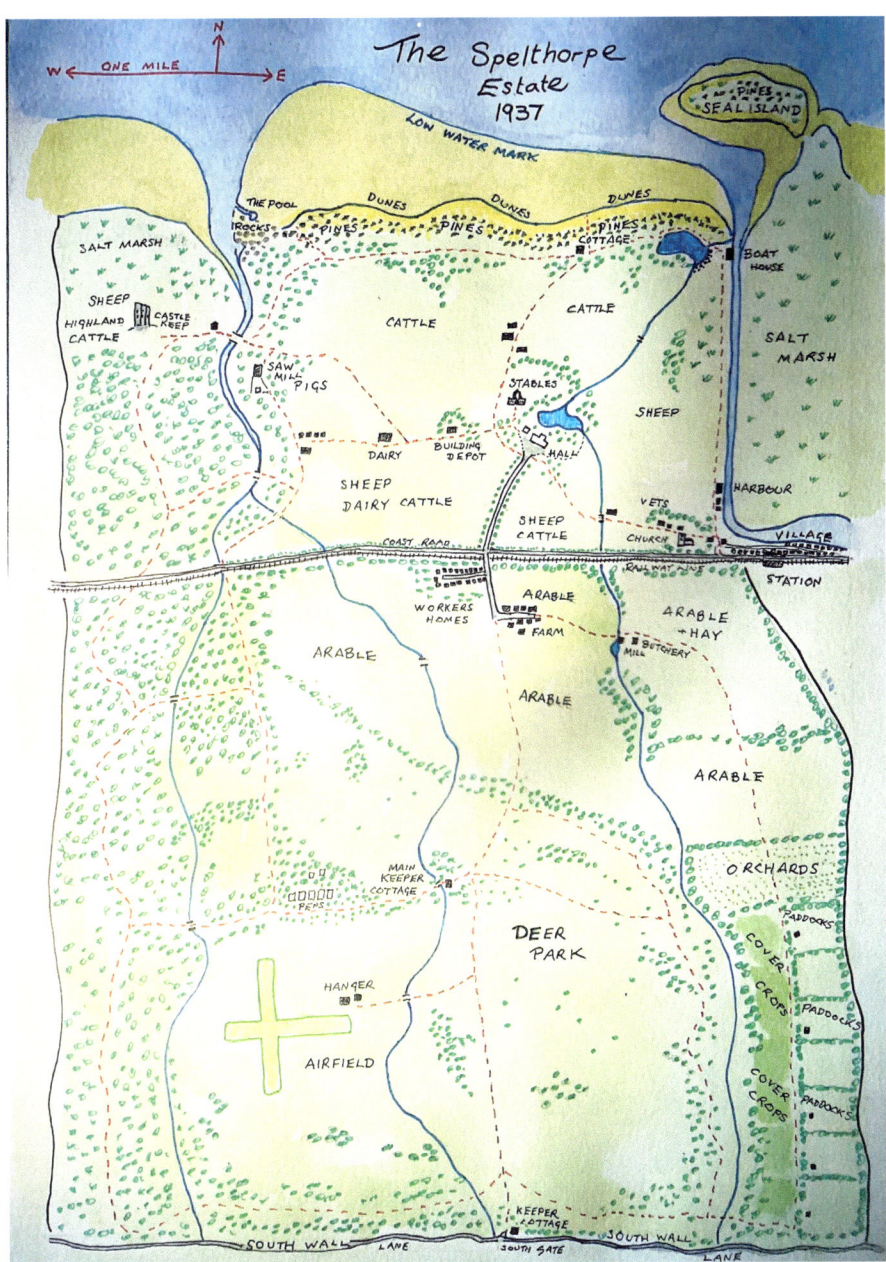

The Spelthorpe Estate 1937

"The day the power of love overrules the love of power, the world will know peace."

– Mahatma Gandhi

1

Poisoned chalice

Michael's decision to resign from the RAF as one of its youngest group captains was not well received. However, once he explained that his wife, now with a hereditary title of Countess of Spelthorpe, had inherited an estate in excess of 9,000 acres in which he was expected to play a major role, there was a greater degree of understanding.

The new Labour government had come to power in July on a landslide, and there were huge expectations of a dramatic change of direction. This would inevitably mean huge reductions in service personnel, and particularly pilots, as had happened following the First World War. Michael saw it very much a case of seizing the moment and going now rather than waiting to be pushed or offered some distant role where he would see himself merely treading water in austerity Britain. The other factor was that aviation was changing, and the future now lay in the jet engine. He had no operational experience in that arena. He took the view that those with jet experience would be the new leaders in training. His contacts with major aircraft manufacturers and designers over recent months had only served to reinforce that view.

Michael had explained that this had not been an easy decision for him or his deputy, Wing Commander Richard Chandler who would be joining him at Spelthorpe. Richard's wife was now the deputy headmistress at the local school. With the writing on the wall neither Michael nor Richard saw any other option. Delaying matters would compromise the future success of their long-term interests and responsibilities. When the nation needed them the most, they had both served with distinction.

The RAF air vice marshal accepted the explanation and saw any insistence that they remain would be counterproductive. He was reluctant because the experience of two highly decorated officers, who could inspire others, would be lost. Both had agreed to stay on until the autumn of 1945 to facilitate any changeover. Their final day was listed as Friday the twelfth of October. Michael mentioned the flying school at Spelthorpe where Richard was earmarked as the manager and instructor with a former flight lieutenant – a Tempest ace, Tom Lyle, as another instructor. Michael would instruct as time permitted. There was also a need for basic training for the newly established Cambridge University Air Squadron, which they could provide as a package with accommodation and board. He reminded the air vice marshal that the Spelthorpe Flying School had provided basic flying training throughout the war, headed by two former First World War aces. Now they had three aces from the recent war who should be able to provide sufficient stimulation, experience and interest. In that way, the close links and experience would be retained.

To the air vice marshal, the offer was certainly tempting, and if firmed up on a contractual basis, it could be mutually beneficial. He undertook to come down to Spelthorpe for a visit to see for himself.

Back at Spelthorpe they were coming to terms with the new regime and the economic reality. In accordance with the terms of her late father's will, Victoria at the age of twenty-five – attained back in January, inherited the estate. After the legalities had taken place, she, with the approval of the king, was now Countess of Spelthorpe. This had involved an Act of Parliament, but with the King's support and all-round consent, it had sailed through. Her mother Helen was officially the dowager countess, but the process had been an evolutionary one and de facto control of the estate rested with Victoria, Helen and her husband, Ash, albeit that now, in the event of any theoretical disagreement, the final decision would rest with Victoria, and they knew that. Victoria's style was very much hands-on, but not in such a way that would undermine her managers. She had learnt much over the last five years and knew the business thoroughly. That gave her the respect of the workers across the board.

Day-to-day running of the farm and retail side rested with Julian Johnson. Ash was back in his old role, pending Michael's departure from the RAF overseeing the coast, port, town rentals, maintenance, forest, game park, holiday lets and airfield. Boynton was happy to be back in his former role as head keeper, head of security and running the newly established turkey farm, which he had initiated.

The veterinary practice came under Major Jeremy de Lisle.

The estate's chief engineer was William Roy, who also oversaw the agricultural equipment dealership. Sales had accelerated over the war years. All these individuals sat on the management board that Victoria had initiated. Michael would join on leaving the RAF. It worked well, maintained communication and fostered positive working relationships. As with any business, profit was a major consideration, but that was tempered with a perceived requirement for benevolence and community harmony within the estate and village. As such, the estate had considerable influence within the local school where Helen chaired the governors.

There was also the doctors' surgery operated by Ash's son-in-law Johann and Julian's daughter Jennifer. The estate also owned the village pub and village stores, and the land on which the church and school were built. Diversification had helped ensure survival through difficult times. There was staunch loyalty from the workers, who were well looked after.

The election had taken place on the fifth of July 1945, but the final result was not known for another three weeks on account of votes by those serving overseas. Tired of war and with hopes of peace, prosperity and a new universal health service, the electorate, whilst recognising the courage and leadership of the old 'warmonger', had opted for a new Labour government under Churchill's deputy from the wartime coalition – Clement Atlee.

Alas, what the new government had inherited turned out to be a poisoned chalice and not because of the previous government, but because of the war. The economic reality was dire. In 1945, defence spending had reached more than fifty percent of GNP, and debt was two and a half times GNP.

Rationing continued, and after a short space of time, bread was added to the ration list as shipments of imported grain were diverted to support and prevent starvation in occupied Germany, which had been left in ruins from Allied bombing. Coal was rationed, and the winters were getting much colder. The quality of coal supplied contained a large element of slag. Smogs developed in the large towns and cities as coal remained the major source of domestic heating. Goods earmarked for domestic consumption were allocated for export to bring in foreign currency. Children's wellingtons were just not available, and petrol rationing continued. Housing was in short supply due to enemy bombing.

While this was going on, there were mutinous acts and poor discipline in the armed forces amongst soldiers who wanted to get home. At the same time, over four hundred thousand prisoners of war (POWs) remained in the UK, and these had to be fed. Rumours about the quality and quantity of food fed to POW's only served to exacerbate public discontent.

The Americans had ended the lend-lease arrangement that had existed throughout the war, and to make matters worse, they had plundered the country of young women. Ships that should have brought soldiers home were used to take GI brides to the States. The Queen Mary took 23,000 to the USA and Canada. In all some 70,000 women had married American servicemen tempted by promises of a wonderful life across the pond. Some came back when they realised they had been deceived. Some had married criminals who were wanted and arrested on their arrival back home. Other descriptions of American home life had been purely 'Walter Mitty'. Wherever the Yanks went, the pattern was the same: in the Philippines, Japan and Australia, but this soldiers' habit was soon to be repeated by British soldiers serving in Germany.

At least Ash was pleased that three years earlier he had managed to avoid the Americans descending en masse to Spelthorpe. The use of the Hall as a RAF convalescent home had thwarted that. As far as Spelthorpe was concerned it was never going to be a case of 'Lock up your daughters.' Local harmony had been preserved.

All this resulted in a picture of total despair, and millions questioned why they had fought and worked such long hours, but there was a chink of light when on the last day of the year, the first boatload of bananas since 1940 was landed at Avonmouth docks. It was allocated to children.

POWs had been put to work on farms, on roads and in other locations, and some opted to remain when they discovered that their home area was now occupied by Russians. At Spelthorpe they had a contingent of Germans and Italians, and that had helped enormously with the harvest, but when Ash, at the instigation of Dr Johann Muller, had their underarms checked for the SS blood group tattoos, four were discovered to be SS men, so Ash had all the Germans removed despite their reputation as good workers.

The Italians were very different and much happier when Italy changed sides in 1943. Across the country, the Italians were regarded as lazy when matched against the Germans. They were the first to go back home, but one who had formed a relationship with a Land Army girl had asked to remain, and Victoria had agreed to that on the basis that he was a good worker unlike some of his countrymen. When the harvest over there was less of an urgent need to retain them as former workers were trickling back after being demobbed.

The Land Army girls had been a major success at Spelthorpe in more ways than one. The deputy headmistress at the school, Linda, had been a qualified teacher and had joined the Land Army to get away from London. When Aggie Boynton – the headmistress at the school, had found out, she swiftly took her on to fill a vacancy. Since then, she had married Wing Commander Richard Chandler (Michael's deputy), who was scheduled to leave the RAF to head up the flying school. Another, called

Molly, had fallen for an Italian POW and would shortly take a trip up the aisle with him. Victoria had agreed to take them both on as they were good workers. Giuseppe was also a superb cook, so that was a bonus.

Victoria had the ear of all on the estate. They were loyal to her, and in July, she discovered that one of the agricultural engineering fitters Brian Jones, who had been exempted conscription as a reserved occupation, had secretly married another Land Army girl called Suzy. Again, both were excellent workers. Suzy had worked in the dairy. Victoria called both up to her office at the Hall and demanded an explanation. They were very nervous, and Brian explained that if they found out she was married, they would throw her out of the Land Army, and they would be separated. Brian had a one-room bedsit in the village and Suzy had carried on living with the other four girls in the allocated accommodation.

Victoria said, "This is absolutely intolerable." Brian and Suzy quivered.

"Why did you not come and see me? We would have sorted this straight away. I congratulate you both, and I am willing to take you on permanently, Suzy, so you can leave the Land Army with immediate effect, and I will allocate you both one of the tied cottages on the estate. I'll get the maintenance team to check it out today. We can't have you living apart. That would be ridiculous. You are good, loyal workers and that's what I want here. You have been here for at least three years. It's a very simple setup we have. If you are loyal and work hard, we will support you, but you have to tell us, so in future, if you have an issue, come and talk to me or my husband or Mr Johnson. We will listen. And I suggest that you go and see Reverend Paddy if you want a church blessing. There's no need to be extravagant, but at least it will let everybody else on the estate share in your happiness. That's up to you, but we are one big family here, and that means we look after one another."

Brian and Suzy looked at each other in amazement and beamed with palpable joy at Victoria's words. They expressed their appreciation with warmth, and Suzy was in floods of tears of happiness. Victoria went to her drawer and took out some tissues which she handed to Suzy.

"Can't have you walking out of here in tears.," she said. "All the others will think I'm an ogre and here is something for you from the estate as a token of our appreciation and a belated wedding present to help you get started."

With that she handed them an envelope with twenty-five pounds in cash (approximately £1,000 at current prices). She added that if they spoke to Julian Johnson, he might be able to start them off with some basic furniture from the stores. She would call him immediately.

She shook hands with them both and simply said, "Welcome to the Spelthorpe family."

The other four Land Army girls had fallen in love with the place and had all intimated that they wished to stay on for as long as possible. They were living in two neighbouring unoccupied houses on the estate. Victoria told them she was agreeable in principle and would review the situation in the months ahead with a view to creating permanent positions for them if that was what they were seeking. One worked as a 'lumberjill' with the foresters. She was good with the horses and spent much of her time dragging felled tree trunks out through areas inaccessible to vehicles. Two worked in the dairy area, and the other was a competent tractor driver who worked on the land.

Spelthorpe was lucky in that it was able to bypass many of the privations that affected those in urban areas.

There was less need for coal because of the masses of off cuts at the sawmill from the forestry. Timber had been sold in plank or rectangular form for construction work throughout the war, but the increased demand and supply resulted in bits left over from cutting that were unsuitable for construction. This was made available for domestic use to those on the estate or village who wanted to collect it for a token charge that went to local charitable purposes.

An informal system of barter existed for produce grown in the extensive back gardens of the workers' cottages. Many kept chickens, so eggs were plentiful, and there was always enough grain from gleaning as well as that which was unsuitable in terms of quality for sale. All the cattle and sheep were grass-fed, and the hay meadows yielded sufficient hay for the winter months. The pigs feasted on acorns in the woodland alongside scraps collected from the school, village shops and elsewhere on the estate. That was boiled up with grain added to make swill for them. They thrived on it. Wild foraging took place for mushrooms and fruits. Wild rabbits and pigeons were plentiful, and venison was unrestricted. The venison was sold but a quantity was set aside for local consumption after culling by Boynton and his keepers. Venison sausages made from the lesser cuts were proving popular at the village shop. All this supplemented the ration system that was administered by the shop. The shop business was owned by the estate.

Clothing was unaffected as working overalls and boots for agriculture were unrestricted. Most people had a suit or a few dresses and skirts for Sunday best. Many of the women were quite skilled in tailoring and were able to adapt older clothing and any lengths of fabric.

In the warmer months, sea and lake swimming were popular, particularly with Michael, Countess Victoria, Ash, Dowager Countess Helen, Lucy and the other members of the Spelthorpe Company. Regular wild swimming ensured a greater degree of personal cleanliness than most of the population, who were taking a weekly bath or strip wash. A bar of soap could last a long time if used sensibly. Hot water heated with coal was expensive. Petrol rationing still applied. Agricultural use was an exception, although that fuel was dyed to discourage misuse.

There was sufficient housing on the estate as mechanisation between the wars had reduced some former labour requirements. Some had been vacated due to conscription, but if any additional housing was needed, they just built it and at a fraction of commercial costs. The estate had an in-house building and maintenance team that had escaped call-up on age or reserved occupation grounds. There was a stockpile of bricks and other building materials. They had a standard architectural plan that they used. They had done it so many times that they could build a house blindfolded. As a general rule, senior managers and technical specialists got a four-bedroom detached house or cottage. Agricultural workers got a three-bedroomed semi, and pensioners had a two-bedroomed house in a terrace. Land was available for any additional requirements. Additional infrastructure for utilities had been installed between the wars.

On occasions, there might be an imaginative interpretation of the rules. Provided this was done for community benefit, blind eyes could be turned but any suggestion of personal gain, profiteering or supplying a thriving black market in the urban areas was stamped on from the outset.

In the third week of August, Michael flew down from Cranwell with the air vice marshal in a Harvard trainer. Michael had prearranged a buffet lunch at the airfield. Countess Victoria, Sir Ash Cromwell and Dowager Countess Helen were there along with Richard and his wife (who were both on leave), Tom and his wife and the air mechanic. Despite all the titles, the air marshal warmed to them as they were friendly and down to earth with him and answered all his questions frankly.

They gave him a tour and inspection of the airfield set-up, including the hangars, maintenance facility, classrooms, catering facility, accommodation and the nearby shooting school where he met Boynton and his wife Aggie – the head mistress of the local school, who joined the party. The complex was registered as a hotel and restaurant. That afforded a lighter touch in respect of rationing regulations. They had lunch served by Amrik, the butler from the Hall and his team.

After lunch, Michael, Victoria and Ash gave him a tour of the estate in one of two jeeps that Chief Engineer William Roy had managed to acquire at a knock-down price from the Americans along with a load of spares. When he saw the scale of the operation and the diversity, he was impressed and could then understand why Michael was needed to manage the estate. He was also taken by the beauty of the place, and that would be a draw for any students. They returned to the airfield, where some of the ladies had remained with Boynton and Richard. The air vice marshal thanked them all for their warm welcome.

Prior to departure in the Harvard, he intimated that there were policy issues he might have to overcome, but his view was that it would be unwise not to take up the offer. What was there was tailored to getting first-timers in the air, and it represented a superb facility. He would be back in touch and asked if costings could be prepared on several options, considering what had taken place throughout the wartime facility. Michael undertook to do that alongside Richard.

With that, they returned to Cranwell, and the air vice marshal was pleased at the opportunity to fly the Harvard back on the return.

Towards the end of August, Richard returned to Cranwell from his leave and there was a brief handover before Michael took off the first two weeks in September. Richard and Linda had settled in well at the detached house up by the airfield. Richard had spent some of the time with potential clients, and things were looking up for mid-October when the Flying School would reopen.

At the weekend, when Michael was back, they had involved Boynton in discussions that would provide flying instruction and experience, coupled with shooting instruction at the Shooting School and accommodation at the lakeside cottages. A draft brochure outlining bespoke packages had been prepared for printing and circulation. The good news was that Tom Lyle, the second instructor, had secured his release and would be joining them and moving in with his wife later in September. Despite the austerity that existed amongst the ordinary population, the reality was that some individuals in industry had made a lot of money out of the war, and they wanted leisure that provided a measure of variety and excitement that had not been available during the actual war. Spelthorpe wanted to be the first off the starting blocks to tap into that wealth.

At the same time both Richard and Linda had helped out with the harvest. Things were easier than in the past as William had introduced more machinery, and where better to demonstrate it to clients of the dealership than at Spelthorpe during harvest time? Three of the former workers had been demobbed. It was good to have them back and they were glad to be home. Life in the infantry could mean days of sheer terror, but there was a huge amount of boredom when things were not progressing, and the separation of war only made that worse. Others had found opportunities elsewhere and had decided not to return, and that included some who actually enjoyed service life and chose to make a career out of it. That was mainly true of some who had progressed through the ranks over the course of the war.

The harvest was always busy, but it did afford opportunities for sport amongst some of the estate workers. Some would take it in turns to walk alongside the harvester to shoot the rabbits that dashed out of the cover provided by the cereal crops. The barns were cleared out to take the new straw and hay, and it was here that the estate's terrier men had a field day dealing with the rat population that was ubiquitous on all farms. There were half a dozen workers and their sons, who, between them managed a pack of a dozen terriers who were fanatically competitive ratters. When they worked as a team, there was no escape. The dogs were lightning fast and efficient, and, like the gun dogs, they learnt from one another. They would hunt out rats around the farm buildings at weekends and would assemble in the week if there were specific areas that Julian or Ash wanted cleared. Ash was vehemently against the use of poisons, as a poisoned rat could end up inside another animal with unpleasant consequences. Traps were used, but only in places where songbirds had no access. The use of terriers, ferrets and the estate's cat population provided an effective rodent control system, and as it worked well there was no need to fix it. Old and contaminated bales were set aside and taken down to the castle keep where they were placed under a tarpaulin in readiness for the November fifth bonfire. Now the dreaded blackout was over, this year's fire was destined to be a big one.

What Michael wanted most of all was to be with the family down at the cottage and his two weeks of leave afforded that. Lisette and Simon were now five and four respectively. Both could swim well but a careful watch was maintained.

There was nothing better than getting up at six in the morning and going down to the lake with the dogs for a swim. Shackleton and Hardy were approaching their prime. Shackleton was now the lead dog with Nimrod and Kipling in retirement, now they were approaching sixteen years of age. Ash believed that their good and varied diet had got them this far, and there still seemed a bit of time left. They both still swam.

The lake provided privacy and total relaxation, and the little cove with the springboard where they entered the water was fenced, signed and screened with willows and coppiced alders.

Swimming costumes were only worn on more public occasions, and it was not unusual for other close members of the younger Spelthorpe Company to adopt the same habits. Lucy was a regular with Johann and both Joanna and Jennifer would come along with their young families. George and his girlfriend, Emma, would do the same. Ash and Helen were veterans and probably came the most. It had all become totally natural to them all. An early morning swim in the sunrise with just the swans and ducks coming in and out of the mist over the water was a form of paradise that provided the perfect escape from the realities of post-war Britain that reverberated in the columns of the tabloid press.

2

Fishing

October – November 1945

October came around quickly, and on Friday the twelfth, Michael and Richard took their leave of the RAF.

When they saw the air vice marshal at Cranwell prior to their departure, they both reflected a degree of sadness at leaving an organisation that had treated them kindly over the years. The air vice marshal was sufficiently candid to admit that with the grey clouds of decommissioning ahead, if he were in their shoes, he would have done exactly the same.

He indicated that the use of Spelthorpe as a training facility had been approved and following the examination of costings, they had agreed to four six-week courses on an annual basis to commence from March 1946 with six students on each course. The RAF would supply one Harvard and one Tiger Moth to run alongside the Spelthorpe aircraft. The charges would match the commercial prices that Spelthorpe would charge, including board and lodging with a discount at an agreed level to cater for the additional aircraft and fuel supplied. There would be a separate agreement for the University Air Squadron, with hourly rates for air experience and basic flying training. The agreement would be subject to annual review. Contracts would be drafted for approval in four weeks' time. Up-to-date RAF manuals would be supplied to ensure corporate compliance.

By leaving before retirement a lump sum would be paid in lieu of a pension. They would not be able to use their rank titles, but neither were concerned, given the stack of medals both held. Privately Michael thought retention of rank titles smacked of undue pomposity. In terms of credibility, it was better to be a Mr with a DSO and bar and a DFC rather than a group captain with nothing of the sort. Michael was just keen to get back to real work at Spelthorpe.

After the estate handover, Ash was now freed up to take trips away with Helen. Both Ash and Helen were to remain on Victoria's board as consultants. The title fitted perfectly with their new role. Their experience and wisdom were valued, although much of that had been absorbed and passed on to Victoria and Michael over the years.

Michael's first action, once back at Spelthorpe, was to do rounds of the entire estate, and he made sure he knew everybody's Christian names before he did that. As their manager, he told them he would remain open to ideas and would talk matters through with them, so at the very least if the idea was not adopted, they would feel that they had been listened to and would understand the reason why. He thanked them for their loyalty and service during the difficult times. Most knew how much more difficult things were outside of the Spelthorpe community. At the same time, he made it known that if he wanted something done, the expectation was that it would be done with alacrity. His experience in leading men and machines through difficult times over the last six years came shining through.

When Michael's cheque arrived, the lump sum was considerable. With the country in the state it was, he had little confidence in banks or the socialist way of thinking. It sounded like a perfect system, but those who were in control rarely had any sense as to how to make money, and without wealth creation, even the poor became poorer which meant that governments merely sold off the family silver that they held in trust or borrowed money to pass on their woes to the next generation.

Michael felt it was a mistake to put all his eggs in one financial basket. His bank balance was very sound as he had spent so little of his service pay over the years, so with a few visits to a bullion dealer he put the entire sum into gold sovereigns, which he buried at a secret location known only to him, Victoria, Lucy and Boynton with whom who he held total trust. That way, in the years ahead the state would know nothing, but Lisette and Simon would have a safety net beyond any state provision.

As November the fifth approached there was considerable excitement for the one event that dominated the Spelthorpe calendar: bonfire night. The weather forecast was good, and the bonfire was the biggest they had ever built. They needed ladders to finish it. Consisting of a wall of bad straw and hay filled with the brash from the forestry and trash from around the farm that had gathered over the war years, it had provided a golden opportunity for a massive tidy up across the estate. Much of the brash was pine with its flammable oils.

The apple harvest had been good, and all the drops had been gathered in September and pressed. There were now several barrels of cider, and one with fifty gallons had been set aside. Bread rolls had been baked, chestnuts had been collected for roasting, and Boynton had shot a large wild pig that he encountered in the woods. Without the usual tags and markings, it was not part of the herd, and there were a few others that wandered the woods in this way, which was very convenient. The torch-lit procession took off to the castle keep as it did back in the 30s, with Paddy in the lead after giving the declaration from the old prayer book. The Guys had now reverted to the traditional Guy Fawkes, which served to reinforce the fact that the war was over. There were no Hitler Guys which had featured in the wartime processions held in the afternoon because of the blackout.

The locals had gone overboard with a full turnout in seventeenth century dress that had stayed in the attics over recent years, and the armour from the Hall decorated the Cromwellian troopers on horseback, mounted on the Suffolk Punch horses. There was Ash, Michael, Lucy, Joanna, William, Jennifer and Major de Lisle on his Arab gelding. Some of the foresters and keepers wore breastplates with helmets and carried long pikes. Helen, Victoria, Emma and Aggie and some of the other ladies, despite the evening chill, came as serving wenches in low-cut blouses.

It was well attended by the estate and village. PC Carter and his wife had entered into the spirit, arriving in period costume. For Spelthorpe, it signalled the end of the blackout, the end of the war and a determination to make merry with a new beginning as the young men were demobbed and started to come home.

The spit-roasted pig was devoured along with some fifty gallons of cider. The fireworks allocated to 1939 had been kept dry, and a super display ensued. On the following day there were a few sore heads, but everyone turned out for work.

Two days later, Michael was in the office at the cottage at 10.30am when he took a call from the harbour master indicating a serious problem. Michael jumped in the truck and was there in five minutes.

The harbour master explained that one of the trawlers had caught something in their net. They thought it was a mine, so rather than haul it in close to the boat where contact might detonate it, they had let the net out and dragged it in thirty yards behind the boat up the channel where they had unhitched the net. The object, about four feet in diameter, was floating still in the net a few yards the harbour side of the boathouse. Michael walked up and recognised it instantly as a sea mine with projecting lugs, which in the event of solid contact with a heavy object would detonate with a massive explosion.

Michael asked, "Have you told anyone else?"

The harbour master responded, "No, I thought I should speak to you first!"

Michael then issued instructions. He ordered the harbour master to seal off the channel at both ends, 200 yards from the object, along with the road and footpath. There were 'Harbour Closed' signs that unfolded near the channel entrance, and these were to be displayed. The channel must be roped off on the other side of the boathouse with access to the other side by using a rowing boat.

Michael then rang the police office from the harbour office and fortunately, PC Carter was in. He explained the situation and asked him to ring his force headquarters to get bomb disposal to attend. He told him that a 200-yard cordon was in place, but if any more signs were available, that would help. He went back to the boathouse and when the rowing boat returned having roped off and buoyed the entrance with danger buoys, he jumped in the boat, and they tied two lengths of rope to the net, securing each length to posts on each side of the channel to keep the mine mid-channel so that any contact would only be with soft mud as the tide went down. High tide had been at 10am and the following day it was scheduled for 10.45 am.

When more signage arrived with the police an hour later, Michael extended the exclusion zone down to the start of the road and footpath that came up the channel from the village. All that could be done had been done, so it was now a case of waiting for the Royal Engineers bomb disposal, who were coming up from London. PC Carter came down with a colleague, and his orders were to maintain the cordon on the village side until the matter was dealt with.

Michael said, "Well, Dave, you are going to be here a while because the bomb disposal won't get here for at least another two hours. From what I can see, their only option is to blow it, but if they do it here, that will cause a lot of damage so they will want to tow it out to sea and blow it there. They can't do that in the dark, so it will be on the high tide tomorrow."

PC Carter rang his HQ to let them know, and they arranged for night-time cover. In the meantime, Michael rang the office to let Victoria and Julian know.

Ash and Helen were in London for a few days in Theatreland.

At 2.30pm the bomb disposal team arrived in two Austin Tilly trucks. A lieutenant got out of the lead vehicle and walked straight up to Michael. "Hello, Michael," he shouted.

"Crikey, George, I hardly recognised you with your clothes on," said Michael. "The last time I saw you was in the lake with your Emma back in the summer. How come it's you here?"

George updated Michael on events. On completion of his additional training back in March, he was offered a chance to spend a period on bomb disposal which was a key role for Royal Engineers and with a lot of work. He volunteered and undertook another three-month course, and since July he had been running a small team. He had a Royal Navy experienced chief petty officer (CPO) on attachment as a deputy and two corporal technicians. They knew far more about things than he, and he bowed to their experience on many occasions. When the call came in, George jumped at it, and when they knew he was totally familiar with the location, he and his team won the job.

He introduced Michael to his team as his stepbrother who had recently left the RAF as one of its youngest group captains and was now running the estate. George, Michael and the CPO walked up to assess the situation. Michael filled them in on the background. After conferring, George and the CPO agreed that the best course of action would be to tow it out to sea and blow it at a safe distance. Michael took them into the boathouse where they had a powerful thirty-foot work and fishing boat. It would be ideal for the purpose. Michael had used it on many occasions. He fired it up. There was half a tank of diesel. The estate had purchased this from the compensation received from the boat that Michael's father and Boynton had lost at Dunkirk. It was a good all-round vessel which they had used for night fishing to avoid any possibility of air attacks, and since May it had been used quite often in the day as well.

By 3.30pm they had a plan.

The CPO said, "Oh dear. We will have to stay the night! That's a shame." He grinned and the two corporals seemed equally happy.

George explained, "They get a generous allowance for an overnight stop for their food and accommodation."

Michael said, "Leave it with me!"

He went into the harbour office and called the village pub, then returned.

"I've booked the three of you in at the village pub. We own it. The landlord will sort you out with an evening meal and a Norfolk breakfast, and you have got a room each, so no problems with the snorers. There's nothing worse than having to share a room with some noisy bastard who just wants to snore and fart all night. And to make you feel at home the landlord is an ex-navy man so he will look after you."

George said, "Right, chaps. I think we can call it a day. The

21

police will maintain the cordon. I'll point out the pub as we go past. We can park the vehicles up at the Hall, where they will be safe and out of the way. If you grab your bags, it's only ten minutes to the pub where he will expect you, and as hotel guests, the bar will be open. I trust you are agreeable to that. I'll see you back at the vehicles at 0900 hours."

George's team were very happy indeed.

A few minutes later the vehicles were parked at the back of the Hall. George went in and tipped off Amrik. Then Michael and George walked around to the office at the annexe. On the way Michael gave George the option: "I know you won't be sleeping alone tonight, so if you and Emma want, you can stay at the cottage with us, or of course you have your room at the Hall."

"We'd be delighted to stay with you two. We need to catch up and I'd like to see Victoria, Lisette, Simon and the dogs. You have to seize the moment," replied George.

George crept into the office. Emma was busy at her desk. He put his finger up to his mouth, signalling to Victoria. He got up to the back of her chair, put his arms around her and kissed her on the neck. Emma instinctively wriggled and turned to see George whom she hadn't seen for a month. She threw her arms around him and kissed him passionately. There was no doubt about the way they felt.

Michael said, "I can see you two are pleased to see each other. George has said he'd like you both to stay with us at the cottage tonight, so you might want to let your Mum know, Emma."

Then Victoria added, "You've kissed Emma but what about me? It's been a long time, George."

He hugged his sister.

Victoria continued, "Well, after all that excitement, I declare the working day over. Let's go back to the cottage."

They collected Lisette and Simon from the nursery at the

annex where Julia still had her hands full with Jack, James, Juliet and Mattie, with Joanna, Jennifer and Lucy expected to return within the hour. George explained the reason for his unexpected visit and said that he would try and get around to seeing all or some as time might allow. He might be there for another night, depending on the events of the following day.

Back at the cottage, Victoria and Emma set about preparing a meal whilst Michael and George took the dogs out onto the beach in the dark. Even Kipling and Nimrod were pleased to come along.

George explained that he had been busy in his new role with unexploded bombs, mainly from the clearance of bomb sites, and rebuilding in the London area. On occasions, they would get jobs further afield, but they were sought after because of the change in scenery, overnight stops and a chance of a few beers with the lads. In the main, there were a lot of incendiaries that were simple to deal with. His confidence had grown with experience in taking out the fuses from the bigger bombs. That made them much safer, so the actual bomb could be taken away and blown up in a safe area.

If something could be blown up in situ without causing significant problems that was often the quickest way to deal with them, but some of the later bombs had bobby trapped fuses and if he had any doubts, he would call on a real expert. There were no prizes in showing off.

In the open countryside people would sometimes come across small butterfly mines which were often best blown in situ with a cordon or surrounded with sandbags to make things safer.

He liked the work. It was a challenge and would stand him in good stead for future promotion to captain. It was a far more relaxed way that the teams worked. Whilst he was the officer, he was on Christian name terms with his team, and they just called him 'Boss' but that was so often the way in the army with specialist teams without all the bawling and shouting that tended to be the case with the infantry. He found the role stimulating because there was always something new to learn and thanked Michael for steering him in that direction a few years earlier.

They walked for almost an hour, then got back to the cottage where they fed the dogs with pigeon and vegetable stew with biscuit.

Everyone shared a venison casserole with mashed potatoes that Victoria had made at lunchtime. There was enough to go round, as she always made extra because the dogs would normally get a share of it. They washed it down with a bottle of red wine from the Hall cellar.

George told them that he had managed to secure six days leave over Christmas. He and Emma were looking at getting married next August.

Victoria asked, "Where's the engagement ring then?"

George replied, "We just haven't got round to it with all the duty changes around my training. Seeing each other was the most important thing."

His sister replied, "Look, I know you love each other with a real passion, but this Christmas, the first thing you do is to jet into Norwich, go to the jewellers near the cathedral and get your Emma a good ring. You need to go public on this, and Christmas is the right time to tell the rest of the world, and that is an order from the countess, so is that understood?"

"Loud and clear, Sis'. Promise. We will do that."

Emma's visual expression displayed her gratitude.

"That's something to look forward to. We were both a bit mixed up with all the changes and the war ending. When we do get married, we will be in married quarters and we could end up anywhere, even in Germany, but I'm confident about that now. With what I've learnt here, I should find a job anywhere, but I don't really want to leave this place. Most of all, we just want to be together."

"I'm sure you will succeed, and you will come back one day,

but that reminds me. We will need to take on a new apprentice. We are not pushing you out, but it will help if you can train her up a bit before you have to leave. I must speak to Aggie about that. If you know anyone who might be suitable, tell me, but we have a bit of time yet," said Victoria.

"What's the news on Edward then?" asked Michael. "I understand you are talking to him."

"This will surprise you," replied George. "He's got himself married. He was working for almost two years at that secret Bletchley Park place where he met this girl who was as mad about sums as he was. I think they communicated in algebra, and they probably sent out the wedding invitations in Enigma code, but they hit it off and got married at the Cambridge Registry Office. They are both in a room at Cambridge working on their doctorates. I can't see them ever leaving the place. They love it. Mum went there and saw him two weeks ago. Apparently, she is a nice girl. They are well suited."

"I expect your mother is a lot happier now, even though she has not seen fit to tell us yet. I was under the impression for a long time that she was worried that she might have bred an odd one, a Nancy, so at least her fears in that direction have been allayed. It's not for us to judge. We can't all like dogs and horses, blowing things up, pigeon shooting and wild swimming in the buff. I suppose we do need a few brilliant mathematicians, and they have to come from somewhere, so as long as they are happy, that's all that matters. I know he has no liking for this place, but will we ever see him and her?" asked Michael.

"Apparently, he told Mum that he would come for Christmas," said George.

"That's good," said Victoria. "At least we haven't lost him."

It was 10 pm so they called it a day.

George went up and took a quick shower and Emma followed him up. That was the protocol because ladies took their time, but men applying the military method could deal with the essentials in less than two minutes.

Michael went out to see if the dogs and cats had settled in the barn. They much preferred being outside and would all curl up in the straw, and the cats were happy with that too. They would snuggle in the midst of the dogs where it was warmest.

Emma was about to go up when Victoria handed her a small package with two items. "You didn't have a chance to prepare for this so here's something you might need. Michael and I were like a couple of rabbits before we tied the knot."

"You think of everything Victoria. Thanks." said Emma as she smiled, then retired upstairs.

Michael and Victoria cleared the table then took tea and a small glass of Jameson's – a habit they had picked up from Ash and Helen. They spent a few minutes going over the day, then they too went up to bed.

On the following day Michael, George and the team assembled by the vehicles at 9am. They said they'd had the best night ever at the pub and asked if they could stay there again if it got too late to go back to London. George indicated that it could be on the cards because it never paid to rush things in this line of work.

The CPO said, "I expect you had a good time too, Boss, but it would be impolite to expect a response." He made a knowing grin.

"Yes, indeed," said George. "Now let's crack on."

They went up to the boathouse and loaded up with their kit.

Michael enquired, "Have you got all you need?"

George responded, "We will blow it with a plastic charge with a timing pencil. I don't suppose you have any of that."

"Best I say no more on that because I'd be breaching the Official Secrets Act. It's quite surprising what some of the Home Guard specialists left behind," said Michael.

On high tide, they took the workboat out in mid-channel and let out sixty yards of line from the back. Michael was at the helm. In the rowboat, George and one of the corporals attached the line to the net with a shackle, then they released the ropes on either side of the net.

Once George and the corporal were back on the boat, they gently towed the net back out along the centre of the channel. On reaching the open sea, they let the line out another forty yards and Michael increased speed. He took them to a spot two miles out, which he said would be ideal.

On arrival, they shortened the tow rope to twenty yards.

"Now all we want is a volunteer to attach this satchel with a pound of plastic. There's a ten-minute timing pencil.," said George as he stripped off till he was naked. "But as I'm the lieutenant destined to lead from the front, and as a member of the Spelthorpe Polar Bear Club and with a warm bed to go back to with a lady to warm me, it has to be me!" With that, he jumped overboard. They handed him the satchel and he swam the 20 yards to the mine. He released the shackle and then attached the satchel with hooks onto the net next to the mine. Then reaching in, he snapped the timing pencil, swam back to the boat and was hauled on board.

"Eight minutes gentlemen … to get the hell out of here!"

Michael sped off until they were 600 yards away.

As George was putting his uniform back on there was an almighty explosion and much more of a bang than with just a pound of plastic explosive.

"Job done," said George.

"Not quite," said Michael as he drove the boat back to the

site of the explosion "Gentlemen, there are two landing nets under the seats. You blew that over the best fishing spot in the area, and we have some fishing to do."

When they arrived, the surface was littered with fish and some were quite large, a mixture mainly of cod, haddock, whiting and a large conger eel. They spent an hour filling the back of the boat, then headed back to the harbour.

On the way back George outlined the history of the Spelthorpe Polar Bear Club with the annual dip on Boxing Day.

"You are all mad, Boss," said one of the corporals. "That's what happens when you live in the country."

When they got back, PC Carter had lifted the cordon on hearing the noise of the explosion. Michael handed him a six-pound cod.

"Take this for your trouble."

Michael loaded two fish boxes and intimated that he had some deliveries to make on the estate. There were at least another four boxes, so he asked the harbour master and his two assistants to take what they wanted and to give the rest away to any of the villagers. He asked them to sort that, then put the boat away.

It was now 3pm, and by the time George's team had sorted things and made their reports, it would be too late to go back to London.

George said "It's bad news gents. You have won another night at the pub, but we leave tomorrow at 0800 hours sharp!"

George left the CPO in charge. Michael asked George if he could get the truck and bring it up for the fish while he made some phone calls. The CPO quietly said to Michael, "Your stepbrother has all the makings of a bloody good officer. Wish we had more like him, always fair. He looks after the men, and he listens to those with experience."

"That's nice to know. Thank you," said Michael.

Michael rang the office to update Victoria. They agreed that they should all eat at the Hall so Lucy and Johann could be there. He hinted that fish might be on the menu. She would let Amrik know. Emma and George could sleep in his room at the Hall.

There were a dozen good sized cod and haddock, He put aside a 10-pound cod for the cottage and half the conger for the cottage dogs.

With George back, they both went on a delivery run: the keeper at the eastern gate, Joanna, Rufus, Paddy, the Boynton's, Ash's parents, the Johnsons and the Hall. Along the way they sliced off conger steaks for the dogs where they were present. George was pleased to see them all.

At 4.30pm they were back at the cottage, and Michael cut off four large conger steaks for the dogs which he placed in the oven. Then he gutted and filleted the cod to get two three-pound fillets which he put in the fridge. They took the dogs for twenty minutes on the beach, where they left the head and fish guts for the gulls.

On their return, he broke up the conger steaks and mixed them with biscuit and shredded boiled cabbage, which he fed to the dogs when it was cool. The cats sensing good food engaged in leg rubbing until they received raw conger eel in strips. The dogs, in true Labrador style wolfed it all down and settled for the night.

After a quick clean up and shower they headed to the Hall where Victoria, Emma and Lucy were waiting. Johann was still at the surgery but was expected back shortly. The Hall dogs had received their share of the conger eel.

It was good to get everyone together again. They enjoyed a meal of fresh cod in cheese sauce with seasonal vegetables and a couple of bottles of white wine from the cellar. They had all missed George and took advantage of the opportunity to hear his tales of the Royal Engineers.

3

Royal secrets

November 1945

Two days after the incident with the mine, on Saturday at midday, Ash and Helen returned from London. Michael collected them from the railway station at King's Lynn.

They had elected to make it an exceptional visit of pure indulgence to mark the end of the war and had chosen to stay at Claridge's in Mayfair. Although Helen no longer owned the estate, she and Ash had built up a large nest egg of personal wealth, much of which was held in Swiss accounts away from prying eyes. Most of their money had come to Helen from her father's estates in Kenya but with a socialist government at the helm, grasping at every opportunity, things could not be left to mere chance.

At the same time together with Victoria they had appointed top London lawyers to draw up a Spelthorpe Trust to which the whole estate would be transferred to ensure its continuity and to future-proof it against inheritance tax. The trustees would be those who displayed total loyalty to the Spelthorpe estate and company and apart from Helen, Ash and Victoria would include Michael, George and Lucy with one or two outside of the immediate family like Julian Johnson and Boynton. Over the years, they would be replaced by those with a similar mindset. Part of their visit was to check on the lawyers' progress, and the other part was to visit the museums and galleries and to see a few of the top London theatre shows.

On Saturday evening, they partook of a fish supper at the cottage with Michael and Victoria. They were impressed with the way the mine incident had been dealt with and were delighted to hear of George and Emma's plans for the future, including their formal engagement set for Christmas.

The plans for the trust were agreed with the trust deed scheduled to be signed at Spelthorpe in four weeks' time. Ash undertook to ensure that Julian and Boynton were in agreement to act as external trustees. He also told Michael and Victoria that he had been in touch with Lisette's parents in Normandy. Both were well. Ash had told them they would fly over in the Dragon Rapide for a visit after April when there was more daylight available. The king would be coming for an informal shoot day on Wednesday the twenty first of November and he would be bringing Elizabeth and both girls. Elizabeth got on well with Helen and Aggie and the princesses would go riding with Victoria, Lucy and Joanna while Ash, Michael and Boynton would sort out the shooting side.

The war had made things difficult, and the large-scale shoots had not taken place. Family shoots had taken place at Spelthorpe and Sandringham. There were enough residual pheasants and partridges to allow that. The king who wanted to set an example, had applied the same discipline at Sandringham, where the younger keepers had gone to fight. He had kept in touch throughout that time, and they always managed a day at Spelthorpe in November or early December, with a return visit to Sandringham in January.

Boynton had started to build up the game bird stocks in the spring and they had managed two commercial days for this season as a taster for former clients, but he was keeping it low profile so as not to attract any undue attention as direct feeding of game birds was still restricted. Accordingly, the game bags were low compared to the pre-war years.

The following day was Remembrance Sunday at the church and just before 1045 the Reverend Paddy led the congregation out into the churchyard where the Act of Remembrance and silence took place by the memorial.

Whereas previously they had concentrated on the Great War, now they had the Second World War to think about. The Great War had cost far more in military lives from Britain and the empire, but the recent war had cost far more lives across the globe and most of these were civilians. Britain had lost 60,000 civilians due to enemy bombing. Many of the assembly wore decorations from the conflicts. Paddy had selected Lucy to recite from Binyon's 'Ode of Remembrance' for she could represent the women killed in the conflict and those at home who had suffered in waiting and loss. The George Medal she wore on her left breast bore witness to her personal bravery. Many now knew that she had been working undercover in occupied France for over two years and without the protection of the Geneva Convention that was afforded to the majority of combatants. Only a few knew the detail.

Some of those who returned to the estate wore the Military Medal. Any external observer would not have failed to notice the number from the estate and village that bore the signs of personal courage and service. The nearby graves of Earl Simon and Lisette and the names on the memorial were a constant reminder of the high price paid by the Spelthorpe community in the two wars. As part of the service, Ash read out Kipling's poem 'My Boy Jack'. It struck a poignant note given that there were so many from the two wars that would not return, and their final resting place was not known, even more so in a coastal community where many had served in the merchant and regular navies. To those assembled, Jack could be John or David, or Stephen or any name of one who was loved and lost:

"Have you news of my boy Jack?"
  Not this tide.
"When d'you think that he'll come back?"
  Not with this wind blowing, and this tide.

"Has anyone else had word of him?"
  Not this tide.
For what is sunk will hardly swim,
  Not with this wind blowing, and this tide.

"Oh, dear, what comfort can I find?"
  None this tide
  Nor any tide,
Except he did not shame his kind—
  Not even with that wind blowing, and that tide.

Then hold your head up all the more,
  This tide,
  And every tide;
Because he was the son you bore,
And gave to that wind blowing and that tide!

Ash, Helen, Victoria, Michael and Lucy placed an additional wreath on the two graves that lay side by side, adorned by the 'dove of peace' shaped leaves that had fallen from the nearby tulip tree.

On Wednesday the twenty first of November the king and queen turned up. He had brought one of his black Labradors along to help with the picking up. There were two police bodyguards in the car that followed. The King told them to stay back by the Hall, as on the estate, he would be surrounded by armed national heroes who were more than capable of protecting him. Michael asked Amrik if he would look after the two officers.

All wore their simple country clothes. Boynton had asked his two underkeepers to run the beating line with three of the foresters who had been detached for the day. Ash would load for the king and Boynton and Michael would take turns. Three drives were arranged for the morning and one after lunch if that was what the king wanted, although he did suggest that he might like to visit the school on an informal basis.

Aggie put in a quick warning phone call to Linda suggesting that the school choir might like to sing for him but not to tell anyone for definite in case there was a change of plan. She told her not to worry. It would be totally informal, and that is what the king wanted because of his great affection for the people of Norfolk. Aggie and Helen would be picking-up along with Elizabeth. Over the years Aggie had learnt the skills required, and Hund was in the same league as Shackleton and Hardy.

Victoria, Joanna and Lucy took off down to the stables with Lilibet and Margaret Rose. Lucy had her father's Webley revolver in the poacher's pocket of her Barbour just in case. Both were licensed to possess it. The girls all knew each other well from previous visits and trips to Sandringham. After selecting their horses, they took off down to the beach. Joanna was riding her father's Arab gelding. They rode along the surf line towards the castle keep. Both princesses were capable and confident riders, so they cantered along the surf before turning inland, where they dismounted for a short break and a girl talk. At the castle keep Lilibet took Victoria to one side to speak privately about an issue. Lilibet came straight out with it because she knew she could trust Victoria. She told Victoria that she was in love with a young man called Philip who was in the navy. She said she had been in love with him since she was thirteen, when she had met him at Dartmouth Naval College when he was an eighteen-year-old naval cadet. They had met up at Sandringham and Balmoral, but never where they could be really alone. They had been writing to each other right through the war. At the moment, he was in the far east but was coming home in January. She asked if Victoria would let her stay at Spelthorpe for a couple of nights when Philip got back. It was out of the way, and now that she was a qualified driver, she could come on her own and he would come up to Spelthorpe separately. After the visit they would then go on separately to Sandringham. As far as her parents were concerned, it would be their little secret, and she could just be visiting for a bit of riding and a change of scenery as she had done in the past. The problem was that her mother, the queen, was against Lilibet and Philip's relationship. She wanted to arrange a marriage with a British aristocrat. She called Philip 'the Hun' because, although he was of Greek, Danish and German ancestry and was of royal blood, his sisters had married Nazis. Philip lacked funds but was British through and through and had served throughout the war. He had been mentioned in dispatches.

"Don't worry about all that," said Victoria. "My mother was just the same when I was your age, a little before, in fact. She wanted me to do all that debutante stuff, and I wouldn't have it because I was in love with Michael and he with me, and like you, it went back a long way. I just stood firm and told her that if she didn't agree, we would dash off to Gretna Green, and there was nothing she could do about it. In the end, she agreed. We were engaged secretly whilst still at school, and we slept together at the weekends and holidays with parental agreement, but that bit's private between us. Within two months of leaving school, we were married so I say stick to your guns, and you will get there. You are my friend, and I will help anyway I can, but you must keep that bit secret and tell Philip the same because the last thing we want to do is to upset your mother and father. They are our friends too, and they have been good to us over the years. When you want something, just ask me and I will do what I can. I have to say all that Hun stuff is a bit rich coming from your mother because everyone in your family, apart from her have some German ancestry. Mums can be funny at times but that's not really for me to comment."

Lilibet took Victoria's hand and said, "Thank you so much. I knew I could rely on you, and you understand how I feel because you have been there already, and I won't tell anyone what you have just told me."

They mounted up and rode back through the woodland and back to the cottage where they stopped, greeted Kipling and Nimrod and took tea before riding back to the stables for noon.

The shooting went well.

They all started with a sloe gin. Somehow Boynton had arranged it at locations where the king would get plenty of opportunity. In all they shot forty-five pheasants and twenty-two partridges which was good with just two guns but not a huge number overall. They used the two jeeps and the truck. The King was impressed with the jeeps and Michael explained that they managed to get them at a knock-down price from the Americans who couldn't be bothered to take them back.

Bertie commented, "They seem to have done rather well out of the war. I know they lost a lot of brave men, but they are taking a lot of our women back with them. At least we got a few jeeps out of it. Useful little vehicle! It's about time that we came up with something like that, but better and larger. I'm sure we will. We have got the brains here, but we sometimes get held back in developing things. It's a bit like those Mosquitos you used to fly. Absolutely bloody marvellous. Who would have thought that something made of wood in a furniture factory would have been so fast and deadly? Our Geoffrey de Havilland is absolutely brilliant, and I hear he is coming up with all sorts of things."

Michael replied, "I met him a few times over the last year. Some of the planes he is working on particularly with the jet engines will make us world leaders and he's planning a jet passenger aircraft that will take over fifty passengers at more than 400 mph."

"Indeed," said the king. "It's a great shame you left the RAF, but I can understand why. You certainly gave it your all with that tally of enemy kills but this government is going to cut back everything. They do it after every war, and we end up with our pants down, but this place needs good people to make it thrive, and you have the acumen to do that. I fear that a lot of our great estates are going to fade away, but if you do it right like here and look after local people as I have seen with the school and other things over the years you should keep it all intact, so you get my vote."

"Thanks for that Bertie," said Michael. "I haven't given up totally with the RAF because Spelthorpe is now contracted to give them basic flying courses next year and the University Air Squadron too, so we will still do our bit. I was sad to leave, but unfortunately, a dog can't serve two masters. It was a difficult decision."

The ladies worked together on the picking-up and had a marvellous time together, after which they all went back to a shoot lunch at the Hall at 1 pm. It was well received and included some of the Spelthorpe sausages that the king had enjoyed so much in the past. There was also roasted venison and vegetables from the estate and for those who wanted it, some mine-blasted cod in a creamy sauce. The king and queen enjoyed both the fresh cod and the story that went with it. The king had decided he would like to visit the school with the queen.

Aggie shot off down there in advance but before going the King asked for a private fifteen minutes with Lucy. He had heard from Winston Churchill about what she had done, but he was curious and wanted to congratulate her in person.

Lucy and the King went to the library. She knew him and trusted him and told him if he wanted her to tell him the whole story, she would do so. He opted for that and was amazed at what she had done and the risks she had taken. She told him of the SS men and how they dealt with them, and how, with Johann's help they had passed on a huge amount of information. The king realised it had been hard for her to tell him the details.

At the end he just hugged her and said, "Thank you so much for that. This country owes you so much and you were exposed there for so long. You are a very brave young lady. I don't think we have praised you enough, but we will see."

The king and queen opted to go down to the school in one of the jeeps with Helen and Ash who had got his revolver back from Lucy. The king opted not to take his police protection men, knowing that Ash was fully prepared. Both were well impressed with what they saw. Aggie had grabbed Rev Paddy on the way down as he was another school governor and one who regularly called at the school. The children had been rehearsing for Christmas and sang beautifully. They were extremely well mannered. They spoke properly, with confidence and asked intelligent questions when the King and Queen spoke to them. Others demonstrated their French. Aggie explained that Lucy had been teaching them. The King just couldn't believe that this state school was delivering a private school education.

Helen repeated Aggie's maxim that she had used at the interview: "Education is not about filling buckets but lighting fires."

"I like that," said the King, "and if you don't mind, I'll mention this place and quote you when I next see Mr. Atlee. I know he wants to do all sorts of things with education, but he needs to get it right. You are all working wonders here! Congratulations to you all."

Royal permission was sought and gladly given for Aggie to use her Leica to take a few photos of the king and queen with the children.

At just after 4pm they returned to the Hall where they took afternoon tea. Bertie thanked them all for such a marvellous day and said he looked forward to forward to the January visit.

Ash had placed a tray of Spelthorpe sausages in the boot of the king's car. At just after 5 pm, the Royals got in the Rolls. Lilibet couldn't resist a grin and a wink at Victoria, who gave a knowing wink in return. It had been a good day.

4

Return from Hellfire Pass

November – December 1945

In the last week of November, Victoria held a meeting with her managerial board. Julian Johnson and Boynton had agreed to act as trustees of the trust that would take on the ownership of the estate. That was purely a legal device to ensure that the estate survived in the long term without being progressively sliced away by future governments.

The day-to-day strategic management of the estate was quite separate although any new capital assets would go into the ownership of the trust. About 500 additional acres to the south and outside the historic boundary wall of the estate were coming onto the market. One-fifth of this was forest, but the remainder was good productive agricultural land. The profits from the last five years would finance the purchase. Despite the shortage of regular manpower, the estate's income and profits had been boosted by the demands of the war, and this was likely to continue.

Increased mechanisation had helped enormously with that, but everyone recognised that much had been achieved by the efforts of workers who remained in all the areas of the estate's business. That included the women of the Land Army who were paid by the estate at the same rates for the work they did. Some were now in permanent roles, and others had indicated they wanted to remain if positions became available. Victoria felt she could accommodate this. Extra labour had been provided by fourteen-year-old school leavers, many of whom had worked on the farm at weekends and were already familiar with the work. Greater production would only be a good thing, and the extra land would help with this.

Ash pointed out that government policy and pressure were to maximise food production and to cut down on expensive imports. Some government support by way of subsidies was available to all farms, and this included the maintenance of good farm prices. At the same time some of the areas of the deer park could revert to their original designation to rest the soil and to maintain the use of cover crops that could be grazed. The new turkey farm, which was now raising 500 birds annually, was currently on the edge of the woodland using some of the former pheasant pens. It was not large but had huge potential when food rationing might eventually end, but that would need some buildings, and these should not be erected in the historic deer park. Part of the new land on the edge of the woodland might suit that in the long term as the land came with housing, which would help with security. A large amount of timber had been felled to meet war needs, but this had been matched by a planting programme to replace the felled timber. In a lot of areas elsewhere this had resulted in conifer plantations. It was agreed that mixed planting would be the way at Spelthorpe to preserve the character and beauty of the location. The oldest woodland would always be protected.

Michael felt that staff morale and loyalty had been critical to the success but any situation where the estate took it all was hardly just. Spelthorpe paid a higher rate of pay than other farms in the county. This fostered loyalty and ensured that good people stayed on. In addition, it kept the trade unionists at bay. The general feeling was that in many parts of the country, particularly in the urban areas, those running the unions had forgotten what they were formed for, and it was all about money now. The extra pay rate set above national averages should remain but in addition he proposed that all staff from the top to the bottom should receive a productivity bonus in recognition of their efforts to be set at one month's full pay. It should be paid in the second week of the next month.

William was congratulated on the purchase of the jeeps. They served as a useful run around generally to save use on the heavier trucks and would be ideal on shoot days in the rougher areas. William intimated that he had been offered two more. The meeting went well, and all the positive suggestions were taken up.

Victoria met up with Aggie. Emma had remained in a state of ecstasy following George's surprise visit and confirmation that marriage was not too far away, but that would mean her position would soon be vacant. Emma was no longer a mere apprentice. She was now a maturing and confident young woman. She was fully qualified in bookkeeping and had reached entry level in formal accountancy. With two years further study, she could make the grade as a chartered accountant. However, marriage to a busy army officer would mean that she would be moving on in the not-too-distant future. A new apprentice was needed. Emma had suggested her adopted sister who following formal adoption two years earlier, was no longer Emily Solomons but Emily Roy. She was now fourteen – the mandatory school leaving age and was working on a casual basis in the dairy.

Aggie was in no doubt. She had come out of the same stable as her sister and had received the benefit of five years' education with Aggie at the helm. She should be offered the apprenticeship forthwith. Victoria wasted no time. She spoke to Emily's parents Robert and Elsie. They were aware that Emma, had asked on her behalf. Emily was keen to take on the role. So once again, the Roys got a super Christmas present with both daughters in employment.

Robert couldn't resist saying in his friendly but direct Australian way, "That's a right ripper. Victoria. I just can't believe what our three sprogs have achieved here. The boy marries the boss man's daughter. Emma's going to marry your brother George, and now this. We can't thank you enough. You're not just a countess. You're a real darling!"

And with that he gave her a big hug.

The countess was not embarrassed in the slightest.

She just said, "Thanks for that Robert. I'm very happy to be called a 'real darling' in private. Emily can start on the first of January, and we can sort out the day release with the college. I'm sure Emma will show her the ropes to start with."

At the same time as Emily became a Roy, young Harry and Beverley had become Boyntons.

Both were thriving at school and at home. On Saturday mornings, Harry would help the butcher at the village shop and Beverley worked in the dairy. There had been no contact with the natural father. All the evidence pointed to total abandonment, and that was a good thing. It was good that they were working with other people and that taught them that pocket money had to be earnt. They were good kids who had put their past firmly behind them. They loved their new parents and were blissfully happy.

Boynton was aware that Black and Tan his two Labradors were nearing the end of their days like Kipling, Nimrod and Zulu. Hund was now in his prime at five along with Hardy and Mbwa who were bothers, and sons of Hunter. All were instinctively good workers. There was, however, a need for some fresh blood for the estate dogs so with Joanna's agreement he took their bitch Foxie over to Sandringham where she was mated with one of the king's best black Labradors called Winston. This was by way of a return because the king, having seen Shackleton at work, had asked for him to mate with one of his black bitches a year earlier and she had produced four puppies of which two were black and two fox reds. All were retained on the royal estate.

At least the king favoured patriotic names for his dogs. On a visit to Normandy in the previous year the king had met General Bernard Montgomery who at the time was commanding all the land forces. He had two terriers who accompanied him on campaign and their names were Hitler and Rommel. The King felt that was a little odd to name a loyal pet after an enemy. Many officers would own a dog that would accompany them particularly when at work in the barracks area. Labradors seemed the most popular.

On Monday the third of December Daniel Martin returned to Spelthorpe. Daniel had worked in the forestry until 1940 when he was called up at the age of nineteen. He had been a good worker. Nothing was too much trouble, and he got on well with the others in the team. After training in the infantry, he served in North Africa, where he fought the Italians and got a mention in dispatches for his courage, but early in 1941 his battalion went out to Singapore in the Far East.

Alas, in February 1942, Singapore fell to the Japanese who had one-third of the number of troops. The leadership and communication on the British side were poor and the Japanese displayed all the fanatical aggression that the Italians lacked. Daniel found himself amongst approximately 80,000 other POWs from Britain, Australia and India. In Singapore, they were luckier than some 40,000 ethnic Chinese who were rounded up and massacred by the Japanese army. Luckier is not the right word because Daniel next found himself in Thailand working on railway construction near a place called Kanchanaburi, and when that was complete, he was taken to mainland Japan, where he was liberated a few weeks after the Japanese surrender following the dropping of the atomic bombs on Hiroshima and Nagasaki. When Daniel left Spelthorpe, he weighed thirteen stone. At the time of liberation his weight had dropped to just over seven stones. Unfit to return immediately he was hospitalised for a period before being shipped home. He had since gained three stone in weight.

Although he wanted to get back to work, he was still not fit to do so on a full-time basis. He was living with his parents. He had an older sister who was a nurse at the main hospital in Norwich. His father was a stockman, and his mother worked part-time in the village shop.

On the evening of his return, Michael went to see Daniel at his parents' home. Michael insisted that Daniel settle in for the first week, and the following week he would work for a couple of hours each day to ease him back in. He would be paid at the full-time rate. Rationing meant that food was still limited, but Michael handed over a dozen eggs, three pounds of steak and a flitch of bacon to help with the weight gain, and he told them all that if they had any worries that they should contact him immediately. He also arranged for Dr Muller to call the following day to check him over. There would be no doctor's charge for this or any medicines. The estate would pay for that. Dr Muller had been widely accepted in the village. His skills as a doctor were outstanding. When people learnt that he had risked his life resisting the Nazis and helping Lucy, they warmed to him. Above all, Michael told Daniel not to worry.

He was part of the extended Spelthorpe family, and everyone wanted the best for him.

On the following day, Michael went up to the sawmill and met the foresters. He enlightened them as to Daniel's return, and they were pleased he was back. He told them about his physical condition, and that they should make sure he didn't push himself too hard.

Angela Brown was the Women's Land Army girl who had worked in the forest for the last three years. She was twenty-three years of age and came from Gorlestone-on-Sea on the coast just south of Great Yarmouth. Like so many others born close to the sea, the coast was in her blood, and when the opportunity came up to come to Spelthorpe, she jumped at it. She spoke with a strong Norfolk accent that had a charm of its own. She was an attractive, cheerful girl but had made no romantic attachments since her arrival. She worked long hours and with most of the young men away or married, there had been little opportunity for that sort of thing. Angela would visit her parents once a month and had joined the local branch of the St John Ambulance where Ash was actively involved. That made her useful on the estate as one of the nominated first aiders. She looked after the horses at the sawmill and would take them into the forest to drag out logs from the more difficult places.

Michael called her over and spoke to her outside.

"Angela, I wonder if you could do us all a favour. Don't get the wrong idea. I'm not matchmaking, but I think you have got a way about you and that might help Daniel get back into full swing. He's had a hard time as a prisoner of the Japanese, and I don't know the details yet but if you can take him under your wing for the next few weeks working with the horses, I think that would help. I'll let the foreman know. Daniel will start with just a couple of hours a day and build up gradually. How do you feel about that?"

"Consider it done, Mr Cromwell. It seems he's had a hard time, and I will help him all I can. I'll let you know how he's getting on," replied Angela.

"That's very kind. Thank you, Angela. I knew I'd got the right person," said Michael.

Two days later, Michael came across Daniel's father.

"How is he getting on?" asked Michael.

"I'm glad you asked. Dr Muller came to see him. He's very good. I've seen the scars on Daniel's back. I'd like to kill the yellow bastard who did that. If they are all like that, they could drop a few more bombs on them as far as I'm concerned. But what worries me is that at night, he wakes up screaming. He talks about the fires and shouts, 'Don't hit me,' but he bottles things up and won't talk. The doctor gave him some pills, which he is taking and recommended some tinned sardines because of the calcium and oils to help his bones and joints. He's eating quite well so that is good but it's his mind I'm worried about. He saw some doctors about that, but they have so many patients and all they seem to do is to say that he will go through this stage, and then another stage and so on, but that doesn't really help."

"I can understand," said Michael. "I'll be down tonight, and I'll take him to the pub – just the two of us. Leave it with me. I had the same with some of my pilots. It's not easy but I found the best way was to talk to them as a mate and to listen, and that worked so I'll give it a go. I'll be down at seven to pick him up." Michael had read about the pioneering work of Dr Rivers at the Craiglockhart War Hospital in Edinburgh in the First World War. The public perception of many was that the military thought they were all cowards, but that was wrong, and there were genuine attempts to make soldiers better. Some of it was barbaric and involved electric shocks but Dr Rivers found that by occupying soldiers, getting them to do things and just spending time listening and talking their problems through often worked but it needed dedication and time.

Michael called at the sawmills. Angela was in the woods with the horses, so he drove up in the jeep and found her. He let her know what Daniel's father had said, and he told her about Dr Rivers and how he had helped some of his pilots that way in the war. She was appreciative of the advice. She had some heavy logs to chain up, and he told her to make sure she had help. People should never be alone in forestry work in case of accidents. He helped her for half an hour until the heavy logs were dealt with then he sent her back.

Michael had words with the foreman in private:

"John, there is something I have noticed that I need to make quite clear. In the future nobody will work alone anywhere. The job by its nature is dangerous. You have been lucky so far and I know in wartime people take shortcuts. That sort of luck does not last. Injured men can't work, and I don't want anyone injured especially when you are felling. That rule will go out immediately and I will reinforce that with a notice for the board. That notice will include the need to ensure that some basic dressings, bandages and splints are always available, and the safety helmets and gloves supplied are worn. If you need anything in terms of safety equipment I want to know by the end of the day."

The foreman blushed with embarrassment at being caught out.

"I'm sorry," he said. "I've let you down, sir."

"Not just me. You've let them all down. As a foreman, your priority is the safety of the people who work for you, and anyone else who might be in the woods when trees are coming down. You've done a good job throughout the war and your next pay packet will reflect that you are appreciated. I know in the war safety courses and basic instructions got forgotten about, but that is no longer the case, so I will have it done the Spelthorpe way, and that means immediately. Are we clear on that?" said Michael.

"Absolutely sir. I'll see to it straight away!" said the foreman. He knew not to mess with a man who had commanded many men in war, and he wanted to keep his job.

Michael called at the Hall where Victoria was in her office, accompanied by the two Hall dogs, Zulu and Mbwa. They had a chat about Daniel, so she was aware. They also discussed the safety issue, much of which would apply across the board, so they drafted a couple of notices that would go to the printers. Victoria said she would speak to Julian first, as he might wish to add something that related to the farm side of the operation and there might be a training need.

Michael had a quick lunch at the Hall along with Ash and Helen who were now gradually taking more of a back seat. The subject of accommodation came up. Increasingly in the working day and with external contacts Michael and Victoria were finding that more of their time was spent at the Hall. The problem with the cottage was that everyone loved it, but it was hardly the location to run a busy estate. Ash said that he knew Victoria and Michael would not be entirely happy but the desire to swim naked on a regular basis could no longer dictate the running of the estate. For that sort of thing, it was only a two-minute dash in the jeep to the lake anyway if they felt the sudden urge. If it was just a swim, then the lake at the Hall would serve but as that was more open in aspect then costumes were more appropriate. Helen would be sad to leave the Hall but as Dowager Countess, she should not be at the estate Headquarters on a permanent basis. Both she and Ash could easily live at the cottage where they could carry on in the hillbilly lifestyle, which Helen now loved. There, they would look after the garden, the chickens and the dogs and not least of all the grandchildren as and when required. This was not a total retirement but merely an adjustment to suit the new regime and both would be available for any extra work that was needed about the estate. The running of the shoot days would remain flexible. Neither Victoria nor Michael could put up a rational argument to challenge the proposal. In all the circumstances, this was the only wise course and so it was agreed that the official move would take place early in the spring after any minor modifications had taken place to each building, if indeed at all.

Amrik's future was mentioned. He was now sixty-two years of age, and he continued to be in good health and was determined to work on. The same applied to his wife. As Helen had brought both to the estate from Kenya, they agreed that she would discuss succession planning with both on a precautionary basis to ensure that when the time came, identified individuals could take on the roles and could deputise as and when required in the meantime.

Michael picked up Daniel at 7pm. He left the jeep by the eastern gate, and they walked the hundred yards up to the pub. Michael was greeted by the landlord, a jovial ex-navy stoker who thanked him for sending up the three bomb disposal technicians a couple of weeks earlier. He said they had a good time. He pulled a couple of pints of bitter for Michael, who introduced Daniel who was at last back on the estate after his time with the Japanese. He welcomed him back home and refused to take any money after Daniel told him it was the first proper pint he had had in five years.

They sat in a quiet corner and chatted generally for a few minutes. Michael told him to cut out the 'sir' bit. That was for on the estate when working. Here, they were a couple of ex-servicemen mates who had known of fear and danger but were lucky to be home. Daniel started to enjoy his pint and relaxed. Michael got them another, and they carried on.

After about twenty minutes of Michael telling him about his war and how to shoot down aeroplanes which Daniel found quite interesting, Daniel suddenly said, "This is the best thing that has happened to me since getting back. It's nice just to go out and be normal, not like all those loony doctors I saw who just kept using long words I couldn't understand. Not Dr Muller, he was good, and he knew how to talk to me, a bit like you really."

Michael said "I've told you about me, but what about you. I'd like to know what happened. Take your time. There's no rush."

And so, for the next hour, Daniel told him everything, right from leaving Spelthorpe to ending up in the desert where the Italians just wanted not to be there, and how they surrendered in their droves. He told of taking over a hundred on his own when he got to a gun position, and how they just threw their guns down and put their hands up. They were happy to be out of it.

He spoke of going to Singapore and how all hell broke out. He mentioned the attack on the Americans at Pearl Harbor, and then how three days later two of our best battleships were bombed and sunk off east coast of Malaya by the Japanese. Morale plummeted and despite having three times as many troops they surrendered to the Japanese.

"We hardly got a chance to fight. I managed to shoot a couple of them, but the next thing that we got was the order to surrender. It was dreadful. We got marched off to a place called Changi. We didn't get fed for days, but we shared what we had, and after that, all we got was water and a mug of rice. We heard a lot of shooting going on still, and somebody said they were killing the Chinese and when they marched us out, we saw quite a lot of bodies. We went by train into Thailand, where we had to build a camp by a river and then it got really bad. There was hardly any food, and they just started beating us for no real reason. If you forgot to salute, you got hit, and the worst thing was that they thought it was funny. They were sadistic bastards. I saw one guy protest and they just shot him there and then. Some of our chaps got ill quite quickly. There was cholera and malaria, but no medicine. I seemed to do better than most because I was quite fit but some of our guys who came from the towns didn't seem to last. I got on well with the Australians. They used to sing quite a lot, and the Japs didn't know what they were singing. I always remember one song they sang a lot to the tune of 'She'll be coming round the mountain.'"

"What was that?" asked Michael.

"I'll sing it quietly, then," said Daniel.

"They'll be dropping thousand pounders when they come
They'll be dropping thousand pounders when they come
They'll be dropping hard boiled eggs
Around those yellow bastards' legs
Cos they'll be dropping thousand-pounders when they come.'

"The singing kept our spirits up, but it got a lot worse after that. We went into the jungle and had to dig out a pass through solid rock. The Japs were in a hurry, so they got guys out of the hospital set up by our doctors, and they were always arguing with the doctors. They were even hitting the doctors, and I don't know how the doctors didn't get shot because some were very firm with them. They gave us hammers and steel tap drills to make the holes in the rock for the dynamite then we had to clear it by hand after the blast and carry it away, sometimes in a small rail truck but mostly by hand. The sick ones couldn't do it, and they just beat them and when I complained they just kept beating me across my back. They beat some to death. They didn't care. We had to work up to eighteen hours a day, in the dark as well. They lit it with fires with bamboo and oil pot lamps, and with the noise especially at night it was like we were in Hell, so we called it Hellfire Pass. That was in July and August of 1943. I know that because I got a wound on my leg, and it went septic and then it turned into an ulcer, so I ended up in the hospital. They would take me to the river and sit me there and the fish would eat the dead flesh, and that got me better. I was lucky because others lost their legs. The doctors took them off with no anaesthetic."

Hellfire pass – Thailand

"The doctors were brilliant, and they used the skills of those in the camp to help them. There were engineers who would make scalpels and syringes and all the other things they used. They could even do blood transfusions. One told me that other prisoners were going blind and had severe pain in their legs and feet and that was because of a lack of vitamin B, so one guy, who was a chemist made yeast by fermenting corn and rice. They gave us what they called 'camp marmite' and it worked because the yeast in it had loads of vitamin B. One chap was a cat burglar, and he managed to steal equipment and drugs from the Japs. He was lucky they never caught him. The rice we had was full of weevils, but we ate it all, and sometimes we had a tiny bit of meat and some vegetables and fish from the river. We would eat anything to survive but as time went by, we got skinny, as you can see."

"Anyway, after the railway they sent me and some others up to Japan, but a lot didn't make it because the Yank submarines kept sinking the boats and we probably lost more like that than we lost from the Japs. I remember it was bad at night when you saw the flash and the bang, and a boat went down, and for days on end, you kept wondering if you would be next. Then, when we got to Japan, the Yanks were bombing all over the place. It never ended until they dropped the big ones. The guards just walked out and left us. Some of the local people fed us a bit, so they weren't all bad, but the trouble was you never knew who was going to kill you, either the Yanks or the Japs. I got muddled up with it all, and then they came and got us out, but they wouldn't let us go home because they said we were too ill, and then there weren't enough ships, but at least we got some proper food and started to get better."

"On the way back, it was a bit cramped, but at least we didn't have to work, and we weren't continually beaten. I know there is one thing I shall never forgive those yellow bastards who did that to us. I hope they hang the bloody lot of them because they were just cruel for the sake of it, and they laughed about it. I heard from the other prisoners that they used the Indian soldiers for target practice then they bayoneted the ones that weren't dead, and they did the same to nurses or made them into prostitutes. So that's it, but it keeps coming back and at night, it's worse. When it's four in the morning and that's the time, no matter where you are you are, you are always on your own and it's bad, but I'm glad I told you. I found it makes things better with it in the open."

Michael bought him another beer, and then they talked about the future. Daniel said that he just wanted to get back to work as quickly as possible to take his mind off it all.

"It's good you are thinking like that, mate," said Michael. "Take a walk up to the sawmill tomorrow, just to say hello and have a walk in the woods and talk to Angela. I've asked her to work with you for a bit. She's a good girl, quite young like you and she does the horses, dragging the timber out. She will look after you, and you can look after her too. And talk to her like you have spoken to me. You won't be a bore. She will be fascinated by all the medical stuff you talked about because she volunteers for the St John Ambulance in the village. It will make a change for her to be with someone of her own age. I think they are all over forty up there. But don't rush it. Take it easy, at least to start with. You can be like one of those Italians for a couple of weeks. I'll come up and see you because I'm always about. You are safe now with friends all around."

In all, they spent about three hours together. Michael took him home. Daniel seemed much more relaxed and was very appreciative of the visit.

On the following day. Daniel walked up to see the foresters in the afternoon. It was a Friday. He met his former work colleagues, who were pleased to see him back. He took tea with them and spoke about his ordeal because they wanted to know. At least now they knew and could make allowances, and he felt better too. He met Angela and spent a while with her just talking, but she seemed to get a lot out of him, and she showed genuine concern over the nightmares. He walked back with her as it was getting dark, and the house where she lived with one other Land Army girl was quite close to his parents. She was going to see her parents on the Saturday, but she asked him if he wanted to go for a walk on the Sunday when she would be back about 4 pm.

Daniel said, "I'll take you up the pub in the evening for a drink if you like. They were quite nice up there when I went up with Mr. Cromwell. He was good to me."

And so, it was arranged. He would call for her at 7pm.

5

Christmas

December 1945

On the Sunday morning after church, Michael was approached by Daniel's father.

"I don't know what you did to our lad the other night, but you seem to have transformed him. He had no nightmares that night, and ever since he has been one a lot more open about things. He's eating well. It's remarkable. I'd just like to thank you."

"He's one of ours," said Michael. "He's a young man and has got a good future here and we will all work to get him through this. From what you say, he's made a good start. I'm pleased to hear that, but we need to keep it up. Please stay in touch."

In the evening Daniel and Angela met up. They walked to the pub where she told him about her home in Gorleston. She had been working in a shop, but when the opportunity came up to help out, she eagerly volunteered. Angela liked the outdoor life, and the horses responded well to her because she showed them empathy, and over time, they put her in charge of them. Having left school at fourteen, she was conscious that there was still a lot to learn. She had approached Aggie, who was helping her by lending books and spending a little time explaining things.

Daniel and Angela seemed to get on well. Daniel had left school at the same age, and the estate had taken him on as an apprentice forester. He was doing well, but then the war came.

Daniel insisted that he buy all the drinks. He had just collected all his army back pay for the last four years, but he told her that he would rather have saved the money more conventionally. All soldiers were paid a pittance compared to what they would get in civilian life but as a corporal, his was better than most.

They talked about his nightmares. Daniel told her that over the last few nights it had been much better.

Suddenly, Angela put her hand in her coat pocket and said, "I thought about your nightmares and what I can do, so don't laugh."

She gave him a little teddy bear.

"Keep this under your pillow and when you feel all alone hold it and think about how I gave it to you in England, where you are safe. It will help you realise that it's all over. You are safe now and nobody can harm you."

With that she took his hand and held it, and she pecked him on the cheek.

"You are with me, and I am looking forward to working with you tomorrow."

They continued to hold hands. He bought her another drink. Half an hour later, they walked back, holding hands all the way.

On the following day, Michael turned up at the sawmill. He had the truck with him and had come to get a Christmas tree for the front of the Hall. He spoke to John, the foreman having noted that the workers he had seen were all paired up. John told him that Daniel had insisted on staying all day, but he allowed it on condition that he take it easy. He seemed to be getting on well with Angela.

Michael found them both half a mile away and enlisted their

help in selecting and felling an eighteen-foot Norway spruce. Having cut it, they winched it onto the truck and the three of them picked up some wedges and a heavy hammer from the sawmill. They took the tree to the front of the Hall, erecting it in the dedicated slot and driving in the wedges to hold it perfectly upright. He drove them back to where he had found them then returned to the cottage to deal with some correspondence.

As the days went by Daniel and Angela grew closer. Daniel got rapidly stronger and more confident. They were attracted to one another. They held hands when going to and from the sawmill, and after a few more days they kissed one another.

At the end of the week Angela's housemate went home to her parents for ten days over Christmas. Angela invited Daniel in for the evening. They lit a fire, and the house quickly warmed. She cooked them a simple meal with some of the estate's venison sausages.

At 10pm she did not want him to leave. They went upstairs together and became lovers. When Angela saw the scars from the beating on Daniel's back she cried for him. He held her close, and she clung to him. They slept together. A partial vacuum in each other's lives had been filled and they would remain together. The recovery process was going better than expected. Daniel would have no further need for the teddy bear under the pillow. He had finally come home.

A week later, on Friday the twenty-first of December, George came home with ten days' leave. He returned to his room at the Hall and for the next ten days, Emma moved in with him. True to his word, on the following day George took Emma to Norwich where an engagement ring was purchased. Emma had seen Jennifer's ring and selected a similar ring with a bezel setting for which George paid £40 pounds (£1,500 at current rates). Purely by coincidence, while they were in the shop, Daniel walked in with Angela. Emma knew Angela and Daniel because they would come into the office to collect their pay.

Angela was so happy that she could not help announcing that Daniel had popped the question, and she had agreed, and they were at the shop for the same reason. They agreed to meet up in the pub opposite in an hour. Angela too, selected a bezel ring because of the nature of her work, and she found something that looked very robust, priced at ten pounds

It would seem that the magic of Christmas made it a perfect time to celebrate a forthcoming union.

They met up in the pub and congratulated one another. George had not met Daniel for many years, but could remember him from before the war, and as a soldier and former soldier, they were on the same wavelength.

Daniel was quite comfortable talking about things now, and both Emma and George were fascinated and shocked at what he had to tell.

Emma suggested that they speak to Victoria or Michael at the earliest opportunity and felt certain that they would sort out something for them in terms of more permanent accommodation, as well as taking Angela on as a Spelthorpe employee outside of the Land Army umbrella.

It was a spontaneous meeting that went very well, and they all had a bite to eat. All around the centre of Norwich, there were decorations and lights which added to the feel-good factor. The lights demonstrated that despite the post-war hardships there was a determination to move on and seize the moment. As Daniel and Angela had come on the train, George offered them a lift back in the car.

They got back to the Hall at 4pm and George insisted they come in for a pre-Christmas drink and mince pie. Inside Michael and

Victoria and the children had been busy with Helen and Ash doing the decorations.

"To what do we owe this pleasure?" asked Victoria.

George explained how they met up at the jewellers and that this Christmas, there was now a cause for a double celebration.

Michael was the first to shake hands with Daniel in congratulations, and he gave Angela a hug.

"Well," he said, "when I asked you to look after Daniel, I had no idea that you would take him on for life, but I'm absolutely delighted for you both."

Daniel was quick to respond. "Christmas is a time for angels, and I can't thank you enough for finding my Christmas angel, and for everything else you have done. You have all been so kind to me."

Helen was most impressed by Emma's ring and announced, "We are going to have a little drinks party here on Christmas Eve just to celebrate George and Emma's engagement, and I'd like you two to come along too, and that includes your parents, Daniel. It will just be a few of us, but a double engagement is something too good to miss. Just come as you are, straight after the carols outside, which we all enjoy. I trust your parents are aware of your engagement."

"I did mention it yesterday," said Daniel. "They have met Angela, and they are very happy with it all, and we do plan to see Angela's mum and dad in Gorleston after Christmas. It's all happened so quickly."

Ash said, "You are not the first here with a lightning romance. It was just the same with Dr Jennifer and her sister Joanna. We have a theory that there is something in the Spelthorpe water, so my advice to you both is to keep drinking it!"

Angela and Daniel stayed for an hour, but before they left, they had a quiet word with Victoria, who ushered them into the library. They explained the situation to her.

Victoria responded, "Don't worry about accommodation. You can carry on as you are at present. I know my name is Victoria, but we don't do Victorian morals here. You clearly love one another and that's good enough for me. We will take you on as a Spelthorpe employee Angela. That was always on the cards. Your housemate can move next door with the other two girls, as the house has three bedrooms. You have been here three years and have worked hard, and you fit in. I'll have a talk with you in the new year because married couples don't always want to work at the same place because you can end up with nothing to talk about, but we shall see. We are all different in that respect but your position here in any capacity is confirmed. If there are any defects with the current house, we will get them fixed, and if you do need any additional furniture please go to the store. My husband will sort you out, as you both come under him. Come and see me again when you have seen Reverend Paddy. I assume that is what you will want, but clearly that's up to you. He will be at the engagement celebration."

Angela responded, "Thank you ever so much, ma'am. You have all been so kind. We were a little worried, but you have put our minds at ease. And thank you so much for the bonus we both got in our pay packets."

Christmas Eve underlined the community's desire to put the war behind them. The tree was lit up at the front of the Hall. The families of the estate turned out to sing and to be served with mulled wine, sausage rolls and mince pies by Amrik and his staff. There was an upright piano placed outside, which Reverend Paddy's wife Ruth played, ably accompanied by Joanna and Jennifer on the violin and cello. It lasted just over an hour.

As the crowd made their way home, those invited to the engagement party assembled in the Hall: the Cromwell/

Spelthorpe family, along with the Johnsons and their extended family, the Boyntons, Paddy and his wife, Daniel's parents, the foresters and the three remaining Land Army girls.

At the outset, both soon-to-be-weds had a few words of appreciation to say and were warmly congratulated.

Daniel and Angela took the opportunity to speak to Paddy. He said that he would be delighted to join them together, and both intimated that as soon as possible would be ideal. Paddy suggested March, when the weather might be better and there could be a reception in the Memorial Hall. Daniel asked Michael if he would be his best man.

Daniel said, "I haven't been back long, but you have done so much to help me and Angela that there is nobody better I could think to ask."

Michael responded that nothing would please him more. In the three weeks Daniel had been home the transformation and the pace of Daniel's recovery had been quite remarkable. He had put on another eight pounds. The facially drawn look he had initially was now gone. His muscular strength was returning.

George circulated with Emma. His officer training had made him so much more confident and personable. He told Ash and Helen that early in the new year, he was to be moved to a Royal Engineers bomb disposal squadron based near Oxford as the deputy to the captain running the squadron. As they were aware that his marriage was imminent, they had allocated him an officer's house at the barracks from March. In the light of this, they had decided to bring forward their wedding day to Saturday the sixth of April and he had had applied for ten days' leave around that date.

In the meantime, he was still quite busy in London and in other cities, with bombs being discovered as they cleared the bomb sites to start reconstruction. The Christmas lull had given him and his colleagues a little respite. There was some discussion on the wedding, which would take place at the Spelthorpe church and the Hall. George wanted Michael as his best man. Emma wanted her sister Emily as a bridesmaid along with Lisette and Joanna's daughter, Juliet.

Surprise visitors were Edward and his wife, Olivia. Edward surprised them all because he was much more communicative and had emerged somewhat from his introverted shell. Olivia looked a little plain and wore no make-up, but her lively personality more than made up for that, and it was clear that she had drawn out another side to Edward. What did emerge was that they were both perfectly happy with one another and shared a life of academia that they both enjoyed. They had met whilst working at the secret establishment in Bletchley.

Cambridge was where they were now, and that was where they would stay. As well as completing their doctorates, they were engaged in lecturing to the first-year undergraduates and writing textbooks. At present, they were in rooms at one of the colleges, but as a belated wedding present Helen had bought them a comfortable four- bedroomed house in the central area and within easy walking distance of most of the key colleges and they would be moving to it in the spring following a few modifications. They were staying at the Hall where Edward had retained a room.

At 10pm the event ended as some attendees were mindful that on Christmas morning, the managers would be up early to attend to essential duties with the stock, the dairy herd and horses. This was a tradition that had existed for many years to allow the regular staff the morning off on Christmas Day. Julian and his daughter Joanna would see to all the horses. The other duties would fall to Ash, Helen, Michael and Lucy.

On Christmas morning, after their essential duties, breakfast was served at 9am, followed by church at 10.30am. Christmas dinner for the greater Spelthorpe family took place in the Hall starting at 1pm. It followed the pattern of the previous year with a choice of venison or Boynton's Norfolk Turkey which according to Boynton had met with an accident and had to be dealt with – a likely story indeed! Any statistician would have found a close correlation across the entire rural parts of the country between livestock that had met with accidents and days of celebration.

They all listened to the king's Christmas message to the empire. It predictably spoke of the vision of a world at peace and the end of the dark days, remembering those who gave their all to bring that about and recognising the hope and fellowship of all men of goodwill.

Helen handed out presents to all and games followed.

On Boxing Day, a rapid meeting for the polar bear dip was followed by red wine, French onion soup with cheese and croutons and Spelthorpe sausages.

Victoria and Michael spent the rest of the afternoon with Lucy and Johann, and they had agreed to babysit and sleep at the cottage overnight with Mattie, whom Lisette adored, so Michael and Victoria could visit the Boyntons for the evening.

On arrival at the Boynton household, Richard and Linda were already there. As they lived in close proximity up at the airfield, they had become good friends. Linda had been working at the school for some time and was Aggie's deputy. They had a relaxed convivial evening, and because they all knew each other so well there was total openness with none of the posturing that can accompany social events.

Beverley and Harry were present until their bedtime and were the absolute models of politeness. They were confident and impressed them all with their maturity and knowledge, but that was Aggie's influence for you, with her superb ability to bring out the best in all who came into contact with her.

She had cooked a super meal of venison cooked in the same manner as a Beef Bourguignon. It went down superbly well with the two bottles of claret that Victoria had brought along.

Richard was in a good mood because Linda had seen Jennifer a few days earlier and had had it confirmed that she was now three months pregnant. Michael, after congratulating them both, said, "I don't know what's happening here. There are babies popping out all over the place, but I suppose that's what happens after a war. Jennifer announced the other day that their number two will arrive in May."

Gabriel Boynton added, "It's nice to see that at least here, without the help of the Americans, the Spelthorpe Pudding Club is doing well. It's causing all sorts of problems elsewhere with Americans stripping the villages of their young ladies and our lads coming home to find the wife or girlfriend has had plenty of horizontal stimulation while they have been away. It's worse still when the wife says it is theirs, and what pops out is one of coffee and one of cream. Calling that an immaculate conception just won't wash at all!"

Victoria, with her business head on said that unless the estate provided a proper nursery, it could seriously hamper the running of the place, with many mums wanting to work and not being able to do it. She was considering setting up a nursery at the Hall or in part of the annexe where mums could drop off their young ones, and providing the cost of the carers was covered, it should work. She was going to ask one of the Land Army girls if she was interested and with help from one or two of the girl school leavers, it should work for the mums and for the estate. They all thought it was a good idea.

Aggie was a bit concerned about her fourteen-year-olds who were leaving school. Some got work on the estate or in the village, but others with true potential were left high and dry unless they could get into the grammar school for boys or the girls' high school at King's Lynn, and that was quite a hike. She mentioned that changes were afoot to increase the school leaving age to fifteen and to have three types of schools with an exam at eleven to decide who goes where. The brightest would go to the grammar school. Next down the list would go to a technical school aimed at a greater degree of practical skilled work and the others would go to what was called a 'secondary modern', aimed at filling jobs at a more basic level. The village school would revert to a primary, covering children up to eleven. Aggie felt it a bit harsh because children develop at different rates, but as long as there was a possibility for late developers to move up it might work. She said she was minded to get, Beverley who was thirteen, into her old private school because she wanted a nursing career. She was aware that Joanne was similarly minded in respect of James who was now eight years old. Victoria intimated that the estate might help with that because that had been the precedent set by her father for senior managers on the estate. Under Aggie's leadership the school was perfectly adequate for younger children, and the king's recent visit had endorsed that view. They were all aware of government plans to nationalise what seemed like everything, such as a new health service for all and education, but it all seemed rather a lot when the country was broke.

Richard said, "It's all a bit much. They always promise the world and those daft enough to believe them vote for them, but the other side is just as bad. I just can't see all this coming off somehow. We have got servicemen tied up all over the world and all these places want independence from the empire and we end up as the piggy in the middle like in Palestine. That will be a nightmare. We will just have to wait and see, I suppose. At least here we are out of it, and as far as I'm concerned, the further from London the better. It's bad there with the cold weather and all these smogs. Can't beat a bit of Norfolk fresh air. With all the logs we have, we are as warm as toast, but I do feel a bit sorry for them. I hear that coal's gone up and what you get smokes like mad because half of it is slag."

Michael was interested in the airfield.

Richard told him that they now had a dozen private clients on the books, and with the RAF contract, they would be well into profit by the summer. Winter weather, as always, slowed things up a bit but both he and Tom Lyle were busy finalising the program for the University Air Squadron. There were also some clients booked for the holiday chalets for the summer with shooting and flying packages, so it was looking good. Michael told him of a conversation he had with Geoffrey de Havilland. His Canadian subsidiary was developing a monoplane trainer with a cockpit to replace the Tiger Moth, and the RAF were sniffing around on that one. He had asked Geoffrey to put him down for an option on two of them.

"If we stay ahead of the game, they will always come to us!" said Michael.

Boynton told them that Joanna's dog Foxie was due to produce puppies quite soon. Foxie had mated successfully with one of the king's dogs – Winston. There was a need to maintain the estate pack for picking-up purposes, and hopefully, this would achieve that. "Well at least we won't need a nursery for them," said Victoria. "It's always sad when they go but at least here they have had the best life any dog could have, and the older dogs always welcome and take on the new ones. The new ones are not replacements because each one always develops into a character of their own, and I know Michael is after a couple for the Cromwell pack."

She then went on to explain how she and Michael would be moving to the Hall, and Ash and Helen would be back at the cottage.

"We are both envious of them, but unfortunately our new positions have decided that for us, and I suppose one day we might move back there, but none of us is wishing time away."

Apart from putting the nation right, a good time was had by all, and a nightcap of Jameson's best Irish whiskey went down well. Michael and Victoria jumped in the Jeep, but halfway back Michael stopped, and they kissed and cuddled in the dark like they always used to as teenagers. Despite six years of marriage and the extra responsibility of it all, passions remained very high.

Two days later, a measure of normality had returned and most on the estate had gone back to work.

George was at a loose end because Emma had returned to the office, so Michael offered him a flying lesson in the Harvard. With a cockpit canopy, it was somewhat warmer. George had been up before in the Tiger Moth but that was many years ago, and he jumped at the opportunity.

Michael collected George from the Hall at 8.30am in the Jeep. He made a couple of phone calls from the airfield and gave George a quick briefing, then at 10 am they took off flying along the coastline at 1,000 feet. Once up, George flew the aircraft, and they went right around as far as Lowestoft. Then Michael put the plane on a heading of 170 degrees south into the North Sea and across the channel, and half an hour later, they were over the coast at Bray-Dunes to the east of Dunkirk. They turned west along the coast. It was low tide, and they could see the wrecks of the ships and abandoned lorries across the flats and jutting out of the sea.

"This brings back memories, George. Higher up, I was knocking out Stukas and the odd Messerschmitt 109 whilst down there, Dad was with Boynton getting the troops out to the bigger ships. It still looks a mess because after D-Day, as we advanced up the coast, we just left Dunkirk still occupied, but contained, and went on to Germany. It wasn't liberated until the Germans surrendered."

Once over Dunkirk they turned up to the northwest and a few minutes later, they could see the cliffs round from Folkestone to Deal. They flew over Sandwich, at which point Michael called up Manston control and was given permission to land.

Once on the ground and parked up, an officer displaying the rank of wing commander came over to them. Michael knew him well. He had been one of Michael's flight lieutenants when Michael was leading a Mosquito squadron. They shook hands.

"Nice to see you, Charlie," said Michael. "You've done well for yourself. Looks like you have decided to stay on."

"Yes," said Charlie. "I'm here for the duration. A lot have got out for fear of being pushed out, but unlike you I didn't have somewhere to go to. The RAF was all I had, so I stayed on. The wife, kids, and I are settled in Broadstairs, and it looks like this place is staying on, being so close to the continent and having such a long runway which is perfect for jets. I'm acting up, as the station commander left the service recently, so I've got fingers crossed that they will make that permanent."

"You've done well, and you deserve it," said Michael.

Michael introduced his brother George and invited Charlie to go to lunch with them at the Albion Hotel in Broadstairs. It had been a popular watering hole for some of the crews when they were temporarily working out of Manston when Michael was there back at the end of May and early June in 1940. Charlie reluctantly declined as he had a number of visitors scheduled for the day, but he said he would get his driver to take them down and bring them back. It was only about four miles away.

"Make sure you have a cup of tea before you go back," said Charlie.

"Most certainly will," replied Michael.

At just after midday, both were sitting in the Royal Albion

Hotel perched on the edge of the cliff overlooking Viking Bay below them. It was a delightful setting, nicely contained and with a sandy beach. Michael quite liked Broadstairs. It always seemed more homely with more of a village atmosphere than the towns of Margate and Ramsgate sprawled out on either side. Margate could get busy from Easter onwards with its Dreamland Amusement Park and guesthouses that drew in the masses from London with the railway station in close proximity. For less than a pound they had a good lunch of fish and chips and a couple of pints of bitter each to wash it down.

They talked about George and Emma's plans. George was quite pleased to be going to Oxford. It was nicely central for the rest of the country, and there were always bombs to be dealt with elsewhere, away from London. They would make the most of the countryside along the Thames Valley on days off. Uncertainty was a part of military life, and he felt that, at some stage, he would have to spend some time overseas. The problem was that with the war over there were lots of factions who had helped defeat the Germans and the Japs and they all expected their freedom. Many in those nationalist groups had received a lot of military training, so knew how to fight and kill, and that was dangerous. Up to then, there had been little use of explosives, but it was only a matter of time before they did. Ordinary bombs were less of a problem, particularly with the war over, as Britain now had all the blueprints of the various devices but with amateur bombs, that was always difficult because you never knew what you were up against. The only question was where and when. He had spoken to Emma about this. She had accepted it. If things got difficult, she could always go back to Spelthorpe until he came home and there was always work for her there.

Michael asked if he had a service pistol, as he was aware that officers could select their own weapon.

"I've got a Webley. 38 that was issued, but I rarely carry it in the UK. There is little need," said George.

Michael said, "If you go overseas, you can have my Colt .45 automatic. It's slimmer but it packs a lot more punch, and you get an extra shot. The seven-shot magazine can be changed in seconds. If you like, you can try it out tomorrow up at the shooting school. I think you will take to it. It is licensed and I've got a thousand rounds, so you can get a bit of practice."

"I'd like that," said George.

"And you've not had the benefit of Boynton's practical survival training. I had it along with Victoria and Lucy, and it served us all well, so I'll have a chat with him. It's the sort of stuff they never teach you in officer training. You need to know how to play dirty because that's the only way you win against some of the evil bastards you might come up against. Take it from me! And he might have some extra tips on explosives and the like. But you will need to show a blind eye on occasions if you want the full benefit. It will be worth it while Emma's at work and you'll still get the evening for fun and games!" said Michael.

"Don't worry about the blind eye. Those secrets will be safe with me," agreed George.

They enjoyed their meal and then got a lift back at the agreed time. They took tea with Charlie, then took off for Spelthorpe. By 4.30pm they were back home.

On the last day of the year, a Monday, Michael took George up to the shooting school, where at the back they had an area off limits to all but the selected few. This had cable operated pop-up targets and some simple walls and buildings. It was something that Boynton had come up with in the war when he was training up his secret resistance force. Michael stayed while the three of them shot off a couple of magazines each, then Michael left him with Boynton for the rest of the day while he went down to the sawmill and the harbour.

At the forestry they were very happy with the bonus pay they had received. Their felling rate had increased over the war due to the two chainsaws that Ash had ordered and with the spare parts obtained at the same time they were still going strong. Throughout that time, Ash had insisted on planting, and some of the trees planted five years back were starting to grow well. It always took a couple of years for the trees to get going. Watering was critical in the first year if there was no rain for two weeks or more. They had a horse towed bowser that helped them ensure the trees would survive. Michael found Daniel and Angela working with the horses in the deeper part of the wood, dragging out the timber. They were both very happy and told him that they had visited Angela's parents at Gorleston over the weekend. All was well. All they wanted was for their daughter to be happy, and she had achieved that.

New year was never a big occasion on the estate. Victoria and Michael opted to go down to the village pub on New Year's Eve to show a little community solidarity. Ash and Helen had agreed to babysit. Familiarity sometimes breeds contempt but there was nothing of the kind expressed here. News travelled fast locally, and the way they had looked after Daniel and Angela had got about and there was no doubt that the two of them who were now running the show, cared deeply about those who worked for them. They were made most welcome and joined in with the spirit of the party. Victoria ordered a round of drinks on the house, which cost her five pounds, but it was worth it. She knew they would all pull together if required, and they in turn, knew that compared to other estates and farms in the county, they were well looked after.

On Wednesday, the second of January, three letters arrived at the Hall in vellum envelopes, and these were addressed to Ash, Lucy and Boynton. The New Year's honours list had been exceptionally long that year, but most of the awards were dedicated to establishment figures running various government departments. Many of the recipients had never encountered an angry man, but that was the nature of the establishment.

The story of Ash and Boynton's adventure at Dunkirk, where under fire they had taken hundreds from shore to ship, where Boynton had shot down a Stuka with an automatic rifle and where they had made their way through enemy lines in a stolen German truck after dispatching two of the enemy, then to booby trap the truck and to steal a boat in Normandy to get home, had finally emerged from the woodwork. At the time, both were civilians and this type of courage under fire was precisely the reason why the king had created the George Medal. Ash and Boynton would receive that from the king.

Lucy's letter looked initially disappointing as it indicated that her George Medal had been withdrawn. But the letter went on to say that the King had decided after consultation that her extreme courage in the war merited a higher award – in fact the highest award for a civilian and she had been conferred with the award of the George Cross – the civilian equivalent of the Victoria Cross. The citation read as follows:

His Majesty the King is pleased to confer the award of the George Cross to Mrs Lucy Muller (née Cromwell), who served as an Ensign of the First Aid Nursing Yeomanry.

Mrs Muller assumed the identity of a French national and was landed secretly by submarine off the coast of Normandy in 1942. She made contact with the French Resistance and for the next two years, she gathered detailed intelligence on enemy deployments and defence works along the coastline, which she encrypted and arranged to be sent to London. On one such mission, she was challenged and violently assaulted by two SS soldiers. Despite being unarmed, she killed one and, with assistance, disposed of the other. Thereafter, she gained access to an element of the German regular army, and with further assistance over the following year, was able to send back detailed intelligence that proved invaluable in the Normandy landings. Her courage was extreme, and over a protracted period. For all this time she was in constant danger, and was aware that if detected, she faced torture and death.

Lucy was speechless at the honour, and so were many others in the local community, who previously had only received an inkling that she had been undercover in occupied Europe, but now knew the full extent of her activity, and that they were living with the bravest of the brave.

The medals would be presented at Sandringham at a date to be notified.

6

Royal visits

January 1946

In the first week of January Victoria spoke with Angela, who assured her that she was more than happy to continue with the forestry. Whilst she thanked the countess for an offer for her to set up a nursery, she indicated that she loved working outside with the horses, and both she and Daniel were happy with that. With her St John Ambulance activities and Daniel's determination to gain professional qualifications in forestry, there was ample stimulation for them both outside of the marriage.

A wedding date in March had been announced. That being the case the countess handed her the sum of twenty-five pounds as a wedding gift from the estate. Angela was taken aback by such generosity. She hoped that the countess would be coming to the wedding as a guest alongside her husband, who would be the best man.

Later that week, Victoria spoke to the three remaining Land Army girls. She did this after discussing the matter with Julian, who had agreed that all should be retained and placed on the Spelthorpe payroll.

The girl who drove the tractor said she enjoyed that and wanted to remain in that role. She said she was getting used to working with the various attachments like the seed drills and harvesting equipment. These were skills the estate required for profit maximisation.

The young women who worked in the dairy were happy to continue but after Victoria questioned them, she discovered that one was a qualified nurse and had only joined the Land Army because she wanted to do her bit and get out of London. She said she would do anything to remain. When offered the opportunity to set up and run a nursery for the estate she jumped at the opportunity because then she could combine her nurse training with living somewhere that she loved. She could re-register as a nurse. Given that and subject to satisfactory references from her previous hospital, Victoria agreed to offer her the job and at the going qualified nurse rate of pay and holiday allowance. She would, in all likelihood, be assisted by one of the fourteen-year-old girl school leavers who she would interview with the countess on recommendation from the headmistress, Aggie Boynton. It would mean her taking a room at the Hall. She was happy with that.

After due consideration it was decided that the Hall would be the best place to install a nursery. There was ample space at one end downstairs with toilet and washing facilities and two good-sized rooms so there was a quiet space for sleeping, a store and a small office. It had its own external door that would be ideal. The countess intimated that she would like some time to be spent in teaching those from the age of four how to read and basic numeracy. That would help enormously when the children started at school. Aggie would supply some materials.

In the end, it all worked out well. The references were sound, and Aggie indicated a sensible, caring girl who had left the school and was seeking an opening. She had been working part-time in a shop. Charges were set that would cover the employment and maintenance costs. Enrolment from parents on the estate and village gradually built up.

On the farm side, profits were up. The national cereal crisis kept prices high. Low pre-war livestock densities afforded a measure of expansion with adequate grass and hay, meaning there was no need to buy in animal fodder. The cereal fields benefited from the manure from the sheds. This was an autumn and winter job, so the muck could be ploughed in before seeding. Some fields had been sown with winter wheat in the autumn. Robert Roy had increased the numbers of sheep and pigs and the same applied to cattle. Livestock prices remained high, and with the extra productivity, the money was pouring in, but that was not something the estate wanted to boast about. The veterinary practice dominated the local area, with labour charges eradicated for the actual estate, so the only cost was medicine and surgical supplies although the actual amount of labour was notionally counted to demonstrate the value of that part of the business. Rufus, his son and daughter-in-law were happy. They did not seek to make a lot for themselves. They were salaried. They liked where they lived and were comfortably well off.

Similar success applied to the farm machinery dealership. By getting in first Spelthorpe was now the main dealership for all North Norfolk and as there was only one main manufacturer serving the country, it was hardly going to compete against itself. William had shrewdly recruited an American engineer who had married an English girl and wanted to stay in England, and that provided a link for importation of the best models from the US parent company of the main UK manufacturer. With the increased demand for tractors, accessories and servicing, the profits started tumbling in.

In summary, Spelthorpe remained in a buoyant financial position and that was an ideal place to be as they headed into the uncharted waters of 1946.

On the well-charted waters of the Mediterranean, the Royal Navy Destroyer HMS Whelp was heading for home after a long deployment in the Far East. She had been in Tokyo Bay when the formal surrender took place on the second of September, and then onward to Hong Kong with Admiral Fraser, who took the Japanese surrender there on 16th September. After a spell of hunting pirates in the South China Sea, she went to Sydney, Australia, for a quick refit and was now heading for home.

There were mixed feelings on board. The men were going home, so the separation would end. Ships took on a spirit and personality of their own, and as time went by, were held in deep affection by the ship's company.

Alas, despite only having been launched in 1943, HMS Whelp was heading to be decommissioned along with hundreds of others. Many were mothballed, some sold to the navies of emerging nations, but the majority, in their hundreds, were to end up on the scrap heap. Over 700 still being built were abruptly cancelled. Many were taken out to sea and sunk after being used as target practice. Morale was mixed. The greatest navy in the world would be no more and it all happened so suddenly and brutally.

On the bridge and second in command was First Lieutenant Prince Philip of Greece and Denmark. He spoke no Greek, and until joining the navy had been looked after by relations as a boy, spending time in England, France and Greece. He was an impoverished aristocrat of European lineage. Philip had a reputation as a bit of a charmer, but he was very bright having been the top in his class of naval cadets and had served with distinction throughout the war. Whilst at Dartmouth Naval College as an eighteen-year-old cadet, he had met up with thirteen-year-old Princess Elizabeth and they had been corresponding ever since. On his return to Portsmouth, he was to be posted as an instructor at the Petty Officers' School in Wiltshire, but he had a short period of leave prior to that.

On arrival in England on the seventeenth of January he put a call in to Princess Elizabeth at Sandringham and arrangements were made. That same day, Victoria received a call from the Princess to say that she was coming to go riding and would be staying for three nights. Victoria prepared the guest room at the cottage.

On the following day at 10am, Princess Elizabeth arrived at the Hall. She had driven across from Sandringham where the family were still in residence. Both Ash and Helen were away having a further week in London. Ash had business at the Ministry of Agriculture and Fisheries. He knew the minister, Tom Williams, quite well as he had served in the coalition wartime government. As both had risen from humble beginnings, they seemed to hit it off. Ash had a wealth of practical experience that the minister could tap into.

Victoria met Elizabeth at the Hall, and they went down to the cottage. Elizabeth was delighted with the room. She was very excited and told Victoria that Philip would be arriving by car at about 3pm. Her intentions were clear. Victoria hinted that if she needed anything, there might be what she wanted in the drawer of the bedside cabinet.

Elizabeth unpacked, then they took morning coffee together and chatted away. They petted the dogs who had come in to introduce themselves to the special guest. Victoria and Elizabeth knew each other well from regular visits, and they shared the fond memories of Michael and Victoria's honeymoon at Balmoral. At 2pm, Michael came home. He had been with the pigs all morning and apologised for his appearance. Elizabeth found it quite amusing, but she said that she always admired it when the senior managers got stuck in at Sandringham and Windsor and that she, too, was often engaged in mucking out the horses. Michael had a sandwich, then excused himself while he got cleaned up.

Just before 3pm, Victoria and Elizabeth headed back to the Hall in Michael's jeep to meet up with Philip. Victoria had briefed Amrik on what was taking place and the security reasons for keeping the visit low-key. She had also informed Boynton and Lucy. George was now back at work in London. He had decided that he wanted the Colt and would take it when he moved into married quarters near Oxford, as there was a range for practice. Michael kept the Colt handy, not that there was any threat, but just in case. And he remained especially mindful that, for the next few days, they were now looking after the next Queen of England.

Philip arrived just after 3 pm. He explained that it had all been a bit of a rush with everyone wanting to get home. His commander had let him go as he was aware of Philip's unique girlfriend, and that being the case, on Monday, Philip would return to the ship to finish with the decommissioning for the next few days.

Philip was a charmer, and Victoria could understand why Elizabeth was smitten with him. They left Philip's car behind the Hall and went back to the cottage in the Jeep. Back at the cottage, Michael was looking considerably fresher. Introductions were made, then Victoria announced that she and Michael would leave Philip and Elizabeth time to get to know one another again after such a long absence. They told them where everything was and would collect them later for a very informal dinner at the Hall that was arranged for 7pm.

Michael and Victoria fed the dogs, then took off to the annexe to collect the children. The children would stay at the Hall tonight with Lucy's daughter. Lucy and Johann would be attending dinner at the Hall. Michael and Victoria would go back to the cottage at first light. All the children were totally familiar and relaxed with the nomadic lifestyle between the Hall and the cottage, as they had their own space at each location. The dogs were in a similar migratory situation with Mbwa and Zulu at the Hall, but often staying with the four at the cottage and vice versa.

Just before 7 pm Michael collected the lovers from the cottage and drove back to the Hall. They both seemed very happy with one another, and Elizabeth clung to her man as an indication that she had finally got him, and she would not let him go.

They had dinner in the small dining room. Amrik had pulled all the stops out, and they shared a superb meal together. They had much to talk about, and Philip swiftly became at ease with Victoria who was running a very successful estate alongside two war heroes and another unsung war hero who had stood up to the Nazi regime and was now one of the two village doctors.

Philip was direct and outspoken, and Michael who was similarly minded, warmed to that approach. They discussed the wider political issues, and it was evident that Philip was saddened by the destruction of the navy, although he could understand the rationale behind that. It was just the suddenness and the lack of explanation to the loyal crews that he found most galling. His plans were to continue with his naval career, which evidently was the second love of his life.

Victoria and Lucy took it in turns to check on the children as the evening went on. Elizabeth was quite open in disclosing her personal ambitions as she felt she was amongst company where she could totally relax. She and Philip were going to marry come what may, and she outlined her mother's objections. Victoria explained how she and Michael had experienced the same thing years back, but assured both her and Philip that love would ultimately triumph, but they would probably have to keep things quiet for a while, whilst the establishment was able to come to terms with things and create a path for them that was acceptable.

Michael was keen to point out that no mention would be made of Philip's visit as the estate had a good relationship with the King and he would not wish to besmirch that. He mentioned that they had been invited to shoot with the King at Sandringham in a week's time. To all intents and purposes, the estate would remain neutral. Once the King had agreed in principle, then Spelthorpe would be a sheltered haven where they could meet before things became official. Both would be most welcome at any time. They appreciated that.

As the following day was a Saturday, they agreed on a late start. Victoria and Michael would surface at the cottage at 9am where they would take breakfast. At 10am Lucy would come up with Joanna and take Elizabeth for a couple of hours riding with the fitter dogs, and Michael would take Philip up to the airfield for a bit of shooting and flying. For the afternoon and evening, they would leave Philip and Elizabeth entirely on their own and they would cook a snack for themselves.

At 11pm, Michael took the couple back to the cottage and brought the four dogs back for a night at the Hall. He left the cats with a couple of pigeon breast filets, and they were more than happy with that.

On the following day, Lucy, Joanna and Elizabeth selected their horses and took off along the beach with four dogs. Joanna's other dog, Foxie, was heavily pregnant, so she stayed at home. Lucy was discreetly carrying the Colt pistol as a precaution. Victoria remained at the cottage with the children and Nimrod,

Kipling and Zulu who were no longer up for long treks. Elizabeth commented that the puppies at Sandringham that Shackleton had fathered were doing extremely well.

Michael took off with Philip in the jeep up to the airfield.

"I expect you could do with a rest," said Michael with a knowing grin.

"You can say that again," said Philip.

At the airfield there were a couple of clients doing the basics with the Tiger Moth and the Gipsy Moth. They were well wrapped up as it was quite cold. The Harvard was free.

Boynton was up at the shooting school and Michael introduced him.

"I've heard about you," said Philip. "Some people shoot pheasants and clays, but I hear you prefer bigger targets like Stukas."

Harry was up there too, and he was loading the trap. Philip had a go and shot quite well.

"I'm surprised he's got the energy," whispered Boynton to Michael. "The King told me how passionate she was about him so no doubt she's riding by day and night. I expect she will need a rest too, but I can remember what I was like at that age."

"Me too," said Michael. "It will draw you further than gun powder will blow you, but we must respect our future queen so we will have to keep that to ourselves. If the King knew we were helping the romance along, he might not be so happy, so when we go there next week, we'll just have to say that Lilibet spent a lot of time riding, and we will be telling the truth!"

Philip shot off about fifty clays, then Michael took him to the Harvard.

Philip was keen to fly but had never had a go himself.

Michael said," I'll take you up then you can have a go, but

we will keep it simple over the sea. Just a few turns, gentle dives and climbs so you get the feel of it, then if you want, I'll throw it about a bit to give you the idea of what you might be able to get up to when you have mastered the basics."

"Thank you. I'd like that," said Philip.

So up they went. Michael took it up then flew it down the valley winding in and out just above the tree line and out to sea and along the coast and performing a victory roll as they flew in sight of three ladies on horseback with a pack of dogs. He flew along to Sheringham, and on the way back over Blakeney Point, Philip took over. They did a few circuits at 1,000 feet for ten minutes then Michael took over and showed off taking the plane up to 5,000 feet, putting the aircraft in a spin and pulling out at 2,000 feet. That was followed by a couple of loops and a roll, and some stall turns. They buzzed the riders at a hundred feet, then flew up the valley and landed.

"I enjoyed that. I can understand why those Messerschmitts didn't stand a chance when you were about," said Philip.

"Well, I learnt here. An old First World War ace put me through it all before I joined the RAF, and that gave me a head start on the rest. He taught me how to survive, and that's something they didn't teach our new pilots. I passed it on to my chaps, and we lost very few compared to some of the other squadrons, but we shot a lot down. I'm eternally in his debt, and now we are teaching the others the same. We have a contract with the RAF, starting in the spring, to teach them the basics. It's not very often you come to a flying school with three aces as the instructors."

They stopped at the Boyntons on the way back. Michael introduced Philip to Aggie. They took sloe gin with them, then headed back to the cottage. Michael and Philip got on well because they both spoke plainly and that suited them both.

At the cottage, the ladies returned shortly after. They had met nobody on the ride but complained about two maniacs in an aeroplane trying to scare them. Michael fed the chickens and came in with two dozen eggs. He gave Joanna a dozen. They had a quick lunch of soup and the renowned Spelthorpe sausages with crusty rolls.

Victoria pointed out some choices for an evening meal to Elizabeth and told them they would come back in the morning for breakfast. Victoria lit them a fire. On Sunday they would have an evening meal in the Hall, to which the Boyntons were invited. With that they left Elizabeth and Philip to enjoy the tranquillity of the cottage overnight, and that's what they wanted to do.

On the following morning Michael and Victoria turned up at 9am with the dogs. Victoria prepared breakfast with the smoked salmon that Elizabeth had brought with her as a gift. It had come from the Balmoral estate. They had it with scrambled eggs and toast, and it went down extremely well.

Michael offered to take them out in the workboat for a spot of fishing in the afternoon if that was what they wanted. For Victoria and Michael, it would be church in the morning as usual. They left the jeep for Philip and Elizabeth and suggested they might want to visit the castle keep. Victoria handed over the key.

"It's not exactly Windsor, but it's the best we have, and you get splendid views over the whole estate from the top. We like to think of it as casting a spell on the visitors because many enduring relationships on the estate originated there, and I include ours in that, but we were much younger at the time."

"Sounds like a good idea," said Philip. "We'll give it a go and I'll take you up on the fishing. I'm not sure about Elizabeth. She might want to stay here with Victoria or take another horse ride. We'll decide when you are back from church."

Michael and Victoria walked to the church. The children were with Lucy at the Hall. The dogs stayed on guard at the cottage after Michael had fed them with some cooked egg, porridge and venison scraps. He recovered another dozen eggs from the chickens.

They returned at 1pm. Elizabeth was happy to stay with Victoria whilst the boys went fishing. They had rods and some chilled bait in a fridge at the boathouse. It only took ten minutes to get to the fishing area a mile offshore, where they fished the bottom for cod. They managed an hour and a half over the chosen spot and allowing the boat to drift as the current was very gentle. Michael had taken four bottles of beer, which went down well with tales of the navy and air force as they waited for bites.

Winter was normally good because the cod were in, and it paid off. They caught six cod between seven and twelve pounds each, which was good. Michael gutted and filleted them at sea which brought the gulls and the seals around the boat as they took a slow ride back with Phillip at the helm. In all, Michael estimated that they had about thirty-five to forty pounds of good fish because a lot of the weight of the cod is in the head. The seals were very happy. They stopped at three buoys on the way back and checked the lobster pots. Michael took out four good-sized lobsters and two crabs. He rebaited the pots with chunks of cod's head

By 4.30 pm, as it got dark, they were back at the cottage after they had dropped off half of the cod and all the shellfish at the Hall. The rest went in the freezer at the cottage.

Michael explained, "That's how we beat the rationing with the fish and the venison. We stick to the rules, but the country life and the sea does present us with certain advantages. A lot of the villagers fish here too. Nobody goes hungry."

"It's a bit like on the ship," said Philip. "Some of the lads would put out lines if we were going slow and steady. We would get some big tuna on occasions that would feed the entire ship's company – made a nice change!"

Elizabeth and Victoria had enjoyed a lazy afternoon in front of the log fire along with all the dogs.

At 7pm, they dined at the Hall and were joined by Boynton and Aggie, along with Lucy and Johann who lived in a comfortable suite at the end of the upstairs east wing.

Victoria had selected some white wine from the cellar.

Amrik and his team had worked miracles. There were no doubts as to the origin and freshness of the food. For starters they had crab soup followed by a half lobster each with a winter salad. The main course was cod fillet in a white wine sauce with seasonal vegetables.

On the following morning everyone was up quite early. Michael and Victoria turned up at the cottage and cooked a traditional egg and bacon breakfast for their guests.

Philip and Elizabeth went their separate ways after breakfast. Both were lavish in their praise for their welcome and the way they had been accommodated and entertained. Philip had to get back to his ship to finalise the decommissioning process before moving on to Wiltshire. Elizabeth would be returning to Windsor when January came to an end after the final shoot at Sandringham, where the Spelthorpe guests would be entertained, and her father would formally present the medals to Lucy, Ash and Boynton.

She would make no mention of Philip at Spelthorpe. He would be calling on her at Windsor in the months ahead. Philip's uncle had an estate in Hampshire that might serve their need to meet up.

She held Victoria's hand as she was assured that if they wanted to repeat the visit she only had to ask.

On the following Friday, Ash, Helen, Michael, Victoria, Lucy and the Boyntons headed over to Sandringham in response to the

King's invitation. Victoria decided to brief Ash and Helen about Philip's visit just to ensure nothing inadvertently slipped out. With Philip in Wiltshire and Elizabeth returning to Windsor, any contacts were more likely to be down south for the next few months. Philip had intimated that he would pop the question and ask the king in the summer, probably at Balmoral.

The day went well with Boynton loading for Ash, and Michael self-loading whilst Elizabeth, Victoria and Lucy went riding on the estate. The Queen was pleased to see Aggie. They got on well and it seemed that she valued Aggie's advice. The queen was worried about her daughter's relationship.

"I did so much want her to marry a suitable English candidate, but she's absolutely besotted with this Philip. He's not even English. He's a Greek and they have no money, and his sisters married Nazis. They have been writing to one another for years, and he came back to England the other day. She told us she's going to see him in Wiltshire."

"Do you mind if I speak frankly?" asked Aggie.

"Not at all. That's why I asked you. True friends can speak frankly," said the Queen.

Aggie responded, "Well, I see it like this. I've dealt with lots of girls at the school over the years, and I have seen the way they are when they get determined. The more you dig your heels in, the more determined they get and then it all goes wrong, and the family gets torn apart. In your position, you can't have that because the press is getting worse. The answer lies in damage limitation. Helen had the same issue with Victoria, and there was Joanna with a lightning romance of just two or three weeks, but it was dealt with by allowing them to do what they wanted but with conditions, and that way they all ended up on the same side.

"Lilibet will be twenty-one soon, so you wouldn't be able to stop it anyway. Let's look at the positive side. He may be Greek by birth, but so what? You only have to look at the house of Saxe-

Coburg -Gotha, your house, where any damage was limited in the middle of a horrific war by changing your name to Windsor.

"Look at Philip. He must be earnest to keep all those letters up. Men are not great letter writers. He's a handsome chap, so he looks right, and most important of all for the last few years he has risked his life for this country, and he has a good war record. I think we can ignore his sisters' choice of Nazi marriage partners in the same way as you have had to deal with your own brother-in-law, and I know that upsets you particularly when he and the American woman spent all that time with Hitler and his henchmen before the war. Philip can change his name to something more English. He can join the Church of England, and he can renounce those meaningless European titles, so if he does pop the question, you can agree but insist they keep it quiet until you have worked out the best way forward with the establishment. I know there are all these restrictions that apply, but you got through it in the past, and you will do it again. The most important thing is that you must be satisfied that they genuinely love each other, and with his war record, he looks a better bet than some pedigree aristocrat who has hidden away for the last six years. Honestly, I can't say any more than that."

"Thank you for that, Aggie. You analyse everything, and you are always so sensible. I'll have to talk this through with Bertie, so he is prepared if Philip asks. You have helped me a lot."

After the morning drives, they all had a good lunch that went on for a while, so there was just time for one more drive in the afternoon.

At the end of the day, in the main hall at Sandringham, the King formally presented the medals, first to Ash and Boynton, who stood side by side. Then he approached Lucy and presented her George Cross.

"Here is the recognition you deserve. The nation is indebted to you and indeed to your husband. There were many right-thinking, decent and courageous Germans, and at least we both know about one of them. Please extend to him my very best wishes."

They all returned to Spelthorpe. Although Christmas had been done and dusted, a final gift from Foxie arrived while they were at Sandringham. She had produced six puppies: three black and three fox red. As Joanna already had two dogs in their prime, she had no need for anymore. It would be six to eight weeks before they were ready to leave Foxie, but all had been snapped up quickly, and with six, nobody was disappointed.

7

Zorro

March-May 1946

Winter turned into spring at Spelthorpe.

The first lambs started to arrive at the end of February. Robert Roy had it all under control, but Ash was there to help out with the lambing when it started to get really busy as March progressed. Robert had increased the Romney Marsh flock down near the castle keep by another hundred. There was plenty of grazing there, and even with the extra sheep they were still way understocked, but it always paid to have some spare capacity in case of bad weather and poor grass growth.

Daniel and Angela were married in mid-March. Daniel's recovery was virtually total, and all that remained were the scars from the beatings on his back and the mental scars which would always be there but were at least now under control. He was now up to thirteen and a half stone and little of that was fat as the daily exercise in the forest had built him up. He was confident now, and in the absence of the foreman he would take the lead. He was taking City & Guilds qualifications in forestry, arboriculture and the maintenance of farm machinery, which sometimes meant he would be away at college for a week at a time. William, the chief engineer, had steered him in the right direction in those areas. The estate sponsored relevant professional examinations and courses for staff as it improved resilience across the business.

George and Emma got married in April. They managed to dodge the April showers. It was a delightful occasion, not least of all for Helen, who was happy that all three of her children were in stable relationships and careers. Michael flew them in the Dragon Rapide down to the Channel Islands for a five-day honeymoon. They moved into an officer's allocated house within the barracks estate near Oxford.

Emma had discovered that there was a good support system amongst the officers' wives. She had taken up a temporary job overseeing and managing the accounts for the Navy, Army and Air Force Institutes (NAAFI) facilities on the estate. The pay was reasonable, and it kept her occupied, especially when George was away in other parts of the country dealing with explosive finds. He ran one of the three teams that all came under a captain.

They had taken one of the puppies – a fox red bitch, Daisy, with them, as both could take it to work in and around the barracks.

In some ways, it had also been a sad time. Kipling, Nimrod and Zulu had passed on over the last two months and were now resting in the wood on the edge of the dunes with the other dogs. The memorial stone plaque had been updated. They had all made it to the age of sixteen, which was a good age for a labrador. Helen's Siamese cat Simba Jike had also passed on having achieved the age of twenty. She too, was buried with the dogs. The other dogs were now allocated. Helen took a black dog which she called Masai. Boynton took a black dog to keep Hund company. He named him Thor. Jennifer took a fox red bitch called Bella who lived with them in the annexe and would eventually go to work with William on a daily basis. Michael took a fox red dog called Mitch, named after the designer of the Spitfire and a black dog called Mossie, named after the Mosquito.

Ash and Helen took up residence in the cottage with two dogs and Michael and Victoria moved into the very roomy Hall, where they lived with Lucy and Johann with four dogs. In reality, all six dogs remained nomadic between the two locations. Ash and Michael took it upon themselves to train up the new members of the pack over the summer so they would be ready to ease their way into work when the autumn shooting season began. In the meantime, they would have a lot of swimming to do in the two lakes and the sea.

Boynton was up at his cottage on a late May morning. He was loading up the truck with grain to take to the pens where the chicks were growing rapidly. Constable Dave Carter turned up on his bicycle. He would call once a week to take tea and to keep up to speed regarding any issues in the local area, as Boynton always knew what was going on. Over the years they had built up a level of trust. Things got dealt with, and Dave Carter knew when it was best to turn a blind eye.

"Hello, Dave," said Boynton. "How's things?"

They walked inside and Boynton put the kettle on. Aggie was working at the school.

"We've got a bit of a problem. We have got some dog thieves, and these are right bastards. They are nicking dogs from back gardens or where the dog has a collar with an owner's details. Then they put a note through the door saying '£100 or we kill the dog', and they ask for a phone number!" said PC Carter. "I've come up to warn you and the rest of the estate."

"Well thanks for that, but what about catching these buggers. Are people paying up? Do they get the dogs back?" asked Boynton.

"So far, yes, but that's the ones we know about. They are frightened because they tell them that if they suspect the police are involved, the dog dies. They have to put the first message reply and the money in a place that can be overlooked from a distance, so that makes it difficult for us because of the risk of getting spotted. We haven't got radios or enough people. It's always the towns that are getting the police attention and they are overrun with crime because of all the black-market gangs, and it's getting nasty, so a few dogs are never going to be a priority. The bad thing is that when they get the dogs back, they haven't been fed, and one died of kidney failure because it had no water."

"Where's it happening?" asked Boynton.

"It started over Cromer way. We had a couple there, and it was just fifty pounds they wanted but then they came to around Sheringham. We have had four there all for £100, and they paid up and got the dogs back but as I said, one died. The latest is closer to here, at Stiffkey, and they are asking £200, so that is seven altogether. It's mainly gun dogs, spaniels and lap dogs that are unlikely to be aggressive towards them. The owners are devastated, and they pay. With two, they broke into the houses and took stuff as well as the dog," said the constable.

" I can understand how they must feel," said Boynton. "This sort of thing is beyond evil as far as I'm concerned, and a lot of others too. It's like stealing a child, and for some, that's all they have."

Boynton poured out the tea and slid the biscuit barrel across the table.

"It looks to me that you are after a bit of help. I'll see what I can do, but usual conditions apply. You know what I mean. Ask no questions. All I want from you is the key details of the crime reports: names, addresses, dog breeds, timings and so on. I won't speak to any of them, but I need to build up a picture. Will you do that?"

"I'll get that to you this afternoon, and that's between us," said Dave Carter.

That evening Boynton asked Michael and Lucy to call at the cottage.

Boynton regarded them as part of the original Spelthorpe Company in the sense that they had all killed in war. Their experiences in the war had taught them that sometimes things have to be done outside of established rules in order to get a result. It was he who had trained them up with their father's blessing in what some would regard as the 'Dark Arts'. Ash was still a member of that group along with Julian, but Julian was starting to show his age, and he felt it best that Ash was kept out of it given his elevated position as a knight of the realm, husband of the dowager countess and chair of the local magistrates. Boynton explained in some detail what had transpired in his conversation with PC Carter, and he was looking for inspiration and ideas. They went through the information gleaned from the crime reports.

Lucy said, "It looks like they are targeting those who are wealthy and those who live alone because they see them as vulnerable and more likely to pay."

Michael was silent, but like his father he was a deep thinker and was always several moves ahead. After a couple of minutes, he spoke.

"These people are getting overconfident and greedy, and when they get greedy, they make mistakes. All they will see is the money, so we need to put temptation their way with a nice juicy easy target. That would be someone who is rich and on their own. My plan is this. The estate is intent on buying another 500 acres of land to the south of us, beyond, but continuous to our southern boundary. There are about a hundred acres of woodland and the rest is good arable land, which is perfect for cereals and sugar beet, but it includes two cottages one of which is in a very good state of repair. It's down the lane that goes to Fakenham, and that is directly opposite our southern gatehouse. It's about 500 yards down on the left. I have a key, which the agent has lent me because I don't think anyone else is after it and they want a sale.

"We will create a fictitious person who lives in the cottage. She will be wealthy. She has a dog which she leaves there every Wednesday morning when she goes to see her stockbroker in Norwich. Her husband is working overseas. All we do is to put this story out in the local pubs, the rough ones. We will go in for a drink as couples. I'm sure Aggie is up to it. We each take a dog saying we have heard of the thefts, and we won't let the dog out of our sight, and we talk about this silly woman who is dripping in money but just leaves her dog behind every Wednesday morning. We have got five days before next Wednesday. We will leave a car on the drive on Tuesday night without the rotor arm. We will all sneak in via the back and Lucy will leave in the car at 8.30 am leaving Boynton and me behind to deal with the thieves and that's where you come in, Boynton, for the next part. That will be getting the truth out of them and recovering the dogs and any money. What do you think?"

"Sounds pretty good to me. You always were a bit of a smart arse, Michael. It's a plan, and it might well work. Like you said, they are getting greedy, and this will be too good to ignore. Might be worthwhile if Lucy has a dark wig, a headscarf and some sunglasses. I can supply the other items," said Boynton. "You don't need to worry about that, and I've got somewhere safe to put them, and in the meantime, can you perfect your Irish accents?"

"How will you get the truth out of them?" asked Lucy.

"Don't worry about that, darling. Just a slight variation on a trick I learnt with the Black and Tans. They will talk!" said Boynton.

Lucy was looking forward to it. Peace time was fine, but she realised that after her time undercover and living on the edge, she was still addicted to her own adrenaline, and she needed something to satisfy that need.

And so, for the next three nights the four of them did the rough pubs all the way to Cromer. Boynton and Aggie took Hund with them, and Michael and Lucy took Shackleton.

They played it cool by not saying too much but making sure anyone who looked a bit dodgy was in earshot when they spoke of the rich, silly lady from Swallow Cottage who always went out on a Wednesday morning, leaving her spaniel behind. Having a good-looking dog in a pub was always a magnet to get strangers to talk, so the dogs were just made out as family pets. One or two suggested that the dogs might make good gun dogs, and it was quite amusing to listen to some of the drivel that came out from the dog 'experts' they encountered.

Victoria and Johann were curious particularly when they were told that what they were engaged in was on a need-to-know basis but were reassured that it was Michael and Lucy working together with Boynton and Aggie, but they did agree to let them in on it if they got a successful result.

On Tuesday night, Boynton drove a car up to Swallow Cottage and parked it on the driveway. He took out the rotor arm and then walked home.

At 5am, he returned with Michael and Lucy in an old truck with a tarpaulin over the load area. They parked the truck on the driveway of the other cottage, which was a hundred yards further down the road, then walked down to the cottage which they entered via the back door. Boynton carried a holdall. Lucy walked out the front door and replaced the rotor arm then came back in. She tied up her blonde hair and put on the dark wig over the top, a headscarf and the sunglasses. It was just about to get light. They waited upstairs with the lights off watching through a gap in the curtains that were drawn. About 8am a car went slowly past. They turned and came back and parked up on the edge of the lane about fifty yards away. There were two male occupants.

At 08.30am, Lucy went out through the front door, got in the car and drove off, taking it back to Boynton's cottage. Boynton handed Michael a loaded Mauser pistol and kept one for himself with the silencer fitted. He got out two black hoods with eye slits and two sets of handcuffs. Assuming they would break in by the back door Boynton hid in the pantry and Michael went into the living room. Ten minutes later, they heard voices by the back door. A pane of glass was smashed and a hand reached through to turn the key on the inside to gain entry. They heard a voice.

"I wonder where she keeps the dog. I bet it's upstairs."

With that they walked towards the hall.

Michael emerged with the pistol drawn. "Stop right there or you will get this!" They turned to run to see Boynton hooded up blocking their exit. He put a shot in the floor just in front of the first man.

"Get on the floor. The next shot will be the to the head!"

The men froze.

"Get down now. I won't say that again. Face down. Now!" The men dropped to the floor. They were in their thirties and looked facially quite similar. "Hands behind your backs. Any movement and I fire."

Michael came forward and applied the handcuffs, so both were handcuffed with their hands behind their backs. He removed their shoes, socks and trousers, then he hooded both and tied the hoods with drawstrings sufficiently tight to stop the hoods coming off but loose enough for them to breathe.

"Stay as you are. Do not say a word. Do not move!" said Boynton in a strong Northern Irish accent.

Michael went out and came back five minutes later having retrieved the truck that he backed onto the drive. He came back in and lifted them by the collars to a standing position.

Boynton barked out the orders, "Do exactly as we say or else. And you won't be the first. Your lives will depend on what you tell us." Clearly, they were in fear. Tell-tell signs indicated that one had shit himself. They led them out and forced them, one at a time, into the back of the truck, where they told them to lie down. Michael stayed in the back. Boynton drove back onto the estate and onto a track that led deep into the woods. After a couple of miles. He parked up. They pulled the men out, then walked them for 150 yards on a winding path. Boynton went ahead and lifted a camouflaged trap door on the edge of a bramble patch. There were stairs going down about twenty feet with a locked steel door at the bottom. Boynton went down and undid the door. He went inside where he lit a hurricane lamp.

He came back up and they walked the prisoners down. The room was about fifteen feet square with a locked steel door leading off it. The prisoners were sat on a small bench. Michael took of the hoods.

"Where are we?" asked the older looking man.

"Let's get this right from the start. I ask the questions. You answer. And if you don't, then you suffer the consequences, which matter not to us. You will just disappear!" said Boynton.

They told Boynton their names. They were brothers. They admitted taking the dogs but would not say where the dogs were being kept.

Bonyton said, "It looks like I am going to have to give you boys a lesson."

And with that he took out a metallic pencil-like object out of his pocket.

"Do you know what this is?"

They didn't know.

"This," he said, "is a timing pencil with a detonator. When I snap it, there is a chemical reaction inside and after two minutes, it goes off. It won't kill you, but you will suffer excruciating pain because I am going to stick it in your underpants right under your bollocks." Boynton took out an apple from his pocket. He snapped the pencil and put it on the bench beside the prisoners with the apple on top. They watched and waited, then suddenly there was a deafening explosion. The apple had ceased to exist, but they were both covered in bits of apple and juice.

"Who is first?" asked Boynton, as he took out another timing pencil.

"Alright we will tell you?" said the older brother. He gave them an address on the outskirts of Sheringham. It was on a short-term three-month rental. He said there were three dogs in the shed. He didn't want to say because his wife was at the property. There were no children. When asked about the money, he said it was under the bookcase. There was about £400. "Who looks after the dogs?" asked Michael.

"The wife does all that. We just nick them and get the money," said the older man.

Boynton said, "When we have the dogs safe, we will let you go. But just to make to make sure you don't move around too much; I have my little friend here who I call Himmler." Boynton went to a cloth bag in the corner and emptied a large adder onto the floor. Michael tied the black hoods back on the two men.

"Who are you?" asked one of the hooded men.

"My name is Zorro," said Boynton.

Boynton and Michael left them in complete darkness and locked the steel door. They walked back to the truck.

"I knew I would find a use for those secret bunkers. We dug them out in 1940, and I've got loads of those pencils – all supposed to be top secret so we could take on the Hun after the invasion, so it's only you, me and the two underkeepers that know about them and they are sworn to secrecy too," said Boynton.

They went back to Boynton's cottage where they met up with

Lucy. They told her the outcome and now it would be her who would lead on dealing with the wife and recovering the dogs and the money. The cottage was in an isolated spot two miles inland from Sheringham. First, they went back to Swallow Cottage, where they tidied up and got rid of the trousers and shoes. They put a board over the broken windowpane. Michael took the offender's car and Boynton and Lucy followed in the truck.

After five miles, Michael drove onto an old abandoned industrial site. The car had half a tank of petrol. Boynton dropped a five-minute timing pencil into the tank, and they took off. They heard an explosion as they headed along to Sheringham. Twenty minutes later, they found the cottage. Boynton stayed in the truck. Lucy and Michael skirted around. There was nobody about. Lucy had the Mauser and silencer. She wore the wig, headscarf and sunglasses and knocked on the door. A woman came to the door. She was in her mid-thirties, somewhat overweight and had a cigarette dangling from her lip.

"I've come to see Charlie and Keith," said Lucy.

"Well, they are out at work. Won't be back till tonight."

At this, Lucy punched the woman hard, sending her sprawling backwards into the hall. Her nose was broken. Lucy stood over her with the Mauser.

"We have them both. If you want to see them alive you will answer me straight away. I'm in no mood for you to mess me around. Where are the dogs?"

"They are in the shed," said the woman. Lucy pushed the woman back into the downstairs toilet.

"And the money?"

"I don't know about that."

Lucy fired a shot that shattered the toilet cistern.

The woman screamed. "Alright. It's under the bookcase."

"Get it. All of it. I want £400. Any less and you cop it."

The woman went into the lounge, moved the bookcase and handed over a large wad of five-pound notes. Lucy directed her back to the toilet.

"Stay here. If you move, you know what will happen!"

Lucy went to the front door and opened it. She saw Michael with two spaniels and a whippet on leads. He gave her the thumbs up.

Lucy went back into the hall. She noticed the phone which she ripped out of the wall. Then she went back to the toilet. The woman was sitting there in tears. She was terrified. Lucy spoke very softly but with her practised Irish accent.

"You stay here. You do not go out. You killed one of those dogs. You gave it no water. It would please me to kill you. I will be watching you. If I see you with a dog, I will kill you. That is not a threat. That is a promise. If I see your husband or his brother with a dog, I will kill you. If you talk to the police, I will be back. You will move away from Norfolk. I will be watching you and I will come for you at any time, day or night. Do you understand?"

The woman was shaking visibly. She sobbed, "I'm sorry. I'm very, very sorry."

Lucy turned and walked out. She turned and walked down the lane. A few moments later Boynton passed her and stopped. They drove straight back to Spelthorpe and were back at Boynton's cottage in twenty-five minutes, where they watered and fed the dogs. Lucy counted the money. There was £550 in total. They took tea together and Lucy described what had taken place. She confessed that she wanted to kneecap her because of the dead dog, but that would have involved hospitalisation and the police, so a broken nose was better than nothing. She handed Boynton the gloves she had worn, and they went on the fire. Michael and Boynton decided they would let the two men stew until it was dark.

At 8am the following morning a crowd had gathered around a lamp post on the main road through Sheringham. There were two men completely naked and tied back-to-back around the post to which there was a large piece of cardboard attached with the words 'Dog Thieves', and after that there was a large letter 'Z'. The police attended and took the men away. Six addresses had been visited in the night, and envelopes marked with typed words reading 'Dog Money' had been put through letterboxes.

Joanna went to open the veterinary surgery at 8.30 am and discovered three dogs tied up outside. They appeared in good health. She called PC Carter as the police were responsible for dealing with lost and found dogs. When she said she had two spaniels and a whippet he realised that these had been taken in the last three days. He collected the dogs and placed them in the kennel, which he had at the back of his police office.

The two men were still shaking in terror several hours later. They fully admitted what they had done in respect of the dog stealing and made statements under caution that were sufficient to charge them with offences of theft and demanding with menaces. The wife refused to talk to the police. The rest of their story remained incredulous, about how they were taken by two Irishmen, one of whom was called Zorro, and a snake called Himmler.

A week later PC Carter called on Boynton. They took tea together. He mentioned that they had caught the dog thieves. He asked if he knew an Irishman called Zorro. "'fraid not," said Boynton. "The only Zorro I know was the one at the cinema, but I think he was Mexican!"

Carter grinned and simply said, "Well, if you come across him, please give him our thanks."

"I'll do that," said Boynton and the subject was never mentioned again.

Michael and Lucy went back to being themselves. They gathered with Victoria and Johann when Boynton told them the police had caught the dog thieves. They went for a swim in the lake with the dogs and the two elder children, who were totally aquatic. Even young Mattie at eighteen months was fast heading in that direction. They ate together at the cottage and told the tale of Zorro.

Victoria and Johann understood the need for secrecy and were delighted that the dogs of Spelthorpe were safe. They chose not to tell Ash and Helen although when the news got out Ash commented to Michael, "I don't know who this bloke Zorro and his friends are, but they've done a bloody good job there and I know the king and queen are delighted."

"You never know," said Michael, "they might be closer than you think!" and he left it at that.

Ash remembered several years back when an Irishman had dealt with the sheep killers, and he smiled.

In three months' time the dog thieves would appear at Norfolk Assizes and plead guilty to all offences. Each would receive five years imprisonment with hard labour. The judge would be a dog owner.

Following the press reports, Zorro became a North Norfolk hero. The local cinemas put the film on again to packed audiences.

8

Return to Pegasus

June 1946

On Wednesday 5th of June, Ash, Michael, Victoria, Lucy and Johann met up at the airfield at 6am. Lucy had made all the bookings and had spoken to the airfield at Carpiquet, near Caen to get permission to land and secure fuel. She had also arranged to hire a car and for overnight accommodation. On this day they were going back to Normandy to see the grandparents, and to satisfy a curiosity relating to the changes that had taken place since liberation, coupled with a desire to face up to the memories that still haunted them. Helen had agreed to remain and would look after the pack of dogs and the children, although the dogs seemed to look after the children for much of the time and they had included them as part of the pack.

They took off in the Dragon Rapide at 6.15am. Although they were on the plane, Michael had no need of charts as he knew the whole area so well, he could have flown it in his sleep. The weather was good with summertime fluffy cumulus clouds at 2,000 feet. He flew below them to afford the best view. He flew at cruising speed to save fuel, and in an hour and a half, they landed with just over half a tank remaining. Michael put in twenty gallons for the return. With Michael and Lucy's fluent French, the French authorities didn't bother with the formalities. That was good, as it saved Michael from having to say that they never asked on the last occasion when he landed nearby. They took possession of a Citroen five-seat saloon, which they had hired for the next two days.

The first stop was at the grandparents' house in Ranville. They were overjoyed to see them all after such a long time, and they were all invited to stay for lunch. Lucy and Johann excused themselves and said they would be back before lunch. They drove down to the Café Gondrée and met up with Georges and his wife. They both hugged Lucy, whom they almost saw as a long-lost daughter. The café was doing well as the booming heart of a war tourism industry. The bridge had been renamed Pegasus Bridge after the emblem of the airborne soldiers. The café had the fame of being the first house to be liberated in France. Lucy introduced her husband to them explaining how he had saved her life from the SS men and how they had worked together to gather information and send it on. The lady with the dog was still coming to the café, and Lucy explained they were going to find her. They had a bit of catching up to do and were invited to stay a lot longer, but they explained they were with the family and had so much to do.

The next stop was a house in the rue du Val about half a mile away in Benouville. A lady came to the door and looked like she had seen an apparition. After a few seconds of stunned disbelief, she said, "Lyla".

She hugged Lucy. It was as if all the pressure that had built up over the years was released and there were floods of tears as the two women who had risked all were reunited. They were invited in. She gave them a coffee and a brandy. Over the next hour, they went through it all from each other's perspectives and the gaps were filled. In the war, neither knew any more than the absolute minimum because they operated in a cell structure to minimise damage to the network in the event of arrest and torture. She still had the radio set, which she had used to send Lucy's encrypted messages about which she had no knowledge other than it was vital. She found out after the war that others in the network had been taken by the Nazis and had just disappeared, but she was thrilled to hear how Lucy and Johann had dealt with the SS men, whom she hated. After an hour they left, and Lucy gave her full details and told her that if she ever came to England, she could always stay a few days at Spelthorpe.

Lucy and Johann got back to the house where the others had passed on the news. Lucy's grandfather described the situation. The house had suffered no damage despite all the bombing which was more than could be said about Caen. The RAF had flattened it resulting in hundreds of French deaths, and that sadly was the story all over Normandy with the battles that raged in the two months before the eventual breakout. Despite all that, the French had largely forgiven the Allies. As far as they were concerned it was all the fault of the dreaded 'Boche' whom they hated. The Allies had been heralded as saviours with many roads renamed after Allied Generals and leaders, with one nearby village now named Colleville-Montgomery after the British general. There were still shortages all over France and the épuration or 'cleansing' continued. Some collaborators had been rightly shot, but the way that some of the women had been treated was a blot on the French nation. For fraternisation and what was often called 'horizontal collaboration' carried out by women desperate to survive and feed their children, the women were stripped, beaten and had their heads shaved. At the same time, hundreds who had traded and made profits from the Germans evaded any penalty. There were others in the south who had helped round up the Jews for deportation, and some of these were now working for the new French government. There were lots of skeletons in the French cupboard, and these would take many years to come out – if at all.

There were other complaints against American soldiers who treated the whole thing as a conquest rather than a liberation. Some women had been raped. Others had claimed rape after excessive familiarisation with the Yanks when French husbands found out. It was messy and often unjust. The Americans had shot some of their own, and most of those had been black soldiers.

Trials had been very rapid with little thorough investigation. Work was ongoing to build the cemeteries and to clear up the debris, but at least it was now taking place, and progress was being made.

They stayed until 3 pm. It had been a short visit after so long, but at least they had made it, and the grandparents indicated they would come to Spelthorpe later in the year as the situation improved. Michael could always come and pick them up. Before they left Ash handed over three pounds of bacon, three pounds of sausages, a dozen eggs, and two pounds of tea, all of which Ash knew to be in short supply. It might remind them of some of the better aspects of home.

They took off after first visiting the Ranville cemetery, where so many of the paratroopers had landed and fought. There was a sixteen-year-old youth who had served as a paratrooper and in the churchyard the grave of Lieutenant Brotheridge, who led the charge to capture Pegasus Bridge. They drove along the coast road for the next twenty miles passing Sword Beach where the

British landed, then Juno Beach where the Canadians had a hard time, and finally Gold Beach which had been stormed by the British. All the way along they saw the debris of the landings with knocked-out tanks and landing craft. There were smashed-up bunkers and craters, but the road was in reasonable condition. At the end of Gold Beach they drove on another four miles until they arrived at Arromanches-les-Bains – a village nestling at the foot of the cliff that had escaped a lot of the damage because it wasn't a landing beach on D-Day, but it was the place where they built a massive harbour – as big as the one at Dover. It had been towed across the channel in sections to be sunk in situ and was built in just four days. Much of the harbour was still there although the weather and storms had taken their toll, and what was left of it stretched out in a massive semi-circle in bits partially absorbed by the shifting sands. The harbour had kept the invasion supplied for months after the landings.

Their hotel was in Arromanches. It was indeed a pleasant place to stop and to walk along the seafront and up to the cliff top on the eastern side to get a good overall view of the remains of the harbour. They took an evening meal there which proved that the French had not lost their gastronomic skills. They had fish soup, coquille St Jacques (scallop in shell covered in a creamy sauce and cheese served in a shell) and mussels with frites as a main course. The following day would be the second anniversary of the landings.

The next day was a little hard, but both Lucy and Johann wanted to come to terms with their past. They drove on for five miles to Longues-sur-mer. The battery was still there with the guns intact. Then they went down the track where Lucy was assaulted and where they had pushed the car with the dead SS man down and over the cliff.

Then they drove back to the farmyard with the well where they had deposited the other SS soldier's body. It was deserted, and the well had not changed. Lucy and Johann held each other at these spots. They had confronted their past and put the ghosts to rest.

On a happier note, they drove inland where they encountered knocked-out German tanks on the way to Bayeux where happy memories came back of the hotel opposite the cathedral where Lucy and Johann had been together. They walked around the cathedral and saw the massive war cemetery under construction. Then they saw the Bayeux Tapestry that had now been returned. The Germans had held it in the Louvre in Paris but had forgotten to remove it when Paris was taken. The French sometimes refer to it as the Tapisserie de la Reine Mathilde. She was the wife of William the Conqueror, who apparently commissioned the tapestry to be made. The final irony was that here they were a few yards from the place where their daughter, Matilda was conceived and at the time they had absolutely no idea. With hindsight, the name now had a more special meaning.

They took a simple lunch at the hotel, then drove on for a quick look at Omaha Beach, which had been the bloodiest on the day. Looking at the cliffs and the bunkers – many still intact, one could understand the difficulties for the Americans. The debris of war still littered the landscape. At the top of the cliff, a massive cemetery was under construction.

They drove back to the airport at Carpiquet where they handed back the car. Ash managed to purchase six bottles of the beloved Calvados and four cases of wine, knowing that there would not be customs officers waiting at Spelthorpe. In less than two hours they were back in England. On the way back, leaving nothing to chance, Michael flew back Mosquito style below the radar for the run across the Channel.

The day had been a revelation to all and, in some ways long overdue. Just to make sure they were home Michael, Victoria, Lucy and Johann took off down to the lake for a swim 'au naturel' with the dogs as the sun went down. France would always be dear to them, but it was good to be home again.

9

Oxford days

June-August 1946

Later in June, Victoria got a sudden phone call. It was Lilibet ringing from Balmoral. Her voice was rushed with excitement.

"We've done it! Philip popped the question to Daddy, and he's agreed, so we will get married. Isn't that exciting?"

"Congratulations to you both from us all," said Victoria. "But is that public?"

"Well, no, not yet. There will be conditions as we expected. We have to keep it secret until I am twenty-one. Between then and now, Philip will change his name to Philip Mountbatten – that's his uncle's name. We have met up there a few times. He must forget his Greek and Danish titles, and he has to join the Church of England but none of that is difficult. I asked Daddy if I could bring Philip to Spelthorpe and providing it is very discreet, it won't be a problem. Daddy knows how careful you are and how you look after us."

"We look forward to that," said Victoria. "You can stay at the Hall with Michael, me, Lucy, Johann and the children. We have plenty of rooms, so officially you can have a room each if you know what I mean, but all the beds are big, and our butler, Amrik, is very discreet. We have had to move out of the cottage now that Michael and I are running the place. Mummy and Ash are there now. We are both jealous of them, but when we are old, we might move back there. You will be able to come and swim in the lake with us. We do that a lot in the summer and the dogs all come in too. I shouldn't say this, but most of the time, we don't wear anything, but we will have to when you are here. You can never be sure with all those newspaper men about."

"That will be wonderful," said Elizabeth. "Philip really enjoyed his time with you, and he gets on with Michael. I expect we will see more of you anyway when the shooting season starts because Daddy is keen to get Philip involved with all that, so he comes across as an English gentleman, not that he isn't already. At least Mummy has stopped calling him 'The Hun'. We should be able to get down to you between now and September and more in the winter, when we are at Sandringham."

Meanwhile George and Emma had settled in at their married quarters near Oxford following their April wedding. As an officer, he got a detached four-bedroomed house with a nice garden for entertaining. Emma had got used to being an officer's lady and she always looked the part because Victoria had given her a couple of evening dresses and some costume jewellery. It was part of what Helen had been assembling for Victoria's coming out as a debutante that never materialised. The subject of debutantes had come up at the time of Philip and Elizabeth's visit. Philip shared Victoria's view saying it was 'bloody daft' and was becoming a parade for 'every London tart'.

George was expected to attend 'mess nights' in his regimental dress, to which, on occasions ladies attended. There were also male-only nights which sometimes ended in cabbage rugby, piggyback jousting and various other activities whilst under the influence of alcohol. Officers right up to the colonel would participate. Invariably, on the following day, the dress uniform had to go off to the dry cleaners.

They worked hard and played hard and needed to let off steam because, despite the high level of practical knowledge that George and the others had gained from attending and dealing with bombs, it was always an emotional strain with the constant worry that it might not go well.

George was often away for one or two days at a time, but Emma felt comfortable. She had her part time work in accounts and their fox red bitch, Daisy, was her constant companion. With German and British munitions, there was rarely a knowledge problem, but that knowledge had come at a huge cost in the war as the Germans booby trapped the fuses and much of the knowledge came about through trial and error. Errors cost lives. It was rare to come across anything unknown. The early bombs just needed the fuse removed but others needed the application of a big magnet to stop the internal clock from working. These bombs were not intended to explode on impact but hours later to maximise disruption. With others, the fuse had to be frozen with liquid oxygen to stop a battery from working or a hardening chemical was injected. Where the fuse could not be removed safely, they had to drill into the casing and steam out all the explosives.

George was the nominated deputy to the captain in charge of the squadron, which was split into a number of sections, each with a lieutenant or subaltern in charge. Under the officer on each section there was a sergeant and then between six and ten corporals and privates. They would do all the preparatory digging and removal once the officer had made the bomb safe.

George had managed to retain his naval chief petty officer who was on attachment. He had two corporals and four privates in his section. They had an unpleasant job on occasions because bombs would tunnel their way deep underground. Bombs never fell vertically because on release from the aircraft, they were still travelling at the speed of the plane. Sometimes they ended up working in houses, in cellars and in sewers, along railway lines and on bomb sites covered in debris. Quite often, they had to deal with quite small butterfly bombs scattered over a large area. They dealt with a few around Ipswich. Some went off on impact, but most were delayed action and could be detonated by farm animals, walkers and curious children who came into contact with them. Periodically they had trips to the coast to deal with land mines that had been placed in 1940 to deal with the threat of invasion. Most of these had been cleared but there were always some that were missed in the clear-up.

George enjoyed his work. It was a challenge and became addictive, but he did feel for Emma, who worried about him. He was always mindful of what Boynton had told him. Survival was the priority, and knowledge was the key to that. From time-to-time, George would meet up with some of the boffins who had worked with bomb disposal Royal Engineers throughout the Blitz to work out ways of defusing the bombs where the Germans had installed booby trap mechanisms. These people used to come and lecture the officers, like George, who had to deal first-hand with the bombs. George found this valuable and would question them in detail to build up his knowledge. They too, valued having an officer who showed so much interest. It was useful to them to deal with somebody who was applying their expertise in a practical way, and they would invite him to their offices and laboratories. George's captain supported him in this because he shared the same view that the more knowledge they had, the greater would be their prospects for survival. The captain had worked through the Blitz. He had seen so many of his colleagues blown to pieces for taking chances and shortcuts.

What concerned George most of all was the future. In the aftermath of the war, people from all the old European empires were seeking their independence. The British army found itself stuck in the middle whilst efforts were made to reach a settlement, but there were always the hotheads who would resort to violent means to get what they wanted. India was a worry and Malaya too, and the French were under pressure in Indochina, but the most imminent threat came from Palestine where things were hotting up. In the main, it was shootings, but in some areas, they were resorting to homemade devices, and these were problematic because each one was different. Some were simple, but others featured timers and anti-handling devices. The simple ones often just involved a detonator or a fuse that might be activated electrically or by lighting the fuse. Others could be activated by clocks, trip wires, pressure mats or mercury tilt switches. These switches were small, with two wires in a tube with a drop of mercury. When the tube was moved, the mercury would allow to circuit to be completed and then, bang! George collected examples of these trigger mechanisms to keep his soldiers up to date.

The easiest and safest way to deal with homemade devices was to visually assess, create a cordon at a safe distance and wait. But this was not always possible or desirable, particularly where there was a lot of explosives that could have a devastating effect on infrastructure like electrical substations, pipelines and water works. George and the boffins had been working on several devices to disrupt timers and switches- the theory being that if you blew the mechanism apart before it had time to react then it would not be able to set off the large explosive. They had experimented with shotguns on tripods that would fire a conventional cartridge with bird shot or a water charge. This often worked but the dangerous bit was setting up the tripod because if the bomb was on a timer, it could go off. What they really needed was a small, tracked vehicle like a mini tank with a disrupter gun that could be controlled from a safe distance, and they were working on that.

The only thing in their favour was that most bombs were set off in the night by lighting a fuse or by an electrical charge or a timing pencil, but quite a few of those devices were in the wrong hands.

On days off George and Emma would explore the countryside, taking Daisy with them. They loved the Thames with walks along the river and visits to glorious pubs that reflected everything that was good about England. They would sit with their drinks in the dappled shade of the willows, watching as the swans glided up and down. Every now and again there was a burst of iridescent blue zigzagging at speed up the river from a kingfisher. There was the activity at the locks and the amusement at some of the novice boat handlers as they crashed into the beautifully kept and polished wooden launches some of which were steam powered. The indignant reaction of the owners was predictable. These boats often came with a navigator who was invariably a pipe smoker with a naval cap and beard and for some reason they always seemed to be accompanied by a bevy of beautiful ladies in very low-cut summer dresses. George was the victim of his own sexuality and had to avert his gaze in case Emma caught him taking too much pleasure in this form of river scenery. In the end, he took to wearing sunglasses.

As May turned into June, they took to swimming with Daisy in the river, and they had their favourite spots. At Clifton Hampden there was a wide bridge with several arches and below that the river was wide and shallow. There, one could walk across.

Below Goring it was hilly on one side, but the water was deeper and slow-moving. Visually, it was stimulating and after the swim they would walk across the meadows to the old St Bartholomew Church and to the grave of Jethro Tull, the pioneering inventor of the seed drill and father of the agricultural revolution, who was laid to rest there in 1741. It was different from Norfolk and about as far from the coast as one could get, but it was every bit as enchanting in its own way. The river was the source of that enchantment.

But the stability they had established in their first few months of marriage was not to last. England was at peace but not the rest of the world. On July the twenty-second, there was a massive explosion at the King David Hotel in Jerusalem. It came after a small device was set off outside. People had gathered outside, and then the main blast took place demolishing much of the building that was the administrative headquarters of the of the British authorities who governed Palestine under an international mandate. Jewish terrorists had placed the bomb in the basement. They had disguised themselves as Arab workers and waiters. There were ninety-one deaths and many more wounded, most of whom were hotel and administrative staff.

Orders came down. George's squadron was to go to Palestine for a six-month tour starting on the twelfth of August. Wives and families would not be going with their husbands. George's section was granted five days' leave prior to departure. George always knew something like this was on the cards, but that was what he had signed up for. Emma knew too, but it did not stop the floods of tears when he broke the news. Emma knew exactly what she would do whilst George was away. On the one hand she could stay, and those around her in the same boat would offer their support. The alternative was to go back to Spelthorpe for the duration, where she could work and would be surrounded by those she loved. It wasn't a hard choice. On the evening before his five-day leave, George turned off the utilities. They packed the car and took off for the four-hour journey to Norfolk.

They arrived at the Hall just after 10pm. Victoria and Michael were both still up. George had travelled in uniform. They broke the news. Victoria and Michael were pleased that they had made the right decision. Emma would work in the office and take her sister under her wing and there was a possibility of day release to college at King's Lynn and home study to gain the next level in her accounting training and examinations. She would reside at the Hall in George's room, which had full facilities. Daisy was delighted to meet up with her brothers Mitch and Mossie.

For the next few days, they would make the most of their time together and with their extended family. They went swimming in the sea and the lake, riding on the beach and in the woods and they helped out with the hay making and the start of the harvest when all hands were required.

George spent some extra time with Boynton, who had spent a couple of years with Lawrence and the Arabs in the Great War. He was able to give him the benefit of some essential words and expressions in Arabic along with basic courtesies and an introduction to Arab thinking that could be very useful. He also passed on some tips on desert survival, dressing like the locals and camouflage techniques. George, like a sponge, soaked it all up. He also had a bit more practice with Michael's Colt until it felt like an extension of his own body. He could strip it, clear it and load it at lightning speed.

The time went very quickly, and the time of departure came. Instead of going on the evening before George stayed until the early morning of day number six. He left the Hall at 5am and went with Michael up to the airfield in the Jeep. Michael, as a former group captain still had a lot of sway with the RAF particularly as they were training their pilots. He had telephoned RAF Benson, which was a stone's throw from the Didcot barracks and secured permission for a landing. They took off in the Harvard and in less than an hour, they had landed. On the evening before, Michael had handed over the Colt and 250 rounds of ammunition which George had placed in his holdall. George had been sad to leave Emma, knowing that it would be at least six months before they were together again. When he left her in the room at the Hall, what he did not know was that he had left not one person, but two, as Dr Jennifer would confirm in a few days' time.

After landing Michael had a polite exchange with the duty officer and a lift was arranged to take George to the barracks. They shook hands and bade each other farewell. Michael spent an hour chatting to the duty officer. He described the Flying School and that they were now teaching new officer recruits how to fly along with the University Air Squadron. He then returned to Spelthorpe.

On return to the barracks George spent the next three days organising the departure. The house would be effectively mothballed pending their return. He did manage a trip into Oxford where he purchased two books, one on basic Arabic and the other, a more recent publication on the history of Palestine.

On Sunday, the eleventh of August, the squadron took off in convoy for Portsmouth docks. Loading took place on arrival. Each section had two Austin Tilly trucks and one Bedford lorry. The squadron had six sections.

10

The Unholy Land

August 1946 – March 1947

On Monday morning, the large landing ship took off. George spent most of the time reading and practising his Arabic and he did spend some time briefing the sections, given that he was the one that had taken the trouble to get a grip on the background. It would take over a week to get to Haifa in Palestine. Some of the soldiers who had received Sunday school indoctrination in their childhood were afflicted with a romantic image of the Holy Land, but George's history book revealed that there was little that was holy about the place from the dawn of time. The problem with the Old Testament was that Sunday schools only used the nice bits and ignored the details of the bloodshed, the butchery, the recommendations for ethnic cleansing and the barbarous and criminal activities of characters heralded in the Bible stories. The Romans had ruled with an iron fist, only to be taken over by the forces of Islam and then the bloody and brutal Christian crusades where butchery and blood lust in the name of Christ went off the scale. And now the butchery continued, piloted by zealots who believed they were God's chosen people, and the land had been given to them centuries ago, so they had an absolute right to take it back regardless of the current occupants.

In the light of the King David Hotel attack, British attitudes hardened. For years there had been trouble with the League of Nations mandate created after the Great War. In the late 1930's, the Arabs had revolted against British rule. They had been defeated. Now it was the turn of fanatical Jewish terrorists who had settled in Palestine and wanted a state of their own. They were cunning, determined and organised. They had widespread Jewish support from other Zionist hotheads. All this originated following the First World War, when the British drove out the Turks. Arabs had fought with the British, and they felt betrayed. Then, in 1917, the British foreign Secretary, Balfour, had made a declaration in support of a homeland for the Jews. This created unrealistic expectations. Thousands of Jews flocked to Palestine and took land by fair means or foul from the Palestinians, who felt let down. The British had the thankless task of trying to keep the two sides apart. With the advent of the Nazis, what had been a steady trickle of Jewish settlers turned into a flood, and that turned into a tsunami as the death camps were liberated. Some Jews had fought with the British, but others, the real fanatics, were only concerned with the use of terrorist violence to get the British out. There were two main groups. The Haganah was more concerned with promoting immigration and initially was cooperative with the British authorities, but not the Irgun, which set about a campaign of assassinations, kidnappings and bombing of railways, military installations and airfields. They cared not who they killed. At the outset, British sympathy was with the Jews because of the holocaust. Some soldiers had liberated the Belsen camp, but as the months went by attitudes changed, and understandably, as soldiers were killed. Others wrongly suggested that Hitler had been right, and sympathies went towards the Arabs. It was a lose-lose situation where the British found themselves the prisoners of history. In rounding up immigrants they played into the hands of the terrorists. Boatloads of Jews were imprisoned in Cyprus, whilst others were intercepted and returned before they got anywhere near Palestine. The Jewish lobby was a vociferous one. Some were very wealthy, and in the United States there were millions of votes at stake, with almost two million Jews living in New York alone.

George's message to his men was a simple one: "We don't do politics. We defuse bombs and make people safe. We act under orders. We don't rush in. We treat as we find. We trust nobody and most important of all, we watch out for each other. We are all going home!"

The captain noticed George's example and leadership. He was pleased to have him as his number two.

They docked at Haifa after nine days at sea. The city backs onto Mount Carmel, where the prophet Elijah was said to have personally slaughtered 450 prophets of the false God Baal.

"Not bad for a morning's work," commented George as he introduced his soldiers to Palestine. It was hot and dusty, and like a lot of ports, noisy and dirty. The men were glad to get off the ship and were escorted by military police to their barracks just outside Tel Aviv. This was very much a Jewish area with a population almost entirely made up of Jewish settlers. Jerusalem was fifty miles inland. There was evidence of commercial activity and much building, which contrasted dramatically with many of the Arab areas that could have done with a facelift.

Over the next few weeks, they settled in. Most of the soldiers swiftly accepted the reality of the place. Barracks had been attacked in the past. They were accommodated with a regiment of infantry. When calls came in, a section would attend but always with a platoon of infantry because of the possibility of a terrorist attack. They covered the area around Tel Aviv and east to Jerusalem. There were large camps that were involved in the resettlement of Jewish refugees. Some still looked drawn by their experience under the Nazis and would display their crude camp tattoo numbers in an effort to gain sympathy. As anywhere, some were positive. Others were bitter and would call the British 'Nazis' when the soldiers were only trying to do their job. Some of the established settlers came across as very arrogant. Generally, George found that the Arabs were more welcoming and would invite him in and welcome him and his team. He greeted them in Arabic and accepted their hospitality because to refuse would have been seen as hostile. George mainly found that the Arabs wanted to carry on in much the same way as they had always done, as subsistence farmers or in the towns engaging in trade or the skills they had. Jews would buy their land and then start developing it, but then they became threatening when the Arabs refused to sell more and so the seeds of ethnic hatred were sown and grew.

Most of George's men thought that the place was a 'shit hole' and said that they wouldn't be coming back for a holiday. In some areas, European style toilets were non-existent. There was just a stinking hole in the ground, and any used toilet paper had to be placed in a metal caged bin that went for incineration. All of this exacerbated the thing that the men hated the most and that was the flies. Leave any food out, and in an instant, it was covered in flies and sickness rates went up. When they got anywhere near a so-called holy site, mainly around Jerusalem, the Arabs would come out selling souvenirs. These were mainly camels and things carved in olive wood, hats and wallets made from goat skins as well as fragments of wood and nails (normally rusted standard British six-inch) sold as nails from the true cross. George did buy several Keffiyehs in red and white. This was the standard headdress of Palestinian farmers and peasants. He also bought some standard cheap woollen robes that might come in useful, and he observed how they were worn. The Jewish areas were very different and almost Western. Attacks did take place, but they were relatively rare, though they still had an effect. Policemen and soldiers were shot and were sometimes kidnapped and caned in response to the British caning of Jewish criminals.

In order to maintain morale, there were odd days when soldiers would go to the Mediterranean Sea in a large group for swimming. This was popular. On the way back they would stop at a stall and buy oranges and dates. George only ate hot food or things he could peel.

On a day's local leave George took two sections down to the Dead Sea for an experience. This was regarded as safer because it was mainly an Arab area. Floating on the sea whilst posing reading a newspaper was good for photos but the excess saltiness could be painful, particularly to anyone suffering from haemorrhoids. It was kill or cure and an agonising one at that. One soldier covered himself in black mud from the sea. It was supposed to be a skin tonic. The shower to wash it off was not working, so he went back in the sea though he couldn't rinse his face in case he got salt in his eyes. He went back to barracks still blacked up and he gained the nickname 'Golly' after that. They went on to the massive rock called Masada that overlooked the Dead Sea. It was several hundred feet to the plateau at the top which was one-third of a mile long. George, two corporals and three privates ran up the snake path to the top. It had been a luxury palace for King Herod, who feared everyone, including his own people. Later in 73 AD, a thousand Jewish Zealots held out for nearly a year against a Roman siege. The Romans built a massive ramp, and with battering rams, broke in. The Jews, including women and children killed one another or committed suicide rather than be taken.

"Now you can understand what we are up against," said George. "That's the mentality. We can never win here, so we just have to do our job until we leave, and then there will be a bloodbath – Jews and Arabs, but what's the point? It will go on and on and on."

They drove back past Jericho and then up through the rocky hills of Judaea to Jerusalem, but they never met any good Samaritans on the way. Then it was through Jerusalem and back to barracks.

As the months went by, George's section carried on with their work. There were many calls relating to suspicious objects, and every now and again there was something to defuse. These were often amateurish attempts to blow up railway lines. Bombs still went off because not all were spotted in time so that was the inevitable result. The section would always go out with a platoon of infantry. When they had the Parachute Regiment, they felt happier. These had a reputation for not messing around, and both Jews and Arabs did not like to mix it with them. George impressed on his men the need for constant observation. It might be just a bomb by a railway line, but the Irgun might be concealed a hundred yards away at the end of the wires linked to the bomb and would blow it if the engineers got too close or it might be that they were waiting for a train to maximise the damage.

George would get regular letters from Emma, and he would write back mainly to reassure her. She was undertaking a course on two days a week that would ultimately lead her to Chartered Accountant status when she had taken all the examinations.

In September, she wrote to tell George that he would become a father in March of the following year. George responded positively but tried to put it out of his mind whilst working. Emma told him that Beverley Boynton who was now fourteen, and Joanne's James who was now nine were both now at the private school that George, Edward and Victoria had attended. Both were bright. The village school had limitations, although with the help of the estate and Aggie's leadership, it was streets ahead of the rest of the state system in both teaching ability and facilities. Education under the state system remained in a parlous state due to a lack of investment and a calamitous shortage of teachers. Spelthorpe, with its superb reputation was where good primary teachers wanted to teach, so there were never problems in recruiting first-rate teachers. The new system with an examination at age eleven had started in 1944, but practical problems hindered full implementation. The Spelthorpe primary was way above the average school performance at this examination, and many ex Spelthorpe pupils were attending the Boys Grammar and Girls High School at King's Lynn. They went to school on the train. In April, the school leaving age would go up to fifteen, but the shortage of teachers exacerbated the difficulties. Emma's sister, Emily, had settled in well at the farm office and Emma's return had helped with this.

December heralded the worst winter in living memory although it didn't get really bad until January. Nationally, there were severe coal shortages with power cuts and the army was being used to help out across the country.

At Spelthorpe the customary vision had mitigated the worst effects. Daniel and Angela had made it their business to ensure that all the pensioners were fully stocked up with logs and off-cuts. Angela and Emma had lots to talk about because Angela was also expecting in March, so the local baby boom was continuing. William had ensured that the farm had several portable generators, and the tractors were adapted to take home-manufactured snow ploughs to keep the estate roads open. The severe winter meant extra problems with livestock. Most fields had access to the streams that ran through the estate from south to north and these were not freezing up like the lakes where the water was still. Water was heated and carried by a tractor-towed bowser to central drinking troughs and to those animals under cover. It meant a lot of extra work. When it got really bad the sheep and cattle were brought under cover although some seemed content to gather at the edge of the woodlands where hay bales were placed. The foresters were active in putting up additional shelters. There was plenty of hay, and the turnips had been harvested from the paddocks in November. The pregnant ewes were driven up to the cover crop zone in January, where they feasted on the kale. There were a few losses, but nothing compared to the national picture. Nothing went to waste. The dogs on the estate never went hungry with the pet mince that was churned out from the small abattoir and butchery. The airfield had come to a stop in January, but they all mucked in on the estate to help out. They helped Boynton feed the deer with hay bales and turnips when the snow got deep. The shooting season had gone well until mid-January, but with only two weeks of the season remaining, that was hardly a problem, but the hens and some cocks had to be gathered and penned in order to provide the eggs for the next season's birds.

There had been a Royal visit in early December when the king was accompanied by his future son-in-law, although the secret of the engagement remained so. In the first week of January, before the winter struck in earnest, Ash, Helen, Victoria, Michael, Lucy and the Boyntons spent a day at Sandringham.

Back in Palestine Christmas came and went. The soldiers managed a Christmas dinner. They were on full alert because the enemy would time attacks during periods when they thought the soldiers' alertness levels might be down. Of course, to the Jews and Arabs, Christmas meant nothing other than increased

Christian visitors in Bethlehem despite the troubles. These gatherings had to be policed in case the Irgun sought to exploit the publicity value.

As the new year came in and the reports of the bad winter back home arrived, the troops were happy to be out of the worst of it. Temperatures were lower but comfortable and the flies were far less active.

In the third week of January, the captain came to George with a special job. It would mean going undercover. A small detachment of the newly reconstituted Special Air Service Regiment was maintaining covert observation positions after it was thought they had spotted a terrorist bomb factory on the hills just to the north of Jerusalem. They had asked for a couple of the Royal Engineers' finest to discreetly check it out. George was heavily tanned. Starchy discipline was not the rule amongst the bomb disposal sections on operations and shaves might get missed for a few days. George was no exception to this. There were far more important things to consider. George's number two, the chief petty officer, Denis Gosling, had a full beard and when they dirtied themselves up, they put on the sandals, woollen robes and keffiyehs they looked the full part. They took off in a battered old Morris. George carried a bag of tools, odds and ends and his Colt. His colleague carried a Sten submachine gun under his robe. They went out at dusk to a rendezvous point just beyond a crossroads. Two minutes later, a figure approached in similar garb to theirs. After introductions, they took off below the ridge line for half a mile to a broken-up disused goat enclosure. There were two men concealed amongst the rubble and covered with an old tarpaulin and rusted corrugated iron sheet. They had an observation hole through a gap in the wall that formed the enclosure. It was a moonlit night. Two hundred yards below was a small barn and a herder's hut. There was no evidence of recent use as such. Above was an olive grove, and old olive trees partially surrounded the shed. The SAS men had spotted regular comings and goings at first light for a few days. Up to four men would go in, stop for an hour and emerge carrying loaded bags. In the day, it was not visited. George said they would check it out, but it might take some time to do a proper assessment. They both had torches but would only use them in the immediate vicinity of the hut to gain entry and search inside.

They went down. It took them ten minutes to cover the 200 yards, but they stopped every twenty-five yards to listen and look. When they got to the barn, they found it unsecured but empty apart from several small milk churns in a corner under some old blankets. They checked these out. They were all empty. They walked around the entire structure looking for trip wires or anything that would indicate a visit. The hut was about ten feet by eight feet. It had a corrugated iron roof, which looked in new condition giving the impression that they wanted it dry inside. There was no window, just a wooden door secured by a padlock. That could be bypassed by unscrewing the hasp. George made a note of the positions of the slots on the screw heads. He looked around the frame and spotted two wedges that would fall out if the door were opened. He took these out and made an exact note of their position and the way each had been placed.

Having unscrewed the hasp, they got in. There was a table and a chair. There were strands of wire on the table. There was a lamp, but they left that undisturbed. Then bingo! Under the table, there was a wooden crate with about twenty pounds of plastic explosive. There was a fertiliser sack full of white powder, which had been finely ground along with five two-pound bags of icing sugar. Another box had several rolls of bell wire, there were batteries, two alarm clocks and half a dozen detonators and four timing pencils. George remembered Boynton's words,

"Sometimes you have to play dirty to get these bastards." He went to work.

"You didn't see this," he said to Denis. "Best you keep watch outside in the dark".

George got a few items from his bag. He wired up a tilt switch and took out a detonator and four ounces of his own plastic explosive, which he embedded into plastic explosive under the bench but out of sight. He attached the tilt switch to the chair leg, and making sure it was safe, and the mercury was in the right place he wired the detonator, one of his batteries (having tested it first), and the tilt switch all together. Any movement of the chair would set the whole lot off, and the chair would have to be moved to get at the crates under the table. George carefully extracted himself from the shed. They then replaced the hasp, padlock and the wedges exactly as they found them.

Twenty minutes later they were back with the SAS team. George confirmed that it was a bomb factory. He asked if they could remain until dawn and told them that nobody other than he should go into the shed because it was too dangerous.

They agreed and asked, "Have you done a naughty?"

"Couldn't possibly comment," said a grinning George, and they grinned back.

They set about concealing themselves, so they had a view and waited in total silence.

About twenty minutes before sunrise, they heard voices in the valley. There were a group of five men. Two at the back were carrying Sten guns. They were in ordinary civilian clothes.

They were looking all around as they went up to the hut. The two with the guns sat down with their backs against the wall. One man went into the barn and retrieved two small milk churns. They checked the wedges then opened the door and the three walked in. Ten seconds later, there was an enormous explosion. The hut and the barn next to it just ceased to exist as it was blown into the air. Debris and body parts were scattered all over the hillside. Some of the smaller bits of debris landed on the iron sheets that covered George, his number two and the three SAS men.

"British army five, Irgun bastards nil," said the SAS leader. "Now I'd call that a good result and the crows will be happy."

He shook hands with George and Denis, and they all headed up back to the road.

"We will let the regular army come and discover that. They will have heard it from miles away," said George.

He and Denis went back to the car, and George checked it all over for devices. A fourth SAS man appeared.

"It's alright mate," he said. "I've been watching that and the road all night. I drew the short straw. I was tail-end Charlie last night."

George and Denis got back to base an hour later. They had the day off and got a few hours shut-eye. They woke and had a late breakfast to be greeted by the captain with a few beers.

"I took a call from Army HQ a couple of hours ago. They are jumping for joy at the fantastic job you two did last night, although officially, they can't say what happened. At the least, it will be a mention in dispatches with the citation kept secret. You've taken out a whole Irgun bombing team. They will be shitting themselves. Officially, it will be that one of our patrols investigated an explosion, and we suspect that it was a clumsy bomb maker who got his comeuppance."

At the end of the month, they were looking forward to going home. Given the fact that they hardly ever got more than one day off in a week they would be given a full month's leave on their return. Then a call came in, and it was allocated to George's team. An improvised device has been spotted under a railway bridge on the main line between Lydda and Jerusalem. This was a key line linking Jerusalem with Tel Aviv and the coast.

It took an hour to get there, and they had a platoon of paratroopers with them. On arrival the paratroopers spread out and maintained a loose cordon 200 yards out from the bridge. The country was quite hilly with rocks, so ideal for an ambush and concealment. The bridge crossed a winding wadi (a dry river valley or ravine), so observation of the whole length was impossible. They had about sixty yards visibility on each side of the bridge. George approached with Denis with the rest of the team a hundred yards back, hiding behind rocks further down the railway track. There were two large milk churns placed against the central support. That was easily enough to blow the bridge. Blowing a railway line was often pointless because the track could be repaired in a day. Bridges and tunnels were the favourite because that meant weeks without use, so this was important.

George could see two wires protruding from the first churn and leading up the wadi. It would appear that somewhere up the wadi was a plunger device or a battery with a timer to set the whole thing off. George and Denis climbed up the side of the wadi and walked along to the first bend then they dropped back down and worked back to where the bridge could be seen, but they were not in direct line of the churns. They swept up both sides and Denis discovered the two wires going further up the wadi. George cut the wires so no person or device further up the wadi could blow the bomb. Then they slowly started walking up the wadi. They heard shots from the hillside. That was like a red rag to a bull and the paras took off to where the shots had come from leaving George and his team behind.

They heard the noise of a train approaching. George just could not understand why the trains had not been stopped. The train passed over the bridge without a problem. George heard shouting from further up the wadi, and shots were fired. Denis was hit in the shoulder and fell. George dived to the ground and rolled behind a rock. He drew the Colt. Three men came running up. One had a Sten, one had a rifle, and the other had a pistol. He was also carrying an electrical plunger.

It was obvious they had tried to blow the bomb when the train went over but failed because of the cut wires. Now they just wanted to connect up and blow the bridge regardless. The shots on the hillside had been a distraction to get the army away.

They got to within ten yards and saw Denis lying wounded on the ground. The man with the Sten raised it to finish him off when George stood up, shouted, and put two shots into the man. The first was in the centre of the chest and the second under his chin which severed his spine at the neck. In a split-second, George put two more shots into the rifleman in the centre and he dropped. The third turned and ran but he made the mistake of not zig zagging. For George, it was an easy shot, carefully aimed, that took him in the back of the head. His brains came out through the large exit hole, and the second shot hit him square between the shoulder blades as he went down.

George ducked down and put another magazine in. He looked up the wadi. It was clear so he got across to Denis. He had taken a 9 mm round in the shoulder but was otherwise alright. He patched him up with a dressing and a sling by which time the paratroopers had returned.

"Jesus," said the lieutenant. "You don't need us. You're a one-man army. We got nobody, and you have just slotted three of the bastards. I don't suppose you will be giving them any first aid. They are beyond it, knocking on the gates of Hell."

The paratrooper lieutenant got two of his chaps down to help Denis up the side of the wadi. He went to the hospital in one of the Austin Tilly trucks with an escort of three paratroopers in a jeep. The rest remained while George dealt with the explosives. They toppled the churns one at a time with rope from a protected spot to make sure there was nothing inside or a grenade wedged behind. Once that was done, they drilled in from each side and flushed the explosive out. It was a homemade mixture of ammonium nitrate and diesel oil. It was the safest way, just in case there was something under the caps of the churn. Then they blasted the churn caps off with a tiny amount of plastic explosive. That was always the problem with an improvised device. There was no design standard, so playing it safe was the only way, with no short cuts. An hour later the military police and Palestine police turned up. An army ambulance took the bodies away after the police had searched them for anything to identify them or anything that might incriminate others. They bagged up what they found in three separate bags. They did the same with the weaponry for fingerprint examination of the weapons and the bullets in the magazines.

After four hours, George and the team returned to base. He completed his report and made a statement for the police, then he went to see Denis who was sitting up in bed with the bullet removed. He was looking good and thanked George for saving his life.

George became a local hero amongst the base but that was not a good thing. In his tour he had been personally responsible for the deaths of eight Irgun terrorists, and they would want revenge. The Irgun were an evil bunch, and they had carried out revenge killings before.

On the following day under orders, he boarded a vessel for Cyprus three days before his team were to take ship. It was a contracted cruise ship. There were lots of women and children on board because they were being evacuated. Palestine had become increasingly dangerous for all British personnel, and even soldiers were spending much more of their relaxation time confined to barracks. Those who ventured out unarmed were taking a risk given the hostage taking and assassinations.

After an evening meal, George went out on deck to take the night air. He encountered a woman who was doing the same. She was a couple of years older – a teacher who had been working at the British school in Jerusalem. She was an attractive woman, full breasted and had brown 'come-to-bed eyes'. George spoke of his tour and the reason for his sudden departure. She was married but said no more on that. Nor for that matter did George. She invited him back to her cabin. Once inside there was no hesitation. Both knew what they wanted, and within seconds they were ripping off their clothes. George was naked and she too, apart from her stockings and they had wild passionate sex against the side of the cabin. After that, she pulled him down onto the bed, where over the rest of the night, they had sex again and again until dawn but as the night moved on the sex became more tender and affectionate. For both, it was a huge relief from the pent-up strains over the last few months. On reflection, George smiled about her being a teacher because she taught him all sorts of things he had never previously experienced.

At first light George said, "I don't know your name."

She responded, "And I don't know yours, but I think it best that we leave it like that."

George kissed her, then got dressed and left the cabin. He never saw her again on the vessel.

Once back in his cabin, George felt guilty. He got a bar of cold tar soap and showered and scrubbed every trace away. He had a stock of penicillin pills that he kept for his soldiers. He took two and then dozed until the ship docked. By then, in George's mind, it was all just a dream and he decided to bury it that way. He had to move on.

Cyprus was a pleasant place to stop over and more so because the constant threat of death and attack was no longer there.

Two days later, Denis joined him. After two more days, both managed to get a lift on an RAF plane heading back to the UK.

They got back to the barracks at Didcot and Denis insisted on staying until the others had returned. George telephoned Spelthorpe just to let them know he was safe back in the UK and would be returning for a month's leave once his tour came to an end. He would have some tales to tell them. He took Denis for several check-ups at the military hospital. He would make a full recovery. George tidied things up in readiness for the return of the squadron.

Back in Palestine there had been a quick handover to the replacement squadron. As time marched on things out there did not get any better but at least George and his squadron had gone home. The Irgun continued to behave in an evil and despicable way. In July, they kidnapped two British sergeants and hanged them in an orchard and to make matters worse, they booby trapped their bodies with explosive. Despite the sympathy for the victims of the holocaust, there was no love amongst many soldiers, for those who in the following year would bring about the creation of the state of Israel.

Progressively matters went downhill, and the following year the British finally got out. The Americans wanted a Jewish state because of the elections. Owing to the dire financial situation, Britain remained firmly under the American thumb. There was no special relationship. It was always politics and money. The Irgun turned its attention to the Palestinians. They massacred a village, Deir Yassin, with some 250 old men, women and children. In retaliation the Arabs massacred a convoy of Jewish doctors and nurses on their way to Jerusalem. As George had predicted the bloodshed would just go on and on and on, but at least the British army was out of it. George vowed never to go back unless under orders and many of the others felt the same.

It was not a proper war with an identifiable enemy – just another thankless task for Kipling's Tommy.

On the third week of February, the rest of the squadron returned. The weather in England had been appalling. For the last week, there was more tidying up to be done.

For their action in dealing with the bomb factory, George and Denis received a mention in dispatches. For dealing with the viaduct bomb and taking out the three armed terrorists whilst protecting his wounded colleague, George received the Military Cross. The citation was kept secret given that the Irgun counted support from some who were resident in the United Kingdom.

The hierarchy in the Royal Engineers were very impressed by George's performance during his tour and as deputy to the squadron commander – normally a major, George had effectively been carrying out a captain's role in a difficult operational environment. He was young but professionally competent and respected by his men. A new squadron with three sections, each with a lieutenant was to be established at a base near Lincoln from May, and they decided that, following a four-week junior Royal Engineer Captain's course at Chatham in April, George should command the new unit. He was offered the post on the last day of February and immediately accepted. His course would start at Chatham on Monday the thirty-first of March and until then he would be on leave. George made just one request, and that was that if any of his crew wished to serve with him there that it be permitted. This was more of a naval tradition than an army one, but in specialist units the army could be more sympathetic.

On the following day, a Saturday, George managed to get a train back home. The roads were still very bad with snow drifts and ice, but the trains somehow kept going. It was a long journey, but he finally got back to Spelthorpe at 5pm. He went straight to the Hall and found Emma sitting with Lucy, Victoria the dogs and children in the downstairs lounge. Daisy recognised him straight away and came bounding over. Emma got up and clung to her hero, who had come back to her. It was too much. She burst into tears. Her bulge was very evident, and according to Jennifer two weeks away from delivery. Victoria and Lucy were similarly emotionally affected. Their brother was back with them after months of the worry of separation, and a regular diet of horror stories in the press.

Victoria excused herself to make a few phone calls and to put into action the plan for George's return. Amrik had been briefed and was ready with his staff. Ash and Michael had been boat fishing in the morning and had caught a dozen large cod and had emptied the pots, getting a good load of crabs and lobster.

Victoria returned to the lounge and told George that a meal had been planned for 8pm with drinks at 7.30pm.

George went upstairs with Emma to freshen up and get out of his uniform. There was a knock at the door after an hour. It was Helen – desperate to hug her darling boy. They came down and went to the large dining room. Everyone was there, the whole greater Spelthorpe family with all the Johnson clan, the Boyntons, Emily and Emma's parents and Reverend Paddy and his wife with all the children and all the dogs. The only one missing was Edward, but the weather had made car journeys difficult in the extreme. George was overcome by the hugs, kisses and handshakes. It occurred to him how many had cared and worried all the time he was away, but now he was back. They had drinks all round. George made a point of going straight up to Boynton and thanking him for the advice and training that got him through.

Amrik's team served up a crab and lobster cocktail to all and this was followed by the most traditional English meal of all: English fish and chips, fried in beef dripping and served up in newspaper – *The Times* rather than *The Mirror*. The cod was superb and contrasted with the whale meat and tins of vile, imported, South African snoek fish that the government was trying to force on the urban masses. With a barrel of bitter ale, it all went down as an absolute treat and was followed by apple pie and cream. The menu was perfect for the mood. Coffees and brandies were served at the end. George said a few words of gratitude and delight to be home, and home for a whole month at that.

It was then that Ash spoke.

"Dear friends, I just want to mention this. Gabriel Boynton has been the guardian angel of the estate for many years. Specifically, he has watched over our children and the Johnson girls, too. Importantly when those children went to war, he gave them training to ensure their survival. That advice had proved itself invaluable time and time again and they have all come home. For that, we are eternally in his debt. I ask you all to join me in a toast – Gabriel Boynton!"

Spontaneously, Michael, Lucy, George and Victoria walked over to Boynton and hugged him. He was genuinely touched by that.

The gentlemen with their drinks retired to the library with George. Following an undertaking that the details would stay in the room, he gave them a warts-and-all rundown on his experiences in Palestine. He would leave it to them to pass on to their ladies that which they felt appropriate. He held nothing back. They were all captivated by what he had to say. Boynton was most impressed. George had won his spurs. The Spelthorpe Company had gained a new member.

Winter at Spelthorpe 1947

11

Summer days

March – September 1947

Throughout the year, central government remained in a state of total chaos. They had taken on far more than they could chew with reforms to education, nationalisation of the railways, steel and coal mines, the creation of the welfare state with the national insurance system, and a universal health service. All this had to be consulted on and negotiated against a background of greed and self-interest from trade unions, the British Medical Association, and other groups whilst any real progress was hampered by labour shortages, rationing, a lack of investment and growing impatience from a public who expected the world. Progressively, this had a telling effect on the health of senior cabinet members. Some died.

At the same time, Britain was shackled to its history with major conflicts as the country sought to rid itself of a massive empire that it could no longer afford. The ruthless haste at which this was implemented, particularly in the Indian sub-continent, resulted in hundreds of thousands of murders from ethnic and sectarian violence.

Meanwhile, money and manpower were directed to feeding, rebuilding and defending Western Europe as former prime minister Winston Churchill spoke of the 'Iron Curtain' that had descended and split the continent in two. In 1947, National Service – another form of conscription for those over 18, was introduced to deal with shortages in the military. Some almost died of boredom as they became imprisoned in barracks after days of spit, polish and square bashing. The lucky ones travelled to exotic parts of the dissolving empire, and others died in the conflicts they were sent to deal with. The Beveridge Report that initiated the Welfare State spoke of the eradication of the five giants of 'Want, Disease, Ignorance, Squalor and Idleness' – none of which applied to those who lived and worked on the Spelthorpe estate.

The one factor that was a constant source of concern was something over which the estate could exercise no direct control: the weather. But here, by good management, preparedness, sheer hard work and determination, the worst effects were mitigated.

The winter months of January and February were the coldest in living memory, but they had got through it with minimal losses. March was extremely wet, but April and May were far hotter than normal. The grass grew prolifically, so they took an early hay cut. Making hay while the sun shone paid off because from July onwards in the east of England there was heat and a widespread drought. Cereal yields were down but not disastrously so. Night-time watering by extraction from the lakes, ponds and reservoirs along the course of the streams allowed a degree of irrigation, and the odd thunderstorm would replenish them rapidly. Consequently, at a national level prices went up, but those with livestock, cereals and reasonable crop yields made money. Predictably, Reverend Paddy would have something to say about it all based on his interpretation of the good book, as he called it. He ignored, as he often did, the bible readings prescribed by the Church of England because he always said he was the vicar of the Church of Spelthorpe. For the Harvest Festival in September, he preached on the subject of the *'Parable of the Wise and Foolish Virgins.'*

On the fifteenth of March Spelthorpe greeted its newest arrival as Emma gave birth to Katie. The newly promoted Captain George Spelthorpe MC was absolutely delighted. On the following day Daniel and Angela Martin were blessed with the arrival of a son, Jonathan.

Daniel and Angela had moved up to the cottage on the new land south of the estate that had been recently purchased. It was a nice, detached three-bedroomed cottage with a good-sized garden. The new land consisted of 500 acres, of which a hundred acres were forest and the rest good arable land. Michael wanted some reliable people up there to keep an eye on it, mainly on the forest zone. Daniel and Angela fitted the bill perfectly and, while Angela had time off with the baby, she would not be alone when Daniel was working. They had a pair of Belgian Malinois shepherd dogs that Daniel had got from a friend as puppies a year earlier. These were superbly athletic, protective and loyal in the extreme. Boynton was impressed and had helped Daniel to train them.

On the edge of the woodland the turkey rearing area was being established, and another 200 pigs were to be stocked. They would occupy parts of the woodland in fenced enclosures. The cottage was only 500 yards from the southern gate where one of the two underkeepers resided. Fifty yards further up and opposite the cottage, was a house that needed some work doing to it. Michael had instructed that this be converted into two three-bedroomed semi-detached cottages so that another two workers and their families could move there. He had two stockmen in mind who had expressed an interest in the turkey and pig projects. This would end any isolation on that part of the estate. The rest of the land would be allocated to cereals, potatoes, beans and sugar beet in rotation.

The construction team had also brought in an excavator to dig out a reservoir pond on the forest side with a dam and overflow across the course of the stream that ran through the land. This would puddle over time in the clay soil to provide additional water should it be required. Similar reservoir ponds existed elsewhere on the estate.

The nursery at the Hall was working well, and owing to the baby boom, it had several new clients. It benefited both the families and the estate but was not run to make a profit. Essentially, it was a self-funding service. The nurse in charge was now in a relationship with one of the estate mechanics having been introduced by William. The two other former land army girls were in a similar position, so the year was likely to proceed with three more weddings.

William had a team of four very competent agricultural engineers and fitters so all servicing could be done on site as well as any servicing needs that came out of the dealership. They had also taken on an apprentice who had just left school. They could turn their hands to most things. They were needed as the farm progressively took on more mechanisation. The estate had recently purchased two self-propelled Massey Fergusson 21 combine harvesters along with two up-to-date balers to replace the existing models that were well over ten years old. This dramatically reduced the need for labour at harvest time, and if not in use locally, the equipment could be contracted out elsewhere to bring in more money.

Alas, the writing was on the wall for the horses, but Michael would have none of it. He insisted that the farm retain a cadre of those (including himself and Victoria) who could work the horses in the traditional way, and he initiated an annual traditional inter-farm ploughing competition for the county of Norfolk. Whilst much of the tedium was removed in ploughing and reaping, the Suffolk punch horses were used daily for carting and in the forest where they still had a clear advantage. Given the volatility across the planet and a government lacking preparedness, he felt it a mistake if the farm were to put all its eggs into the petrol and diesel basket. The dealership was turning in a steady profit.

It was fortunate that the requirement for national service did not extend to miners, farm workers, the merchant navy and lunatics. According to Boynton this was a great shame for the military because, in his experience, it was lunatics who won battles. From Spelthorpe's perspective it would mean that the fourteen-year-olds that the farm had taken on would remain because by the age of eighteen they were getting physically stronger and had developed the skills required.

At the end of the month, George headed for Chatham. He returned Michael's Colt pistol and had ordered the same from a London firearm dealer as officers were permitted to select their own sidearm, not that there was much need in England, but he was expected to keep up his shooting skills at the barracks. This was now his weapon of choice. He, more than most, knew how effective it could be.

He took the car, having built up a stock of petrol coupons while he was in Palestine and would return at weekends. Emma was much happier now with the long separation over and she had a very demanding daughter to think about.

For much of the course, he was going through the motions in respect of the expectations of the rank of an engineer captain, but he did value the time spent on refreshment of some of the basics that all engineers covered in respect of construction, bridge building and road making. He was called upon to lecture the others about bomb disposal and his experience in Palestine. In the meantime, his friend Denis had been in touch. He had taken George's advice and been accepted for an upgrade to be a naval commissioned officer and given his extensive experience, that would only involve a month's course at the Royal Naval College. To put the icing on the cake, he had asked to continue to serve on attachment, and given his practical experience, they had agreed to that. Following George's request, he would be the adjutant in George's command with the rank of naval sub lieutenant (equal to army lieutenant). This was so useful because some of the munitions they encountered were naval mines and torpedoes that had failed to explode, and he could liaise better with the navy on that. In the majority of cases, it would save a navy callout and George's squadron would deal with it.

In April, George started at the barracks in Lincoln. He was happy to be there and delighted that two of his corporals and two privates from his old team would be joining him. Of his three sections two were led by lieutenants, and the other by a subaltern for whom it was his first operational posting. One was married, and both had experience working in London, where it was still varied and busy. The subaltern had a good theoretical knowledge but would need a guiding hand to start with.

On the first day, he interviewed each separately, and once that was done, he took them all out for dinner at a local restaurant where they could get to know each other in a less formal atmosphere. For his sections, there would always be one on duty at each weekend. Periodically, he would step in to lead a section if the lieutenant was on leave, but he would expect sergeants to lead on more routine matters like the smaller munitions and where there was little threat to life or infrastructure. He reiterated his views that he had expressed about caution, survival and looking after one another, and he was sure that those who had followed him up from Oxford would pass that message on informally anyway. There were lots of questions and a lot of interest relating to George's activities in Palestine.

George got his stuff moved up from Oxford and took up residence in the married officer's house that was provided. It was to a good standard with a spacious garden. He would move Emma up to Lincoln when she had fully recovered from the birth, and she had settled with the baby. There was a battalion of infantry based at the Lincoln barracks. Child minding facilities existed for when Emma was ready. Altogether he was looking forward to life here. He liked Lincoln with its splendid cathedral set at the top of a steep hill that dominated the city. Once, with its spire, it had been the tallest building in the world, until a storm in 1548 made the spire collapse. There was plenty of good countryside all around, and Spelthorpe was only a couple of hours away for monthly visits.

In late May, Elizabeth and Philip came and spent a couple of days at the Hall. Victoria and Lucy took Elizabeth for a swim in the lake with all the dogs, which she enjoyed. With the high temperatures the lake was used on a regular basis from April onwards.

While that was going on Philip had a flying lesson with Michael in one of the Tiger Moths. He managed a take-off and did a few circuits and down the coast and back, but Michael did the landing that required more care. Philip would get that in the next lesson.

Elizabeth was excited as the day to make matters public was getting closer, and early in July, Victoria got the call from Elizabeth to say it would shortly be official. When the announcement came, it was the tonic that the country needed. King George and the Queen were popular because of the courage they displayed in the war by staying in the thick of it. Elizabeth had served in the forces towards the end of the war and was shortly to marry a handsome naval officer with an excellent service record. It gave the nation something to look forward to.

The summer heat waves were a mixed blessing, but on balance, they were welcomed following the appalling winter.

Ash and Helen continued to take a back seat, not that they wanted to do so, but because they felt it important to let them all know that Victoria and Michael were now running the show. They gave quiet advice that was always welcome, but above all they enjoyed being together in the cottage with the dogs, enjoying the simple life and looking after the grandchildren on a regular basis. Ash maintained his work as chair of the magistrates' bench, representing farming interests and with the St John Ambulance.

Michael flew over to Carpriquet with Ash and bought the grandparents back for a week's stay at the cottage.

Lucy was happy to enjoy her time with Johann. In July, they left Mattie for a week with the grand parents to go on a touring holiday using the petrol coupons they had saved. Lucy carried on with her work at both schools.

They planned a trip to Paris – the city of light – with Michael and Victoria, for a few days later in the year, to brush up on their French and enjoy the unique style and beauty of the city that had largely avoided the war damage that afflicted so many other parts of Europe.

12

Extortion

October 1947

October brought about the start of the pheasant shooting season and with it the gradual changes as the leaves on the trees changed from green to reds, yellows and browns. In a month's time the autumn colours would be at their best. The nights were drawing in.

Business was picking up, and five commercial days had been booked for the months ahead. There were at least 3,000 birds on the estate. This was less than the pre-war days. Boynton was planning a gradual buildup over the next few years.

North Norfolk had escaped much of the criminality that plagued the rest of the country. Crime remained the curse of the urban areas. Contrary to what many thought, the war may have brought about blood, tears, toil and sweat, but that covered an undercoat of crime. With rationing, there was the inevitable black market, and there were a host of deserters who survived in the underworld. It was easier for them to hide in the towns. With a few exceptions, the war had stripped the police of its most able and reliable officers, and those that remained tended to be the less competent or have a dubious reputation. Some who were recruited to plug the gaps and fulfil extra demands were not of the best quality. Vetting was a lottery, and many with criminal records found their way into policing.

One notorious individual who had spent the 1930s in and out of prison was accepted as a war reserve constable in London. He went on to commit serial killings, hiding the bodies in his flat at 10, Rillington Place in Notting Hill. The killings went undetected for years. His name was John Christie. The good few that remained had their work cut out, and matters were not helped by additional American servicemen who deserted, sold firearms to criminals and supplied the black market. With the end of the war, many demobbed servicemen returned to policing, and others of a sound background were to be recruited, but it was going to take several years before the effect was felt. In the meantime, most resources were still directed to the towns. The rural area was left to look after itself. The past intervention of Zorro did have an effect for a while, but these things never last.

In the village, the estate's shop remained the heart of the community under the management of Amrik's very competent and helpful wife, Jasmir Singh. When it came to the administration of the rationing, she was incorruptible and managed the system without favour or affection. She was seen as totally fair and that made her popular. At the same time because of the existence of the estate she was able to offer non rationed goods in abundance and these included fresh and smoked fish, venison and venison sausages as well as log off-cuts as a substitute for coal. In her endeavours, she was helped by a team of ladies and the estate's butcher.

One late morning in mid-October, a Bentley pulled up outside the store. Two men emerged. One was below average height, balding with greased hair swept back, quite fat and about 50 years of age. He wore a dark overcoat, a trilby hat which he removed on entering the store, and he displayed quite a lot of gold jewellery for a man. He smoked a cigar and carried a bag.

The other was a lot younger and taller and somewhat overweight with flabby cheeks that gave the impression that he did not have a neck. His hands were tattooed.

The older man asked the lady behind the counter if he could speak to the manager, whilst the younger man just looked at the display of the newspapers and magazines. At the time, there were no other customers in the store.

Jasmir came to the counter. "Hello, can I help you, sir?"

"Perhaps we can help you," said the man. "Do you sell Spam or tins of salmon, corned beef, cigars or whisky?"

"Would you like some?" asked Jasmir. "I have a few tins of corned beef and one or two tins of salmon, but it's on the ration, and you will need to register here for me to sell it to you. We do have some other things not on ration."

"You don't understand," he said as he opened the bag and placed a few items on the counter. "I have these, lots of these and you can buy them from me and sell them from under the counter. That way I make money, and you make money, and everyone is happy."

"I couldn't possibly do that," said Jasmir. "I would get into trouble. That would be against the law. You will have to go. I can't possibly help you."

"Listen, you brown bitch!" said the man. "This is England, not Bombay, and we do things differently here. All the other shops buy from me, and with those that don't, things happen. There are accidents, there are breakages and fires, so I'll be back next week, and I'll take your order then!"

With that he turned and walked out of the shop. The other man followed him out like a dog with its master. They got in the car and drove off towards Sheringham. Jasmir had the presence of mind to get the car's number then she called the Hall and spoke to Michael.

Half an hour later Michael turned up at the shop with Boynton. Jasmir told them in detail what had happened. They told her not to worry as they would deal with the pair when they returned the following week.

As they left, Boynton said to Michael, "Looks like we have another job for Zorro. We will put Lucy in the shop next week. I know she loves this sort of thing so we will have her as a dowdy shop girl with a strong Norfolk accent. I'll speak to PC Carter and get an address from the number plate. After Lucy pretends to be all dumb, we will tail them and clock all the places they call at, but we will keep swapping over the lead, so they don't see the same car following them. We know what they look like so we might be able to do a bit of work on them in the meantime."

"Sounds like we have a plan. Best you don't let Himmler start to hibernate quite yet. You'll have to keep him warm and give him a mouse. I'll give Lucy the good news. She won't be able to wait. After those two years undercover, she's still like a cat on hot bricks. It's a shame we haven't got a drama group here because she would steal the show," said Michael.

Later that afternoon Boynton met up with PC Carter.

"This sort of thing is on the rise. Like always, it's mainly in the bigger towns, but clearly they want to spread into our coastal patch, and that's annoying because I can't do it on my own just on a bicycle, and the other village coppers are not up to much. I'll get you the owner of the car, and if I see it, I'll give it a traffic check and glean what I can. I won't get any help from King's

Lynn. It's mainly army deserters and well-established villains and they use the deserters as minders and delivery boys. I'll get back as soon as I can but it's the usual rules and I know nothing. He must have a warehouse somewhere, but if they suspect we are onto them they will evacuate it," said PC Carter.

"Thanks Dave. That will help!" said Boynton.

Four days later Carter came back.

"I've got an address on the outskirts of Fakenham, and I had a drive over there. It's quite a big place with a sidetrack and some large sheds at the end of the track. I saw a small lorry on the drive. I went past a pub called the Royal Oak on the outskirts of Fakenham and saw the Bentley parked in the car park. It's about a mile from the house. I'll leave the rest to you."

That evening, Boynton and Aggie had a drive over to Fakenham. They clocked the name of a house a quarter of a mile from the target house. Then they parked outside, and Aggie went up and knocked the door. She had her hair up and wore glasses. A woman answered. She was in her mid-fifties, heavily made up with a peroxide blonde hairdo and a lot of chunky jewellery.

"I wonder if you can help me. I'm looking for a house called 'Notre Repos'. I've got to go to a party there or rather two houses up from that one. It's a housewarming and they don't have a name up yet."

"Dunno," she said in a London accent. Her speech was slurred, and her breath stank of booze. "We ain't been here that long. My husband might know."

"Could you ask him please?" askedAggie.

"No sorry. He's down the pub. He lives in that bleedin' place. Never takes me. Always says it's business and he don't come home. I think he's got a bit on the side. I don't know how he does it because he's an ugly bastard."

"Well thank you anyway," said Aggie.

She got back to the car and told Boynton, "That was worthwhile. The woman was drunk, and she spilt the beans. He's always at the pub. I don't think she likes him very much. She thinks he's got a fancy piece."

"We'll have a look in the pub then," said Boynton.

Aggie took off the glasses, let her hair down and changed her coat.

Five minutes later, they walked into Royal Oak pub having parked outside quite close to the Bentley. It was quite a new model. The pub was on the quiet edge of the town. There was an alleyway from the car park that led through a lychgate into a churchyard.

Boynton ordered a pint and a bottle of Guinness. They sat at the bar. There were about a dozen people in there. Sat in a corner was the pair they were looking for. They stood out as they didn't look Norfolk types. Boynton got talking to the barman and asked about the Bentley outside. The bar man suggested they go in the snug bar. They both moved.

The bar man whispered, "It belongs to the one in the corner. No one likes him, but because you are from around here, I'll warn you. Bit of a flash bastard – always waving his money about and trying to flog things. Says he wants to buy this place, but no way that's happening. We've been here for centuries."

"Has he been here long?" asked Boynton.

"Came here when the war ended. A lot of shops are buying stuff off him, but I think he makes them. They are scared of him. Police don't do nothing. They are never about, so he gets away with it. We don't have anything off him, but he doesn't threaten us. I think that's because he's seen the size of the boss and his brother. He just goes for the easy ones, and he's always got the goon with him."

"Does he chase women?"

"Too right! Any woman who walks in here on her own and he's like a rat up a drainpipe. He buys them drinks and tries to get them to go for a ride in his car, and I've seen him offering money. He's a dirty sod. I suppose it's the money because every now and again he gets one, not the locals, but I think some of those whores from Norwich come over here, and I suppose they talk to one another. We've never seen his missus, that's if he's got one. We'd rather not have him, but he buys drinks, and we are here to sell drinks and that's it."

Boynton and Aggie had another drink and then went home.

On the following morning Boynton donned a pair of glasses and a deerstalker hat with a field guide to birds and an ordnance survey map. He went for a walk in the vicinity of the fields at the back of the target house. Posing as a bird watcher was always a useful cover when snooping in the countryside. He found a good observation spot in a hedgerow. There was a medium-sized barn at the rear of the property. The perimeter was enclosed with a seven-foot deer fence and a gate, and two Alsatian dogs roamed inside. Outside of the enclosed zone were a couple of small sheds and a lean-to that appeared to be a log store. The sheds appeared unsecured and not in use.

At about 11am a truck drove down. It was driven by the goon. He offloaded what looked like a like cases of whisky, then some cases of tins and finally a dozen jerrycans. Ten minutes later the boss appeared with the Bentley. They loaded two cases of whisky in the back and half a dozen cases of cans. They secured the gate, then both vehicles left.

Boynton walked closer. It was only when he got to the fence that the dogs started barking and snarling. He walked along the track to the side of the house. The truck was on the drive, but the car had gone.

When the second visit was due. Lucy had installed herself in the shop. Michael had arranged for two of his largest foresters to be shopping and had briefed them. Lucy wore a headscarf and glasses and had blackened a couple of her teeth and had padded out her cheeks. She wore a plain canvas dress that was padded out to make her look twice her size. The pair came in as expected and demanded to see the manageress.

"I'm very sorry gentlemen," said Lucy in her best Norfolk accent. "She's sick today so I'm standing in for her."

"Did she give you a list," asked the shorter man.

"What list? I'm sorry, I don't know what you are talking about." said Lucy.

"The list of things to buy from me. She was going to do it," said the man.

"I can't understand. This is a shop. We sell things to customers. We don't buy things from customers, so I will have to leave it at that!" said Lucy. "And now I have to serve these men." She indicated the foresters.

"You tell her to get that list sorted, or accidents will start to happen."

"Are you making a threat to me? I'll call the police," said Lucy.

"Don't do that," said one of the foresters, and with that he grabbed the man putting him in a headlock and walked him out of the shop. Then he kicked him up the backside when he was out on the street.

The goon went to intervene, but the other forester punched him hard in the stomach and knocked the wind out of him. Then he dragged him out into the road.

"Don't you be a threatening her. Not our Miss Molly!" he said, as he barred the doorway.

The two got back in the Bentley and drove off.

The foresters went back into the shop and had a fit of laughter. Lucy got rid of the disguise and Jasmir returned from out the back. The foresters pledged their full support if anything happened.

In the meantime, Michael and Boynton followed the pair as

they made their drops. They did six pubs and eleven shops before returning to Fakenham. A careful note was made of all the drops.

In the late afternoon, Boynton, Michael and Lucy made their plans and equipped themselves for the evening's activity. Michael called on the foresters and thanked them for their robust action.

At 7pm they assembled and got in the truck. Boynton had a small holdall with everything they needed. At 8pm they got to the pub. The Bentley was there. Boynton parked the truck with its back to the alleyway.

"Give us ten minutes before you come in, Lucy!"

Michael and Boynton walked in. There was a different bar man on duty. The two were sitting in the corner. Michael ordered a couple of pints, and they sat near to the door.

Ten minutes later Lucy walked in. Heads turned. She was dressed to kill with black stockings, a red dress that was low cut at the front with, as the French would say, 'the world on her balcony', a black coat and her black wig. She wore auxiliary red lipstick, which had been popular in the war with girls seeking to flaunt their independence. She walked up to the bar and ordered a glass of white wine. She spoke with a French accent. As the drink arrived, she was aware of a presence close to her

"I'll get that," said the man.

"Thank you, monsieur," said Lucy.

"What brings a beautiful lady to a place like this?"

"I am on holiday, monsieur, but I am looking for somewhere to stay. I thought I would have a look around, but it is very quiet here. When I have had my drink, I will go back to the centre. There is a hotel there!"

"I could take you there. My car is outside."

"And why does a man like you want to buy me a drink and take me in his car? I am not stupid. Monsieur but I am very expensive. I know what you want."

"Would five pounds help you decide?" asked the man.

"What do you think I am, monsieur. If you want a quick 'knee trembler' as you English say that will be ten pounds (£330 at current prices), but for the night that will be fifty pounds. That will be a night to remember, but not tonight because I have some things to do. I can give you a quickie outside in the dark where it is quiet."

"That will be good, darling. I'll agree to that."

"You will have to excuse me for a minute while I make myself ready for you. I will be back shortly."

Lucy walked to the ladies' room and, on the way, gave Michael a wink. That was the signal. They drank up and left. In the ladies' room, she removed a pair of lacy black panties from her handbag, which she sprayed with a whiff of perfume. Then she returned to the bar where she took the man's hand and discreetly placed the panties there.

"That is your receipt, Monsieur. Now you pay me."

He took out two five-pound notes which he folded. He handed them to her. His face reddened. She could see his pulse was up. She took a couple of minutes to finish her drink. He walked over to the goon and told him to wait. He would be back shortly. Then he walked back to Lucy.

"What is your name?" he asked.

"My name is Lyla," said Lucy, "and I come from Paris."

"How is your English so good?"

"My father was working here. I went to a convent school where all the girls were very naughty. They taught me how to make money."

They walked out, and he steered her to the car, but she insisted on going to the alley behind the truck.

"The car is too well lit and in the open," said Lucy.

He didn't argue. She leaned back against the wall, and she handed him something.

"I am ready for you, but you are not ready for me. You put that on first. You might give me the cupid's measles and I don't want that, or I might give it to you."

He didn't argue. He was worked up in expectation as he dropped his trousers and underpants and put the item on. He came forward and started pulling up her dress.

With the lightning speed of a puff adder, she struck as her knee came up crushing the man's testicles. He collapsed to the ground in agony. Two hooded figures emerged from the darkness. A chloroform pad was placed over his nose and mouth. He was handcuffed from behind. Trousers, shoes and socks were removed. He was hooded and legs were tied, then he was lifted into the back of the truck.

Lucy went back into the pub and emerged with the goon having told him that his friend had collapsed in the excitement. He followed her up behind the truck. As she pointed to a mass on the ground, his legs were taken from under him, and he fell face down. The pad was applied, and he was secured in the same way as the other and hoisted into the truck.

Michael got in the back with the prisoners then Boynton took off with Lucy in the front.

He dropped Lucy at the end of the drive to the Hall, then went up the slope and into the forest to the secret bunker which was open and prepared. Both had come around and were mumbling under the hoods. Their legs were untied, and they were manhandled down the stairs and made to sit on benches. Boynton and Michael, who were masked, instantly applied their Northern Irish accents. They were made to sit on the benches, and their hoods were removed. Boynton stood in front of them with the Mauser fitted with the silencer, in his hand. In between them was a pumpkin with a face drawn on it. Boynton put a shot right between the eyes of the pumpkin, and a mass of pulp came out the back.

In the meantime, Lucy had got back to the Hall and was reunited with Johann and Victoria. The children were there, and they were all sleeping on the floor curled up with the dogs.

Lucy was starving and grabbed a sandwich and a mug of tea. She gave an account of events to a mixture of amusement and concern but Johann, having worked with Lucy in Normandy was fully aware of what made her tick, and these escapades were a way of coming to terms with that experience. He was pleased to hear that the chloroform had worked well.

Back at the bunker, the two prisoners were in a state of anxiety. They had initially refused to say anything but after Boynton had produced the timing pencil they had a rethink. He placed it in the pumpkin between them and told them where the next pencil was going. After two minutes, it blew the pumpkin apart and splattered them with pulp. The effect reduced them to a trembling state. They disclosed some twenty-five locations that they were supplying. The bulk of their supplies came from an American in Norwich and another in King's Lynn. When pressed they gave names and addresses, and Michael noted it all down.

Initially, they were reluctant to give personal histories. Boynton produced Himmler, who was squirming in a bucket. The larger man admitted he was a deserter from the army. He had come from Liverpool and had deserted from the Cheshire Regiment after Dunkirk. The main man had dodged the draft and gone into the London underworld. Having fallen out with others, he had fled with the proceeds of his criminal activity, and his wife had purchased the property for cash.

Michael hooded the men again. He told them to sit still because Himmler was being released.

"When are you coming back?" asked the bigger man.

"When we are ready," said Michael.

Boynton and Michael left them in the dark for a couple of hours and went back to the cottage. It was midnight, but Aggie had stayed up in expectation. They took a sandwich with tea and a large Jameson's. A placard was written out using a letter template. It simply read 'Black Market Extortioners. Army deserters and London Criminal – Zorro'.

Aggie typed out a note to the police detailing their activity and their suppliers. It was placed in a plain envelope. Boynton loaded a few items into the truck in a wooden crate.

At 2am, they returned to the prisoners. They were led up the stairs and into the back of the truck, where their legs were tied. They drove to Sheringham, where the pair were tied back-to-back to a lamp post at a location that was not overlooked. Whilst still hooded, and when they were secure, the handcuffs were removed.

"Who are you?" asked the shorter man.

"I am Zorro. You will leave Norfolk. If you return, I will kneecap the pair of you." said Boynton.

Michael produced scissors, and the rest of the men's clothing was cut away, so they were naked. The hoods were removed. Boynton poured lukewarm tar over them, then covered them with feathers.

Half an hour later, they parked up near the house. They walked up the sidetrack in the moonlight. The dogs in the compound were sleeping. They would not wake up as Boynton put silenced shots into each of them. They cut through the wire and tapped out the glass on a side window of the barn. Boynton tied a can with a gallon of petrol to the window frame then taped half a pound of plastic explosive to it with a fifteen-minute timing pencil. They dragged the dog corpses to a point below the window then snapped the pencil and made off. This was a blast incendiary. When it went off it would fill the entire building with a fireball, and anything combustible would go up.

Five minutes later they passed the pub car park. The only vehicle was the Bentley. Boynton crept back and dropped a ten-minute timing pencil in the petrol tank. The letter to the police was posted in the police station. The building was in darkness.

Twenty minutes later, they were back at Spelthorpe. They never heard the huge explosion as the barn went up nor the lesser explosion from the car.

At 6am the pair at the lamp post were discovered. It was over an hour before the police got there. The press got there first. All they could say was that a gang of two Irishmen with a snake called Himmler and a French prostitute had kidnapped them. The police were hardly concerned with that and arrested them for indecency and army desertion. When the note surfaced, they raided the suppliers. The offenders admitted their guilt and were remanded in custody. When those threatened were visited, they made statements knowing that they were now safe. The two fires remained a mystery. Nothing was left of the barn because of the petrol and spirits that were stockpiled there.

The press loved it. 'Zorro strikes again' was the headline and the internal pages were full of accounts of the shop keepers who had been threatened by the pair.

A couple of phone calls were received at Spelthorpe. Ash took them both. One was from the King with his Norfolk crown on. He was absolutely delighted and confessed that he wished he knew who Zorro and his associates were. He said he would love to give them a medal. Ash responded, "The problem with that, Bertie, is that it might mean the end of Zorro because his methods seem a little different from the way the police do things, even if they are much more effective. But you never know, they might have medals from you already, but I couldn't possibly comment on that."

The King laughed and said, "If you do find out Ash. Please pass on my congratulations."

A similar phone call was received from Detective Chief Inspector John Skingle. As a result of Zorro, they had made major inroads into the black market and seized goods worth many thousands of pounds. He confirmed they were not looking for Zorro because the two offenders were too frightened to make statements.

Ash replied, "I couldn't possibly comment. All I can say is that those two did try it on at our store but two of our burly foresters picked them up and threw them out in the street. As far as we were concerned it was dealt with."

Two weeks later, on a Saturday, on the strength of her immoral earnings Lucy and Johann invited Victoria, Michael and the Boyntons to participate in a slap-up meal at the appropriately chosen Hotel de Paris at Cromer. At the end of the meal Michael produced a pair of black lace panties that he had recovered from the offender. He presented them to his sister with the words "Eh voilà, madame, le reçu pour tes services formidable." (Here, madam the receipt for your splendid services.)

Aggie responded, "That's one hell of a pair of bloomers, Lucy! You will have to share the secret as to where you got such powerful underwear."

With that she raised her glass and proposed a toast to the two Zorros and Lyla. It was a fitting celebration.

Three months later, the two 'salesmen' appeared before the judge at the assizes. He gave them ten years each with hard labour.

"Selling black market goods is bad enough but forcing those sales with threats and intimidation is unforgiveable," said the judge. The suppliers each received five years.

The lady at the house sold up and moved away. The word got about that Norfolk was not the place to go for a life of crime.

Joanna reported that at the veterinary surgery, she had an influx of new puppies and half of them had been named Zorro. PC Carter came up and had a celebratory Jameson's with Boynton. Nothing was said. It didn't need to be.

13

Honeymoon and honey trap

November 1947- October 1948

The rest of the year 1947 proceeded without any significant changes at Spelthorpe. The harvest here was better than expected after the summer rainfall shortage. Irrigation from the ponds and lakes had helped. Emma had gone up to Lincoln in May and was settling down to life as an officer's wife. There were plenty of other officers' wives on the barracks estate and many of them had babies and young children. She decided to take several months out from work but not from her studies which she was able to continue in Lincoln. By the end of the year, she gained a full chartered accountant qualification. She then started undertaking work from home for some of the local businesses which paid well. George had settled in quickly with his three sections, and Denis was there now. He would take a section every now and again as did George to cover leave and courses. Extra effort went into bringing the subaltern up to speed, but he had an experienced sergeant and had the good sense to listen to him. Daisy would alternate spending the day with George and Emma and became a popular member of the team. The work was varied, and they covered a large area so quite a lot of travelling with overnight stops took place, but it was far less intense than London in the immediate aftermath of the war. Visits to Spelthorpe were limited because of petrol rationing, but judicious use of fuel enabled some coupons to be saved up for longer trips.

Thursday, the twentieth of November, was the highlight of the social year at national level with the wedding of Philip and Elizabeth at Westminster Abbey. On the day before, Philip was accorded the title of Duke of Edinburgh. National austerity continued, to which there was no letup – evidenced by the fact that even the royal wedding dress required ration coupons for the material for Elizabeth's gown. Some 2,000 people were invited to Westminster Abbey for the service, and these included Ash and Helen, Victoria and Michael, Lucy and Johann and the Boyntons. Although protocol dictated that those at the very front would all have royal status, the fact that all eight from Spelthorpe were there and had been seated quite close to the front was an indication of the value that the king and queen had placed on their relationship. Medals were worn, and given the number and quality of the awards, that turned a few heads from the other guests. Despite the ongoing difficulties it was a splendid affair.

The Spelthorpe eight returned home on the same day.

It was a symbolic mark of respect and kindness that on the following day the royal bouquet was returned to the abbey and laid on the tomb of the unknown warrior.

The first night of the honeymoon was spent at Broadlands in Hampshire, the home of Philip's uncle, Lord Louis Mountbatten who had just recently returned from his role as the last Viceroy of India. Thereafter they went to the Balmoral Estate, where almost ten years earlier Michael and Victoria had honeymooned as the guests of the king and queen.

Three weeks later, the king and queen came to Spelthorpe for pheasant shooting. The shooting went well, and they enjoyed the relaxed set-up. Bertie appeared to be coughing rather a lot, and this was not helped by his heavy smoking habit. The Royals would all be spending Christmas at Sandringham as usual, and an invitation for the Spelthorpe team to shoot there early in the new year was extended.

Christmas followed the usual pattern, and on Christmas Day at the Hall, there was a full family attendance. Paris had worked its customary romantic charm at the end of October when Michael, Victoria, Lucy and Johann had made a three-night stay because Lucy announced to them all that she was now expecting baby number two. The Calvados apple brandy that Ash and Michael had brought back from Normandy was well received. Boynton was in a good mood because Aggie had given him a Malinois puppy. She had seen him working and training with Daniel and had been so impressed by the alertness, loyalty and guarding instinct of Daniel's two dogs that she thought it would be a welcome addition and a contrasting companion to Labradors, Hund and Thor. She had bought the puppy along with her and he stole the show. Boynton concluded that it had been a good year despite the challenging weather because all the ladies seemed to be getting pregnant, and nobody had died.

1948 was to be a year of major national importance. After a huge amount of squabbling the heralded National Health Service finally came into existence on the fifth of July. Many of the older doctors did not want it because they felt their independence and ability to earn extra money would be compromised. There was opposition in parliament too, but it was driven through with a compromise. Local doctors would not become state employees. They would continue with practices remaining as private businesses, but they would have a contractual agreement with the government to provide healthcare. Things outside of the contract could be charged privately.

The Spelthorpe practice had worked well. Jennifer and Johann were equal partners. Lucy had bought Johann in, so each had a fifty percent share of the business. By having both a male and female doctor at the practice it brought in more registrations as in the countryside, conservative views still applied in relation to the more personal and delicate conditions. Johann was qualified in surgery and this meant that a lot of minor matters could be attended to locally. Both got on well and NHS patients were registered with the practice i.e. both doctors, but patients would be seen by one or the other if the situation demanded that. Their skilled dedication was recognised and they held the trust of the community. They had taken on a secretary and a nurse to deal with routine issues and some of the paperwork and they had advertised for a pharmacist. In the view of the Spelthorpe partners, it was better for the health of local people and the estate. People's worries could be dealt with immediately and issues nipped in the bud rather than being allowed to fester because of the fees. At the same time, the new arrangements and free service did foster a degree of hypochondria, but both were soon aware of those individuals and a stock of placebo sugar pills of different colours was kept at the surgery to treat them very effectively. Some patients swore by them and would come in to ask for specific colours.

Jennifer supported Voltaire's view:

'The art of medicine consists in amusing the patient while nature cures the disease.'

Hospitals previously run by local authorities or charities were now taken over by health boards, and many of these now provided training for nurses and doctors.

In October, Ash took a call from the newly promoted Detective Superintendent John Skingle asking if he could call at the cottage. An hour later, he turned up. They greeted each other as old friends.

"I'm surprised you are still at it," said Ash. "I thought you lot retired after thirty years, and it's thirty-five years since we first met when you were the local village constable."

"They bribed me to stay on with another rank up so when I do go the pension will be considerably more. The kids are off our hands, and I'd get bored out of my skull at home all the time. There's only so much decorating and gardening one can do but we have a dog now, and he keeps the missus happy. The problem is a lack of experience because we lost so many police officers over the war years, not in the sense that they were killed, but some are still serving having gone up the promotion ladder and have stayed on with the military. With a few exceptions, we were left with the wasters and those we took on were not up to much, and that resulted in crime going up. I must admit that this Zorro character helped us out a lot, particularly in the rural areas because we had to concentrate on the towns, although officially, I can't be seen to applaud his tactical excesses, but none of us will be looking too far into such matters." said John.

"Is there any hope?" asked Ash. "We are not getting anywhere near the cases up before the bench like we used to get before the war, and most of what we get seems to be tedious stuff where people have been a little greedy or not stuck to the rationing rules, but the real criminals must be milking it and getting off scot-free."

"That's the way it has been, but over the last year some very good ones we had previously have come back in after being demobbed, and we have managed to recruit some good new ones with a lot more fire in their bellies. That has helped, and we have got rid of a lot of the idle ones, so I'm optimistic and that's the main reason they asked me to stay on, so they got the right leadership." said John.

"But discussing the current inadequacies of the police is not what you came here for. What do you want John?" asked Ash as he poured out two large measures of Jameson's Irish whiskey to go with the coffees that Helen had served up.

"It's a bit delicate," said John. "We have a honey trap blackmail situation going on. Simply put, there's a couple at it. The woman is very attractive, and she gets a man to get in bed with her, and whilst she is performing, her accomplice takes the photos. Then a week later the man gets the pictures with a demand for cash."

"Do they pay up?" asked Ash. "Sounds like these fools have only got themselves to blame."

"That's the problem," said John. "They only go for the rich and the famous, and we have had three so far. They paid up and it was £500 each, all in cash but, they won't make statements or go to court unless we have an overwhelming case. That's a lot of money they are making, and that's just the ones we know about. We can have our victims in court behind a screen as Mr X, Mr Y and Mr Z. One was a rich businessman with a wife who would take him to the cleaners, another was a circuit judge, and the last one was a bishop."

Ash laughed. "The bishop doesn't surprise me. So, if I'm guessing right, you want me to be their next target and hopefully you will pounce with your heavies before I have to perform, which of course I won't."

"That's about it. We know what they look like and especially the lady, because she holds nothing back in front of the camera. They get a short-term rental of a flat. The last time was in Norwich and as a result of that, we contacted all the agents in Norfolk, and we've just had a confirmed hit in King's Lynn to start in a week. They normally spend a week doing the research in the better type of establishments within 200 yards of the flat. Once they have got a target, they strike and then clear out within a couple of days. At King's Lynn there is another flat next door that is vacant, and the agent has let us have it at no charge for a couple of weeks. We got in and have a concealed microphone wired to the next door flat, so we can listen in. When you say the keyword, we will be in, and the photographer won't escape out of the window because it's three floors up. So, we've done our homework. The question is, will you do it?"

"So, you must think I'm rich and famous. Looks more like a job for Zorro, but I understand he only operates in a black hood. I suppose I must be seen to be supporting the police, and it looks like a bit of fun, but there are two conditions."

"What are they?" asked the superintendent.

"Firstly, that you pick me up and bring me back and I suppose that will be for two evenings because I can't use all my coupons up on the petrol, and secondly and more importantly, you tell Helen what you have just told me."

"Agreed," said John.

Ash called Helen in from the garden. After listening she saw the funny side and told them to go ahead.

"I just can't wait to see the photos! Did the bishop keep his mitre on?"

As agreed, two days later, a car collected Ash, and they went back to the main police station in King's Lynn, where he got a briefing. They showed him the photos of the bishop and the judge so he would know the woman when she approached him. He could understand why she managed to draw them in. The plan was that on the first day that he would go to the selected venue – a large hotel bar – and make it known who he was by having a couple of undercover detectives come in and have conversations with him that could be easily overheard. He would be greeted as Sir Ash. Ash's story would be that he was engaged in meetings with government agricultural officials over a three-day period and he always used this hotel in the evenings. There would always be two detectives, a man and a woman posing as a couple, who would be in the bar, watching and following at a discreet distance to establish if the bait had been taken. Two more would be in the flat next door listening in. It was apparent to Ash that John was determined to pull this one off and was putting the resources in, and probably some of his best detectives. Ash was introduced to all those working on the case.

That evening, Ash went to the bar and spent the time there. After an hour, he spotted the woman who walked in. She appeared tidy but with no make-up and clearly not dressed to seduce. She was with a man of similar age and sat a few feet from the bar where Ash was sitting on a stool. They ordered their drinks. The plan went into action.

John Skingle walked in and boomed, "Hello Sir Ash. I haven't seen you for a while. What brings you up this way?"

"I'm attending conferences with the ministry for the next three days, and I am on my own. I always come here because the beer is quite good and sometimes, they have someone on the piano. The countess can't stand this town, and she gets bored so she's off riding with her friends from Sandringham."

They had a brief conversation about agriculture and the government, then John made his excuses and left. Ash noticed that the couple were listening intently. *Looks like the fish is taking the bait,* he thought to himself.

He spent another half an hour at the bar, then walked out. The suspects remained. The two detectives struck up a conversation with each other that again was overheard.

"Who was that chap?" asked the male.

"Oh, him," said his female companion. "He's Sir Ash Cromwell – one of the richest men in Norfolk. They've got thousands of acres. We don't see him this way very often, but he's the boss at the Magistrate Court. He dishes out the porridge and quite a lot of it from what people have told me."

A few minutes later, the target couple drank up and left. Ash went back to the police station and waited. An hour later, the two who had been in the neighbouring flat returned "It's on for tomorrow," they said. "They have taken the bait. We heard them. She will get you back to the flat and take you to the bedroom while he snaps some pictures of the pair of you."

On the following evening, Ash got to the bar at 8pm. Ten minutes later, the woman walked in. She was made up but not overly so. She wore a short fur coat, heels, black stockings and a very low-cut, knee-length dress, that displayed what was potentially on offer. She ordered a drink and looked around and seeing Ash alone at the bar she sidled over to him.

"Hello, stranger," she said. "You look like you could do with some company."

"It's always nice to talk to an attractive lady." said Ash.

"And you're an attractive man," she said. "You look quite powerful and important. I like that in a man. They say power is the ultimate aphrodisiac."

The conversation continued for another fifteen minutes. He told her that he was engaged in agricultural work with the ministry.

Then she said, "Would you like to continue this conversation elsewhere? My flat is only a couple of minutes away, and if you think I am attractive then I might be able to let you see a little more of me."

"With an offer like that how can I refuse. It seems very interesting."

With that he stood up. She took his arm, and they walked out.

They walked the two minutes to the flat. Ash felt he would have to make things a little bit more realistic *Forgive me, Helen,* he thought to himself, and as they walked up the stairs his hand dropped, and he caressed her bottom. As they got to the door of the flat, he kissed her, and she reached up and responded passionately. Then he cupped her right breast and fondled it.

They went inside. He sat on a large settee whilst she stood in front of him.

"Are you going to take me to bed then?" she asked.

"Not straight away," said Ash as he removed his jacket and tie and kicked off his shoes.

"I normally like the lady to slowly disrobe. I'd like to see and appreciate you visually first. It turns me on."

"As you command, sir."

And with that she pulled up a chair and proceeded to perform a striptease in front of him. With her dress and brassiere removed, she slowly took of her stockings and suspender belt then finally removed her panties, which she tossed towards him. Then she stood in front of him completely naked. Ash was aware of a shuffling noise from behind a door that presumably led into a kitchen area.

"Do you like what you see?" she asked.

"You are very beautiful," said Ash.

"Well, come and enjoy me!" she said as she reached down took his hand and led him into the bedroom. She left the door wide open. She directed him over to the bed where he lay looking up at her. She lay on the bed beside him then straddled him and started to undo the buttons on his shirt.

"Heaven." he said. "I think I've just arrived in heaven."

'Heaven' was the key trigger word and a second later, the door burst open. There was a struggle as one detective jumped on the photographer and another grabbed the camera. Then a policewoman in uniform burst into the bedroom, grabbing the woman. She put a set of handcuffs on the woman and covered her with a blanket from the bed.

The woman screamed, "You bastard. You're not just a bastard. You're a first-class bastard!" She spat at Ash.

The policewoman gave her a firm slap and said, "That's enough of that. You are nicked, madam!"

They took the two away in separate vehicles then searched the flat. John Skingle walked in.

"And just when I was starting to enjoy my evening," said Ash. "She put on such a good striptease. Worthy of Mata Hari that was, but at least you will get the photos of it for the CID office. I'd heard him snapping away, but I had better things to look at! At least on this occasion you didn't find the word 'Zorro' written on the lady's backside."

John was pleased in the extreme.

"You played that brilliantly," he said. "I was next door listening. Now I suppose we had better get you home to your lawful wedded wife, and I expect after all that stimulation she will suffer for it."

Ash got home just after midnight and related the story. Helen thought it was hilarious, but she did note that he was exceptionally passionate that night!

On the following day in the afternoon John Skingle phoned.

"We have got them. Hook, line and sinker," he said. "They have both put their hands up to it all. They had pictures with the bishop, the judge and the businessman, and with three others too, so they got about £3,000 at least over the last few months. We have recovered just under £2,000 of that. And to cap it all, we got the film developed and I've got about twenty shots of you and the stripper. The only problem is that you are either an Oscar-worthy actor or you genuinely were enjoying yourself. My guess is that you would rather not have Helen see them, but next time you are this way pop in, and you can have a look. We have charged them with conspiracy to demand with menaces. Should be a guilty plea because if they upset another judge, they will never see the light of day. He was a deserter from the army, and she was a showgirl that he hooked up with in London."

Three months later they appeared before the assizes. They both got seven years imprisonment. With a bishop and a judge as the victims, it was clear that the establishment always looks after its own.

For Ash, it was a good story. Michael and Lucy were delighted that their dad still had it in him, despite missing out on a part in the Zorro escapades. Victoria and the Boyntons shared in the hilarity.

14

George Cross Island

May 1950 – May 1951

The years passed by, and at Spelthorpe the worst excesses of austerity were averted. With petrol for agricultural use there were few difficulties and limitations, so all the tractors, trucks and jeeps managed well. The fuel was marked with a red dye to discourage abuse. They managed within the rationing system by cutting out non-essential journeys and saving up coupons for private use, but a secret stock remained, as it had from 1939 for emergencies.

In 1948 bread rationing ended, and this was followed by the end of clothes rationing the following year. Public discontent with rationing resulted in a Labour win in the February 1950 election but with a very narrow majority of only five seats which meant that their days were numbered. Finally, in May of 1950 petrol rationing came to an end.

For the Spelthorpe family there had been additions. Lucy's second baby, a boy named Leo, had arrived in June of 1948. Emma gave birth to a second daughter, Elizabeth who was known as Betty from day one, and Dr Jennifer produced Josephine – a sister for Jack, in September. A similar rate of productivity occurred throughout the estate and village leading to a succession of christenings for Reverend Paddy to perform as well as guaranteeing the future of the Spelthorpe Primary School and the nursery at the Hall.

Aggie was approaching her sixtieth year but was not slowing down, and she was not inclined to do so.

In 1949, Beverley Boynton left school and commenced her training as a state-registered nurse at Norwich Hospital. Her brother, Harry had been taken on as an apprentice butcher by the estate. He had been working at the shop informally since the age of eleven and already had many of the skills needed. In his spare time, he worked closely with his father in gamekeeping. As expected, he was an excellent shot.

George's three-year stint at Lincoln was scheduled to come to an end. He was offered an overseas posting for a further three years to the Mediterranean island of Malta to replace the post holder who was to retire. Given the strong naval connection, Denis would accompany him along with one of the Lincoln sections. Two would remain as it was felt that with reduced demand levels, they would cope. The senior lieutenant remaining would be promoted to captain. The Malta position had five sections in total and involved working closely with their naval counterparts. Denis would help in that respect, for it meant promotion. George would be promoted to major and Denis to a full naval lieutenant (equivalent to an army captain). Denis had married a local girl from Lincoln. Both jumped at the opportunity. It was a plum posting with excellent family facilities. All-year-round sunshine was the icing on the cake.

Malta was a leading defence establishment for all three services with several barracks around the island. It was key to defending British interests in the Mediterranean and the route to Suez. Between 1940 and 1942, it was probably the most bombed location on the planet as it had been a vital naval and air force base critical to cutting off German and Italian supplies to North Africa, and that was followed by the invasion of Italy. For their courage under fire with heavy civilian losses, the people of Malta had been awarded the George Cross by the king. As a result of the continual bombardment, the island and seas around were littered with bombs, shells and mines, so there was always something to do.

In the third week of April, George, Emma and the children sailed from Southampton to arrive a week later. Emma had made the most of the end of clothing rationing and had topped up her wardrobe so she would be able to play the part of the major's wife with elegance. She was now totally familiar with expectations and military traditions towards the ladies. Daisy had been deposited at Spelthorpe under the care of Lucy, and she seemed very content to be back with her brothers. There would be no issues as Joanna had spayed her six months earlier. The draconian quarantine requirements made the accompaniment of dogs impractical. Victoria had maintained contact with Princess Elizabeth and Philip, with visits and brief stays over the last two years to Spelthorpe, Sandringham and Balmoral. Philip and Elizabeth were now based in Malta as Philip continued with his naval career. She wrote to Elizabeth informing her of her brother's impending arrival.

On arrival in Malta, George and Emma were allocated a senior officer's house within the St George's barracks. It was well appointed, and their own effects were already waiting for them within the barracks stores, having been shipped out a few days before their departure. This was all part of the massive Pembroke Garrison, where there were two other barracks: St Andrew's and St Patrick's. It was a good location, some five miles out from the busy capital, Valletta. There was a school, a NAAFI shop, medical and sports facilities. It was a stone's throw from St George's Bay where there was a dedicated beach club for forces personnel and their families – the Robb Lido. The only minor snag was the noise from the shooting ranges at the rear, but they were only operated during the day and not every day.

George and Denis settled in quickly with their new team, but having a section go with them provided a useful informal introduction from those who knew him and his methods. One could not help but think that the island was a mixture of a massive base and a holiday camp for service personnel. The social life was good with sporting and social events along with the usual officers' mess functions. Once away from the barrack areas, the countryside with huge areas of karst limestone with parts farmed was not unpleasant, although it lacked the number of trees they were used to. The harbours were colourful with traditional, brightly painted fishing boats, and the year-round climate and sea temperatures were a marked contrast to the Norfolk Coast – in fact, George found it easy to swim all year round.

The people were generally kind and welcoming, particularly if one took the time to engage with them. It was just simple courtesy. The only thing that irritated George was the habit of Maltese men who would blast songbirds and migrating birds with shotguns at each and every opportunity. Most were far too small to eat. It seemed pointless and cruel.

The capital, Valletta, was built on the Sciberras peninsular with harbours on each side. There were ancient forts, and the area was steeped in history, some of which was bloody in the extreme. In medieval times, the island was occupied by the knights of St

John, whose origin went back to the crusades. The island was besieged by Turks in 1565 who, after capturing Fort St Elmo at the end of the peninsula beheaded some of the knights and floated their bodies on crosses across the Grand Harbour towards Fort St Angelo. The Christian knights responded by beheading their Turkish prisoners and using their heads as cannon balls, firing them at the Turks who held the peninsula. At the end of a long siege, the knights finally triumphed.

Frequently, there were visiting naval ships, and others were based at Malta. For the crews, their place of entertainment was Strait Street, one of the many steep, narrow streets in the capital with tall buildings on both sides. To the sailors, the place was known as 'The Gut'. Here a sailor could get a meal and get drunk for ten shillings in bars like Dirty Dicks or the Galvanised Donkey (real name – the Silver Horse) and there were other distractions to which cost more money and often a visit to the ships' surgeons for some penicillin. Others would head back to the ships drunk only to discover on the following day that they had acquired quite offensive tattoos. At one bar, the ladies would pick up half crowns from the corner edge of the table using a part of the anatomy that was not usually visible. The experienced ladies would feel the coins first because many a drunken sailor would get thrown out for heating up the coins with their lighters.

Emma decided to settle in properly before seeking any work. She had children to look after and had made contacts and friends at the local nursery. At the end of the afternoon on a late July day, three months after their arrival, George came home to find Emma with Katie and Betty and a little boy who was almost a year younger than Katie.

"This is George," said Emma. "He is Katie's best friend. They seem to spend all their time together, and it's odd. I think he looks quite like you. They could be brother and sister. His mum is coming to pick him up. I have got to know her quite well. She works here, but a year ago, her husband, who was high up in the navy and a lot older than her, was killed in a car crash. You will like her. We get on very well together, and she seems to be coping with it all."

George thought nothing of it. His mind was full of dealing with bombs located in the harbour – a project he was working on with the navy. He sat down then, Katie joined him to be followed onto the sofa by young George. There was a knock at the door, and Emma went to answer.

"Come in, Caroline," said Emma. "They are both on the sofa with my husband. He got home a little earlier today."

Caroline walked in and saw George and stood there in silence and realisation. She blushed, and George looked like he had seen a ghost.

Emma suddenly exclaimed, "I was going to make you a cup of tea, but I've run out of milk. I'll only be ten minutes at the NAAFI. You two get to know one another," and she dashed out.

George stood up and walked over to Caroline. She looked shocked but happy. She held out her hands, and George took them both, and they just gazed at one another as they had done just over three years earlier. A spark had been reignited. He loved Emma but now he felt he loved Caroline too, because she was the mother of his son. It all made sense to him.

"Emma said to me they are like brother and sister, and now I know why. I thought I would never see you again." said George.

"Me too. I got back here two days after we parted. Then I discovered I was pregnant, but I knew it wasn't my husband's because we had tried, and the tests showed that he couldn't be a dad. But he accepted things, and he always knew George wasn't his, but never said anything and when George came along, he just took him totally as his own."

They moved into the hallway just out of sight of the children, and they kissed affectionately. It wasn't sexual, it was just affection, a deep affection brought about by their brief encounter and fate.

"Why did you call him George?" asked George.

"It was because of you. After we parted I told myself it was just a dream, but I had feelings, and when I saw the London Gazette entry with your name against the Military Cross for 'extreme courage in Palestine'. I knew who you were. So, when he was born on the George Cross Island at the hospital overlooking St George's Bay, George was the obvious choice, and I wanted his real father's name just to keep the link. It probably sounds a bit odd to you."

"What are we going to do?" asked George.

"I don't know," she said. "I like Emma. She's been kind to me, and we get on, and I won't do anything to spoil that. And George loves his older sister. It's so odd. Of all the children in the nursery it was those two who paired up and they ignore the rest of them. It's uncanny. And I know how close you and Emma are. She's told me, although at the time I didn't put the two together because we only used Christian names."

"We'll just have to see how it goes. If fate brought us together then fate will sort it out," said George. They gripped each other's hands, then kissed again, then went into the lounge and sat on the settee with the children. George picked up his son and sat him on his lap. He was joined by Katie on the other side.

Emma returned and they took tea together. Caroline explained how she was the headmistress at the primary school, and that after her husband's death, she had decided to stay on. She had moved out of the large, allocated house and now had a flat overlooking the bay only 200 yards from where George and Emma now lived.

As the months went by, the three got closer and whilst from the outside it might have seemed odd, it was as if Emma wanted George to be close to Caroline, and when they were close, she showed not the slightest jealousy. It was as if some greater force was guiding them to be together. George and Caroline knew they would tell Emma, but the time had to be right, and they would know when that was, but to leave it too long would jeopardise the trust that existed between them.

George enjoyed Malta. The work was varied. They were dealing with both German and Italian munitions. They tended to find that the Italian bombs were less sophisticated and without the built-in booby traps, but caution was the rule of the day, and nobody wished to add to the victim list. Many bombs were found at or near the surface because the rock did not lend itself to penetration in the same way as London clay, so there was less digging for the NCO's and privates. As a rule, if there was sufficient distance and a safe cordon the safest bet was to blow them in situ, and if they were in a hollow that was better because the blast went up rather than out. The same applied to those at sea. In harbours, it was critical because boats or dragging anchor chains could set them off. They could lift the bomb by flotation, then tow it out to sea and blow it or just let it go in deep water. Both options were practical.

George and his team worked with their naval counterparts. It was a case of working hand in hand and getting the job done. Relations were good. The navy tended to use the well-tried and tested hard copper hat divers with heavy weights and heavy boots, with air fed down a hose from a pump on the surface. This was alright, but it took time to set up. As most of their work was shallow, George preferred to use a simple re-breather closed-circuit set where the diver breathed from a bag that was at the same pressure as the water around him. It would be topped up by an oxygen cylinder and the carbon dioxide would be scrubbed chemically. It was ideal for shallow work and had been used for sabotage in the war when limpet mines were attached to ships – something the Italians had used successfully at Alexandria in Egypt in December 1941 when they sank two British battleships, a tanker and a destroyer when frogmen rode specially adapted slow torpedoes. The re-breather sets did not emit 'give away' bubbles.

The only downside was that the oxygen could become poisonous, particularly if used at any depth.

In the war, in Vichy France, two Frenchmen, Jaques Cousteau and Émile Gagnan had perfected a demand valve which allowed breathing from a compressed air cylinder. The system was just being marketed, and George managed to get two sets, which they tried out. The diver wore a weight belt which could be dumped if there was an issue, but the vitally important thing was to exhale on the way up because if you held your breath, your lungs could blow up. It was important not to stay down too long and to come up slowly to prevent one from getting the bends that could paralyse a diver. There were tables for this, which had to be strictly applied. Using this method was far more flexible. A diver could go down, rope a bomb and fill a bag with the exhaust air from the mouthpiece, and this would lift the bomb so it could be gently towed away. In many cases it was a five-to-ten-minute job so there was no risk of the bends.

George and Denis started using this equipment for pleasure purposes, and they got quite good. They were self-taught because there was no one to train them, but like his brother and sisters, he had a good French knowledge, so he was able to translate instructions and published advice from Cousteau, who was carrying out pioneering work. They always dived as a pair and never went below twenty metres and limited their dives to twenty-five minutes, but as they got more experienced and relaxed, they found that their air lasted a lot longer. Keeping it shallow helped in that way as well and it was pointless going too deep because the reds and yellows of the marine life turned to monotonous shades of blue as these colours were absorbed by the depth of water. There were plenty of fish, and sometimes they would encounter quite large groupers. The only thing to watch for was the numerous sea urchins with sharp spines that could pierce the skin and snap off. These were like little black hedgehogs and plagued the rocks just offshore from some beaches. One would end up applying lemon juice to dissolve the calcium carbonate which was the main component of the spine.

George sent regular reports of the diving activity back to the Royal Engineer Headquarters at Chatham as he felt this was an area that would be of benefit to the Royal Engineers where divers were engaged on construction work on bridges, piers and harbours. Considerable interest was generated. He was asked to develop matters and purchase items as he saw fit and to work with others and the Royal Army Medical Corps on the safety side in order to produce a draft manual for Royal Engineer operations.

The social side worked brilliantly too. There were beach parties with water skiing, and sailing and by arrangement, George and Emma would meet up with Philip and Princess Elizabeth. Caroline would also come along. Philip had been acquainted with Caroline's husband who had been based in Malta, Cyprus and Palestine. He had been considerably older than her and held the rank of commodore. George, Emma and Caroline would tend to avoid the very big social events although on occasions George was expected to attend and did so alone. They would attend more local mess nights where ladies and guests were invited. Philip and Elizabeth were very happy in Malta and took a great delight in doing the ordinary things. On occasions George and Emma were invited to dine with them. Philip took a keen interest in George's diving activities and had a couple of goes himself. They were aware that Michael and Victoria were likely to be coming out the following year and were looking forward to that. Elizabeth remarked how helpful and kind they had been in the period before the engagement.

In early December, it became apparent that Caroline was spending much of her time with George and Emma, and young George had been accepted as part of the family. It was an unusual arrangement, but it worked, so Emma suggested she and young George just move in as there was plenty of room in the large four bedroomed house that had been provided. That is what happened. They became intimate, and George would quite often hug and kiss Caroline along with Emma.

On Christmas day they went to church in the morning and Denis and his wife Anna, came round for Christmas lunch. It was a fine lunch that Emma and Caroline had prepared, and fortunately there were no call-outs. Denis and Anna left at 7pm, and the children were put to bed an hour later. They all shared the same room because that was what they wanted.

The three retired to the settee. George had put on some Christmas music on the record player, and they relaxed with George in the middle with an arm round each of them on either side and their heads nestled into his shoulder.

Emma said, "I've noticed that George keeps calling you Daddy."

George replied, "I think I have to tell you something. Both Caroline and I wanted to tell you for a long time, and if you are angry, then you are right to be so. You should know that I am George's Daddy."

"How come?" asked Emma, who was obviously shocked at the revelation.

It was then that George explained exactly how it all happened. He talked of the daily fear in Palestine that had haunted them whilst there, of the bombs and the killings and the body parts and the separation and having to deal with those fears in the soldiers for whom he was responsible. Caroline explained the same about her teaching experience, the fear in a British school in Jerusalem, and for her too, the separation.

And George explained why he was on the boat and leaving early because he was a prime target for the terrorists, because he had wiped out eight of their bombers. He told how they had met and had something in common, and what happened was out of a relief from the fear and a reaction to the separation, and how they had both buried it, or so they thought, until fate took a hand.

Caroline said, "I know how you love George, and he loves you and I love you too in a sisterly way, but we had to tell you and to beg your forgiveness. But we have young George, and I know George would not run away from that like so many others."

George said, "This might sound strange, but I love you both, and I want to look after you both. We have discovered something that works, and because it works, I had to tell you. I know we'll have to go along with what you decide, but whatever you decide, there is one thing you have to know; I will never forsake Katie, nor Betty and nor George and seeing them together, I feel they have decided for us."

Emma sat in a stunned silence for a moment, then asked them for time to think. She had an excellent analytical mind and could evaluate options in a very rational way.

After thinking things over, Emma said, "There is nothing to decide. I should have realised this because of the way you hit it off with young George and treated him like the others, and how you got on with Caroline right from the start. I'm just as stuck because I love you both. I don't care what people think, and I know that even with Caroline, you don't love me any less, George. It is not as if it is the first time that something like this has happened, and it has worked with others, and in some parts of the world, it is totally normal, but don't let that give you any ideas George. You can have Caroline and me but no more. Your name is George, not Abdul. So that is it. We carry on as we are and that is my decision because I do not want to lose either of you, and young George can carry on calling you Daddy."

They both hugged Emma. George kissed them both. He went out and came back with three glasses of Jameson's whiskey, which they drank after toasting the three of them and the children.

George and Emma then talked at length about Spelthorpe and that from now on Caroline should consider herself a member of the Spelthorpe family. They told her of how at Spelthorpe they had ignored convention in their relationships and that the only thing that was important was love, human kindness and a fierce loyalty to one another. They didn't need to worry about what others thought in terms of their conventional standards. If they wanted a Bohemian lifestyle that was up to them. The Royals had been doing things like that for centuries. She would meet Victoria and Michael in the following year.

"Promise us one thing," said George.

"What is that?" asked Caroline.

"That when my time ends here in Malta, that you will come back and live at Spelthorpe."

"I will," said Caroline.

It was late so they retired to bed, but they wanted to be close, so that night the three slept together with George in the middle. At 6am they found three more had joined them.

With the new year, there was a greater degree of optimism at Spelthorpe. After the 1947 winter, nothing could be as bad and now petrol rationing was over, things started to look better for the flying school, the chalet lettings and the shooting. Boynton was intending to double the numbers of pheasants and partridges to be reared for the next season. The new lands were in full production and the additional pig and turkey project had taken off. The two stockmen had taken up residence in the semi-detached cottages and were looking after that side of the business area on a day-to-day basis. Daniel was fully recovered from the war, and would always bear the mental scars, but with Angela's attention all was fully under control. However, if any purchase of Japanese-manufactured items came to his attention, his anger came out. The head forester had retired, and Daniel who had gained several qualifications had been selected by Michael to replace him. The others respected that.

Back on Malta, the ménage à trois was working seamlessly. Emma had taken on accounting work, auditing and certifying accounts as required by law for several companies. Caroline continued at the primary school with some 300 pupils. It could be tiring at times, but between them it worked for childcare and job satisfaction. George was intimate with both of them, but always separately, so any physical needs in that area received adequate attention.

Professionally it was going well for George, with considerable interest in the diving side of his work. A basic manual had been produced with the seal of approval from both the army and navy, with George and Denis as co-writers. There were also regular updates as new items were produced commercially, and companies were keen to have their products tested by the British army and navy. George was mindful of the way companies could behave when seeking contracts, so he always ensured that an independent civil servant was present to make notes and to safeguard against accusations. It meant, however, that new products got tested and were provided at no cost to the defence budget. George established a cadre of army and navy divers who were approved users of the new equipment. Most of the bomb and shell disposal work could be left to the sections and when there was no call on their services George insisted that they work alongside the construction engineers on the island to maintain their skills in that area. George too, would participate. He had to spend more time on the paperwork but would always attend if there were tricky ones, and he was keen to arrange beach parties for the squadron and their families with plenty of games and beer for the adults.

In May, Michael, Victoria, and Lucy came out to Malta for a week and flew in the Dragon Rapide stopping at Paris, Nice and Rome for refuelling, with an overnight stop in Nice. They planned to divide their time between Princess Elizabeth and George and had booked a hotel in St Julian's.

George, in uniform, met them at Malta's Luqa airport. The major's uniform opened lots of doors.

He took them for a drink at a quiet but exclusive bar overlooking the harbour and Fort St Angelo to explain that they had a three-year-old nephew called George. Initially they were somewhat aghast, but when George reminded them of how unorthodox they had been in their own lives he had them convinced that this was only another variation on that theme of unorthodoxy that characterised the 'Spelthorpe way'.

Michael said, "George, you were always one to surprise us particularly when you came out of your shell. Does Mum know yet? She might take a bit of convincing, but she's changed over the years, and she and Dad are always swimming naked in the lake. She would never have dreamt about that a few years back. I have to say that you have really pulled this off with two women, but from what you say they get on brilliantly, so we won't knock it. I'd like to say I'm envious, but I'll get thumped for that and there's no way Victoria is going to get another husband, not unless she wants a Boynton done on him."

George did impress on them the need to keep their arrangement quiet with any locals they met. Officially, it remained a lodging arrangement to facilitate mutual childcare.

They checked in at the hotel then went up to George's, where Emma and Caroline had prepared a slap-up welcoming meal. As the meal went on and the wine flowed, they got on like a house on fire, and Michael could see why George had been smitten by Caroline and why he was determined to hang on to the pair of them. After swearing them all to secrecy, they regaled Caroline with tales of Zorro, Lucy's powerful underwear and a snake called Himmler – tales of which even Emma was totally unaware. Caroline realised that she had joined a family of totally courageous English eccentrics who engaged in a hillbilly lifestyle, went fishing with sea mines, mixed with Royalty and put on the best genteel society could offer but only when absolutely essential. She was delighted to have having stumbled upon them. They welcomed her on board with open arms and no indications of being in the slightest way judgemental.

On the following day they went up to the northwest tip of the island and caught a boat to the small island of Comino which lies between Malta and its smaller sister island, Gozo. They went to the Blue Lagoon, renowned for its crystal-clear azure, blue waters. George had bought two tanks with the breathing apparatus and gave them all a demonstration and an opportunity to dive down to about twelve feet. For them it was a remarkable new and almost unbelievable experience, and they were hooked. They took a late lunch at the restaurant and then returned home.

For the following two days, the visitors spent time with Elizabeth and Philip who were residing at the Villa Guardamangia just outside Valletta. They wined and dined them in style and gave them a full tour of the city, where, at the harbour they went on board Philip's ship.

On the final day they all participated in a beach picnic. Whilst the ladies were making sandcastles with Katie and George, Philip introduced Michael and George to water skiing, which they all enjoyed. By the end of the day, they were getting extremely competitive and weaving left and right and trying to overtake the boat. For Philip and Elizabeth, it was soon to be a farewell to Malta. They loved just being ordinary but royal duties would soon dominate. They were aware of difficulties with the King's health, and stand-ins were anticipated.

After fond farewells, Michael, Victoria and Lucy boarded the Dragon Rapide and headed for home. They left at 7am and stopped in Nice for overnight as to just stop for refuelling was a little over ambitious with a cruising speed of 130 mph. On the following day they landed at Spelthorpe at 4pm. All the children and dogs had been staying at the cottage over the previous week, and all were well. George had consented to Victoria explaining matters to Helen and Ash regarding his Bohemian lifestyle and their new grandson. As expected, there was an initial shock, but this was soon followed by acceptance.

Helen and Ash were glad of a safe return because in just over a month's time they were heading off on an adventure of their own, along with the Boyntons. They would be away for six weeks in July and August.

15

Karibu Kenya

July – September 1951

Ash, Helen and the Boyntons landed at Nairobi Airport at
3pm on Wednesday, the twenty-fifth of July 1951 having
left England two days earlier. There had been refuelling stops
at Rome, Cairo and Khartoum, but they got there in the end.
Over the preceding weeks Jennifer had inoculated them against
every infection under the sun. They carried a jar of anti-malarial
pills and on a visit to a London specialist store they had kitted
themselves out in classic safari clothing. The first surprise was
the temperature. With Nairobi being only a hundred miles from
the equator, they had been expecting a furnace, but at just under
6,000 feet above sea-level, Nairobi was a place of permanent
English summer, and as they had made a wide sweep south of the
capital on the right-hand side of the aircraft, they had witnessed
the snow covered peak of Mount Kilimanjaro at 19,000 feet –
the highest mountain in Africa.

The second surprise was the sky. It just seemed so big as they
gazed all around at different fluffy cloud patterns.

For Helen, her arrival back to what she saw as her homeland after nearly forty years of absence was a momentous occasion. Her father owned a massive and highly profitable tea and coffee plantation on an estate of 25,000 acres, the Armstrong Estate, – more than double the size of Spelthorpe, which he farmed with one of her younger brothers and sister. An earlier return had not been possible because of home commitments, children, the two wars and a lack of transport other than long sea voyages but she had written regularly and some of the estate profits had been diverted into her Swiss bank account to make up for the fact that her younger brothers and sister would inherit the estate.

Helen had a huge affection for the land, its wildlife and its people and as a child had learnt Swahili – hence the names of her cats and dogs. She was hoping that over the next few weeks it would all come back to her. They had decided to invite the Boynton's to go with them as they were the same age, good company and, over the years had shown great loyalty to them and the estate. Aggie had spent some of her childhood in what had been German Southwest Africa and like German East Africa – now the neighbouring territory of Tanganyika had been taken over by the British Empire at the end of the Great War.

They were met at the airport by Arthur, Helen's young brother, who was now fifty years of age, although as she had not seen him, other than in photos, since he was eight years old. It took a while to get used to one another. Arthur was married to Jean, and they had two sons, Tom and Richard, aged twenty-five and twenty-three, and a daughter Harriet aged twenty-two, who all had roles on the estate. The eldest, Tom had been married for the last three years. Helen's father, Albert Armstrong was over eighty. Her mother, Alice, had died five years earlier. Helen's other brother Steven was forty-five and lived on the coast near Mombasa. He ran a fishery business that was part of the estate and was married to Sophia, whose father owned three hotels along the coast. They had four children: three daughters and a son. Helen's sister Barbara was forty-two. She had lost her husband fighting the Italians in the war. She ran the estate shop but was now in a relationship with a solicitor based in Nyeri. An engagement was expected.

They drove sixty miles north towards Nyeri- an area that was noted for its deep, loamy, fertile soils. It was sandwiched between Mount Kenya to the northeast and the Aberdare mountains to the west on the edge of the Great African Rift Valley that ran for over 4,000 miles from Turkey down to the Red Sea and right the way down the eastern side of Africa. Volcanic activity on each side of the rift had produced fertile soils and there were several spectacular lakes along its length. This is where Helen's father had come from India when she was a young child and had claimed the land to grow tea and coffee. Of the 25,000 acres some 15.000 acres were taken up by tea and coffee with 5,000 acres for dairy activity, a tea and coffee processing plant and the growth of crops for local needs and the 300 workers who lived on the estate with their families. There was a school, a church and a clinic with a dispensary, where Harriet worked as a trained nurse alongside a young doctor who had been sent by the London Missionary Society.

About 4,000 acres were unsuitable for agriculture, so this was left as woodland, grass and bush and served as a small nature reserve with antelope, zebra, baboons, vervet monkeys and a small population of black rhino. This was open to other wilderness areas. The only major predators were leopards. These were ubiquitous but generally avoided contact with humans. There were no elephants because of their destructive nature, and no lions.

Around the large house were about 200 acres of parkland and a lake, one of several on the estate fed by streams that ran down from Mount Kenya.

As they drove up the front drive, two large Rhodesian Ridgeback dogs appeared and ran up alongside the car. They looked frightening, but as soon as Arthur alighted, they were all over him and the visitors because Arthur introduced them. Unaccompanied strangers would get the hostile treatment. Albert was sitting on the veranda, and on seeing the car, he was up and walked rapidly towards it. He threw his arms around his daughter, and they hugged for over a minute. Both were in tears. It had been so long. They separated, looked each other up and down, then hugged again. Helen introduced her husband whom Albert had never met but had heard plenty. They shook hands firmly and then the Boyntons. He had heard much in the letters although it had never been admitted back at Spelthorpe.

"Ah, finally, I meet Zorro," he said. "We could do with you round here!"

"I couldn't possibly comment on that," said Boynton as he grinned broadly.

Albert called out, "Moses," to one of the houseboys as they mounted the veranda and sat around a table. Moses appeared two minutes later with a tray.

"Jambo," he said to the guests "Your drinks Bwana. Do you need anything else?"

"Asante sana, Moses. That will be all for now," said Albert.

Albert asked about the journey and outlined the accommodation arrangements. All would be staying in the main house with its six large bedrooms. Albert had lined up a safari and a trip to the coast. Two other houseboys, Joseph and Benjamin, were unloading the cases from the car boot and roof rack. While this was going on Aggie and Helen found they were being sniffed and rubbed against. Both jumped when they saw two female cheetahs who had crept up on them.

"Don't worry about the girls," said Albert. "We've had them since they were kittens. Their mother was killed by a truck, and one of the farm foremen found them. We hand-reared them and they have been here ever since. They have the run of the place so shut your doors tonight because they will try to sleep with you."

At the same time, a family of banded mongooses trotted across the lawn.

"Are they pets too?" asked Boynton.

"We have a dozen around the house. They deal with any snakes. We used to get the occasional mamba and cobra, but I haven't seen one anywhere around here for years. If on the farm they see any they just kill them but off the estate always be aware, especially at night. Some of the smaller adders have a habit of lying on footpaths. We lost a dog to a mamba twenty years back, but nothing since. I hate them. They can be aggressive at certain times of the year, and although there is an anti-venom, by the time you get to the hospital it's too late in most cases. We keep some in the clinic. Every year across the colony, we get a few deaths, mainly children and farm workers. Black mambas are quite a long snakes, but they're grey and sometimes brownish, not black. But they call them black mambas because the inside of their mouths is always black. There are tree mambas too. They are green. Killing the snakes means we get a few rats, but the servals and mongooses deal with them. But you just have to look at it and accept things. Back in England, people accept road deaths, but you wouldn't run blindly in the road, just as here you wouldn't go into the bush without looking around and making a noise because most avoid contact."

"Is there anything that we should watch for?" asked Boynton.

"Puff adders in rocky areas. There aren't many around here, but the lower you go, like on the coast, snakes are more numerous because it is warmer. Puff adders are nasty fat bastards. They just don't move, and they strike at lightning speed and with long fangs, so if we see them, it's a quick swipe with a long panga or a blast with the shotgun. That always works!"

"What about mosquito nets?" asked Ash.

"Always, even though at this altitude and away from water it's far less of a problem. You might have your pills but the best way to stop malaria is not to get bitten in the first place. We spray around here, but the mosquito is the most dangerous animal in Africa with thousands of deaths every year," said Albert. "But now I've frightened the bejesus out of you, I'm sure you will have a good stay. We will eat at seven after you have had time to wash off the travel dust and don't drink the tap water. There is boiled cold water in bottles in your rooms."

They went inside. It was beautiful – constructed from tropical hardwoods, with wood panelling on the wall and stone. There was a big open stone fireplace in the centre. The roof was tiled but beneath was open to the outside with shutters that could be closed. There were some trophy heads like a massive buffalo and some ivory tusks on the walls – some carved, along with some African carvings and a very large dining table that matched, with carvings around the edge. The floor was wood with massive carpets, zebra and other animal skin rugs. Paintings on the walls were of the landscape and wildlife with one large painting of Albert and Alice along with some treasured family photos including some of Spelthorpe and the family growing up. The rooms were similarly furnished with ensuite facilities.

For the evening meal the whole family turned out apart from Steven and his family, who were down in Mombasa. The food was excellent with big juicy steaks from the farm washed down with South African red wine.

"We don't worry about rationing here," said Albert. "Most of us are self-sufficient and we are so far spread out that they just haven't got the officials to enforce it. The servants and the workers eat well because we look after them, and they know that.

Compared to those who live on the outside, they stay loyal and there is no shortage of those who want to work, unlike on the bad farms where they can't get the workers. They have a school and a clinic, and their housing has all the basics. They have football pitches. They have a church. We pay more than the going rate, and they have a shop. They are happy or so it would seem because they don't complain but I suppose that might be because they know the response, but seriously, we find that with good care, they work well. It's a bit like in England in Victorian times where some of the best industrialists gave their workers the best like the Quaker Cadbury family. They built Bournville near Birmingham for their workers. The farmers who abuse their labourers don't seem to keep them, and they show no loyalty. There are still some out here who think it is OK to flog their natives, and these idiots are making it bad for the rest of us. Here on our farm, it is different. It all pays off with the profits we have made over the years."

"That's exactly the same as we have done at Spelthorpe for years," said Helen, "and it has served us well. The only issue we have had is to keep the government at bay because they do little for us in terms of education, law and order, and now the health business that has just started up. Aggie runs the school, and it knocks spots off what the state provides. Gabriel here and his team do the law-and-order bit, but in a way that is effective and it's not the fault of the village constable. Their leadership at the top is poor, and during the war, they recruited some rotten apples. The government just takes it for granted, but between us we get it done and the same with the medical side with Lucy's husband and Jennifer. They are brilliant, and it's the same with our vets. And it's not as if we ignore the national need. We have produced tons of agricultural produce and timber. We have been training the RAF's next generation of pilots. The pile of medals that Spelthorpe people have personally gained over the years speaks volumes about our contribution."

For the next three hours as the drinks flowed, they all brought each other up to speed on what the families had been up to over the years and how, at Spelthorpe all the key families had merged into one over time. Albert admitted that Helen had got out before things went downhill with the Happy Valley set. Albert explained:

"They really let us down and at a time when England was fighting for its survival, there they were, getting drunk, getting high on cocaine and openly having sex with each other's husbands and wives and corrupting anyone who got within reach. It all came to a head with a court case ten years back. There was this debauched, dodgy old gambler Sir Jock Delves Broughton who had lost most of the family fortune to gambling. He turned up with his trophy wife, thirty years his junior. She started seeking her pleasures with others, including this Scottish Lord Errol, who was similarly inclined, and they had a very open affair. They found him shot dead in his car. It was obvious who was responsible but Delves got away with it because of not finding the murder weapon. Coincidentally, Delves had reported two of his pistols stolen a few days earlier. After the trial, Delves went back to London and topped himself with a drug overdose the following year. The trouble was that the press was all over it. There's nothing like a bit of raunchy sex to sell the papers and the general conclusion was that we were all at it here in Kenya. Didn't do us any good at all."

Kenya was facing problems ahead with this huge push to get rid of the colonies. India had gone, and now some of the others who had fought in the war wanted the same.

The government was less sure about Africa. The Foreign Secretary, Herbert Morrison had said that giving the African colonies their freedom would be 'like giving a child of ten a latch key, a bank account and a shotgun', and there were some who had thought that they should create a British Raj for Africa. At the same time a lot of pressure was being placed on landowners to give up land and transfer it to the Kikuyu tribe people so they could get started in farming. Understandably, the landowners were not sympathetic particularly those like Albert who had put the time in and created something that was working well only to have it wrecked by the tribes' people herding goats on their former plantations. The Kikuyu were the largest tribe, but there were others, and they didn't all get on. Some had served and stayed in the British Army as members of the King's African Rifles.

"We are all getting worried," said Albert. "To make matters worse there are educated Kikuyu like this Jomo Kenyatta who went to university in London and now leads this Kenya African Union. He's stirring it all up, and now we have these hotheads that call themselves Mau Mau – that's Swahili for Mzungu Arudi Ulaya, Mwafrika Apate Uhuru which means 'Whites go back to Europe, so we get our freedom', and these people are getting violent. We have had a few killings, and they are getting others from the tribe who are working to take part in traditional secret oath ceremonies. I suppose it's a bit like some of your Trade Unions but the only thing here is if they don't join, things happen to them, and the hyenas and marabou storks get fed. I suppose in the long term we will have to give up some land, and that's why we are diversifying to spread our options. That was behind the fisheries venture. We are probably the largest tea and coffee producer, and we aim to stay that way. We can probably lose two to three thousand acres, so we still have enough for our own needs and the dairy side which is profitable.

"Have any whites been killed?" asked Boynton.

"Not so far," said Albert.

"Then it's only a matter of time and you need to be prepared for that. What guns have you got here?" asked Boynton.

"We have a couple of heavy calibre hunting rifles, two shotguns and a couple of Webley pistols – a .38 and a .455."

"That's not a lot of use apart from the .455, but it's a bit heavy for the ladies. You need to upgrade and urgently," said Boynton.

"Perhaps you could help me with that. Helen, in her letters told me how you gave, Michael, Lucy and George extra tuition and how that paid off. If you could do the same with Arthur and the two boys, that would help us."

Boynton responded. "If it's heating up, you don't want to be the first or the last. I'll give them a couple of days, and the ladies too, because on their own, they are vulnerable. And I suggest you get on to your gun dealer. I suggest at least half a dozen Colt .45 automatics with stopping power close up. Once you put one or two down, the rest will run. That's what George had in Palestine, and it served him well. Get a couple of American M1 carbines. They are light, compact and reliable with a fifteen-shot magazine with not a lot of recoil. Get a couple of pump shotguns with buckshot and solid slug ammunition. Get a Bren if you can. That's real firepower, but I expect the rules won't allow that one. And you need security, so if you get a break-in, they won't steal them. I'll review all that. I'm sorry to ruin the meal with all this talk, but you did ask."

"No, not at all. You're right and we will get straight on to it. Arthur, can you go down to Nairobi with Gabriel first thing tomorrow?"

"We'll do that while the boys and Harriet look over the estate with the others," said Arthur.

The conversation went on for another hour, and they got comfortable with each other. They all slept well under the nets and woke at 6am to a cacophony of bird noises. They breakfasted with the cheetahs on the veranda.

While the group toured the estate, Boynton and Arthur went into Nairobi. It was quite busy in the centre. The city had grown around the railway that stretched from the coast up to Uganda. The railway was the main reason for the creation of Kenya as a viable colony. The government wanted a link between Uganda and the coast because they saw the rich land around the massive Lake Victoria as the jewel in the African crown. They also felt that as the source of the Nile, it was strategically important even though the Nile was not readily navigable because of cataracts in the Sudan and the fact that, closer to Uganda it disappeared into a vast swamp called the Sudd. Between Nairobi and the coast was just a mass of acacia scrub and semi-desert that would green up following most of annual rainfall in May. There were rivers that crossed it and a few small lakes with populations of hippos and crocodiles but generally it was not fit for agriculture, just wildlife.

They went to the only gun dealer. As expected, he had a massive display of twin-barrel express heavy hunting rifles, and a good number of Webley revolvers. There were no Bren light machine guns, and the dealer suggested the only way was to bribe a soldier of the King's African Rifles to steal one, as they were seen as for military use only. He did have two Colts – both were new, so they took them along with 1,000 rounds. Both came with two magazines each. He also had several pump-up shotguns that had been imported from South Africa. They took two five-shot pumps with 250 cartridges of buckshot and another 250 of solid rifled slugs.

He said he could get more Colts so they ordered four, and he could probably get the M1 carbines via South Africa. He knew a dealer who had a contact with the USA, so they ordered two with 1,000 rounds. It would probably take a couple of months for the rest of the order to arrive. They also took some cleaning kits for the shotgun and pistols.

"Are you expecting a war?" asked the dealer.

"I'm afraid so," said Arthur.

"So are a lot of others," said the dealer. "But you seem to be the first who know what you really need. Most are just buying .38 Webleys with fifty rounds each – amateurs!"

"Have you got anything else that we have not seen on the display? We are not shooting elephants," said Boynton.

"I've got a couple of Stens." said the dealer.

"Condition?"

"Brand new, still in the factory grease and with two spare mags for each and basic cleaning kits."

"Where from?"

"Let's just say an old army contact who wanted to enhance his demob pay," said the dealer.

They went to a room at the back where Boynton inspected them thoroughly. They were as described. Boynton assembled both, checked the pins and dry-fired them. They agreed a price on a sale or return basis along with 1,000 rounds of 9 mm ammunition. They would not be going through the books.

Having checked the weapons at the farm earlier, they took another one hundred .38 rounds for the one of the Webleys. There was adequate ammunition for the express rifles and the .455 Webley.

At least they had been partially successful.

Boynton explained, "We can make a good start with what you have here. I feel a lot happier for you all now. At least with the pistols, you will have something when you are out and about, and the Stens would be valuable if you get a mass attack on the house. They are good for a hundred yards but better at fifty, and you can knock a lot down on automatic with a 32-round magazine. Those rifled slugs will crack an engine block and stop a car so can imagine what they will do to a fanatical tribesman with a panga.

'The civilised European, if wounded will lie down and wait for a stretcher and a medic, but the uncivilised dervish, if merely wounded, will carry on and cut your head off unless you blow him away'. That's what they first taught us when I was in Egypt with Lawrence. You are fighting a different enemy here!"

On chatting with Arthur, it came across that he was dealing

with a very nice man, a gentleman coffee farmer, but he would need to install a bit of killer instinct to make sure they all survive.

For the next few days, they stayed on the estate apart from a one afternoon trip up into the Aberdare forested area to take tea at the famous Treetops observation platform in a large tree, which had very limited accommodation. This was only ten miles from Nyeri. It was over a waterhole, and they saw elephants coming to drink along with antelopes and wart hogs. They took tea served up with cakes and cheese and cucumber sandwiches. Then the screaming started. Alas, the other guests fled in terror as a troop of baboons raided to help themselves to some of the sandwiches. It was hilarious to see the others panic and scatter, but the guests from Spelthorpe sat there stoically, knowing that once the sandwiches were gone, the raiders would move on. They knew not that in six months' time, Treetops would become world-renowned.

For the second week a safari had been arranged. They took two modified trucks with improved suspension that would seat three in the front of each. Arthur and his eldest son were going and would drive to start. Later, the others would take their turn. Albert, who remained at the farm had decided that they should go across into the neighbouring territory of Tanganyika to see the best the world had to offer. There would still be time to visit other closer wildlife areas in Kenya on a day basis.

They drove through Nairobi and crossed the border at Namanga and thence to Arusha – a tiring 200 miles. They spent the night at a hotel in Arusha. It was, to say the least basic, but they were only there to sleep and take a few beers.

At the crack of dawn, they drove the fifty miles to Lake Manyara which appeared partially pink in colour, but that was the thousands of flamingos that fed there. They drove around the lake and spotted lions uniquely in the trees. The tree-climbing lions here were quite famous so parking under the trees was never advisable. They took lunch on the edge of the lake and watched a group of hippos bobbing up and down in the water.

"These, apart from the mosquito are the most dangerous animals in Africa," said Arthur. "They kill more people than any other. In the water they are safe but get between them and the water and they can go berserk. They emerge at night to graze along the banks, so it is not good to be here early when they are heading back."

After lunch they drove thirty miles on rough roads getting higher and higher. They spotted lions but these were huge with black manes almost twice the size of those at Lake Manyara.

And then they arrived. They alighted from the vehicles and stood on the rim of a massive crater. The hairs on the back of their necks stood upright in amazement. It was like they had gone back to the dawn of time. They all felt the same and nothing had prepared them for this. Spread out below them was the Ngorongoro crater, like Arthur Conan Doyle's Lost World but inverted. The crater was twelve miles across, and it was 2,000 feet to the bottom where there was a lake, grassland and woodland. They drove down as far as it was safe, as a roadway was under construction. They saw massive herds of zebra, and wildebeest. There were giraffes, black rhinos, elephants and buffalo, in fact everything in the guidebook, and with so much game about it was obvious why these lions were so huge and never went hungry. There were ten log cabins on the crater rim, and they had booked three. Such was the awe and magnetism of the spectacle they felt as the sun went down, they were late for dinner.

On the following day they drove down into the Serengeti – a massive grassy plain with scattered granite kopjes, with rounded huge rocks. They were like islands in the sea of grass that fed the never-ending herds of zebra, wildebeest, buffalo and elephant. Here at the kopjes, there were trees and shelter and occasionally the sight of the King of the Jungle on the huge rock boulders majestically surveying his domain. As they drove over the plains they came across cheetahs, often a female with full-grown cubs and they watched as they brought down a Thompson's gazelle. They came across a lion kill – a zebra. The lions moved on after their fill leaving it to the hyenas, the black backed jackals and the vultures. A large lion came back, and they all scattered.

They spent the night at a small lodge built around a kopje. Again, it was primitive, and the meal consisted of zebra steaks. There were baths – black, as the enamel had worn off and the water was brown but who cared after the sea and lake swimming at Spelthorpe. It was just magical to be there, and they were glad because they had seen something before the masses arrived.

Ash said, "We have seen no other vehicles today, but I bet you that as soon as travel opens up, they will see the value here and they will exploit it. They need to keep some parts left alone, but I suppose it's all about greed and money and in twenty or thirty years we will end up with thirty trucks all around some poor bloody lion. They won't be able to hunt and feed naturally. I can see it coming, but at least we have seen it as it should be. They will need to manage this so carefully otherwise it will end up like Skegness with lions."

They spent another full day in the Serengeti. They watched the herds of migrating wildebeest in their thousands as they crossed rivers where the massive crocodiles took their fill of the struggling wildebeest. It was sad in some ways, and they took no delight in that. Under those huge African skies, the sights had been spectacular. They were sad to be leaving. Aggie had taken roll after roll of film. The following morning, they were up early and headed for home.

When they got to the border at Namanga, they turned right and drove the fifty miles to the lodge at Amboseli game reserve, where they spent the next two nights. At dawn on the following day, they were up early to catch the best of the wildlife. Amboseli was a mix of scrub, grass, woodland and swamp with lakes. Some areas were sandy dust bowls where the wind would whip up miniature tornadoes. They saw masses of wildlife, but above all were the large herds of elephant – many with impressive full-sized tusks and all with the spectacular snowcapped Mount Kilimanjaro as a backdrop. At the end of the day, they had a good meal at the lodge and downed a few bottles of the suitably named Tusker local beer. After a further early morning drive in the reserve and breakfast, they took a slow drive back to Nyeri arriving at 5pm.

As they drove up the drive to the front of the house, they saw two figures sitting with the cheetahs on the veranda. One was in military uniform, and the other was Albert.

As they got closer Helen said, "I don't know who that is next to Daddy, but he is the spitting image of George."

A couple of seconds later she exclaimed, "My God, it is George. I thought he was supposed to be in Malta. I don't know what he's doing here, but it doesn't look like he has bought his harem with him."

All was revealed when they met up. The government was getting in a panic because of the Mau Mau activity and was anticipating a major deployment in the next few months. It was the copycat syndrome. There had been Palestine, then Malaya and that was still going on and there were rumblings around Egypt and Suez. Getting rid of the empire was getting expensive. Such was the hierarchy's confidence in George's ability that they had sent him out with one of his lieutenants to scope what might be needed to be done and in what order with respect to Royal Engineer involvement in the event of a major deployment. They had given him two weeks out here and another two weeks to come up with a report. They had been flown out from Malta via Egypt. He was out here liaising with current military units, the King's African Rifles and the police. He was tasked with looking at roads, communications and suitable sites for internment camps and forward bases and forts in areas where the Mau Mau were likely to be active. This was expected to be in the area around Nairobi, Nyeri and the Rift Valley because that was where the best land was located, and the ideal terrorist operating bases would be in the Aberdare Hills and forest. He had come up to the estate to meet his grandfather and the rest of the family and to pick their brains on such local issues, and he had visited some of the villages to see for himself. George had arrived four days earlier and had wasted no time. He only had to ask for the Armstrong Estate and was directed there easily and had been staying up here ever since, with his colleague and himself accommodated in one of the small bungalows at the back of the house which was far better than what the military had to offer. His lieutenant was delighted and was engaged in the preparation of some maps with key locations for Royal Engineer activity.

George was getting on well with his grandfather, who had been made aware of George's domestic arrangements. His grandfather was impressed.

"Nice to see you are doing it the Kenyan way. They have had multiple wives out here for centuries," said Albert. "There's one chap out here with at least a dozen wives and about thirty children, but I don't suggest you go that far. The custom is that the first wife must consent, and from what I understand you have that. Out here, it's all about cattle. The more cattle you have the more wives you can get. How many cattle are there at Spelthorpe?"

"About a thousand," said George.

"You have no problems. You'll have to move out here then!" said his grandfather.

They had a week before the next trip to the coast, and in that time, Boynton was able to impart his wisdom to the whole family. They were initially shocked but were very grateful for what he was able to say. George was usefully able to back him up on the use of the Colt .45 pistol. They made sure they had plenty of practice and got into the habit of always carrying one if they were away from the immediate vicinity of the house, and they got some shoulder holsters made up. They did the same with the Stens, and these worked well. They kept these hidden in the house. Boynton demonstrated the devastating effect of the pump shotguns on some old petrol barrels filled with water having loaded the weapon with alternative cartridges of buck shot and solid slugs, and they tried it out for themselves. After that their confidence increased.

The missionary doctor was shocked most of all, but after talking over some real experiences with Boynton and recognising the importance of protecting his flock, his views changed somewhat, and he too was minded to keep a pump shotgun under his robes or hidden but available in the clinic.

Helen was pleased to see her son and intimated that she and Ash intended a visit in the autumn as she wanted to meet Caroline and see all three grandchildren. Everything she had heard from Victoria had impressed her.

A week later, and after a few days out, the four visitors took the train from Nairobi down to Mombasa. This was the line built fifty years earlier that put Nairobi on the map and had brought about the rapid development. During construction, many lives had been lost to the man-eating lions of Tsavo who were now stuffed and in a museum. The journey took some six hours, passing through a mass of acacia scrub with the occasional sightings of wildlife, but nowhere like the densities they had witnessed in Tanganyika and Amboseli.

At Mombasa they were met at 3pm by Steven and his wife, Sophia, and after a quick tour of the fishing facility at the port, they took them on a two hour journey up the coast to a hotel owned by Sophia's father at a delightful place called Watamu.

The location was like Eden on Sea. One could walk for miles on the coral white sand with the coconut palms swaying in the breeze. In front of the hotel was a lagoon that went up and down with the tides. There was always a depth of up to thirty feet further out, but the shallows and rock pools were interesting to walk in shoes, avoiding the stone fish that looked just like a lump of rock. They didn't move, safe in the knowledge that the hollow spines in their dorsal fin would pump in a dose of venom into the foot of an unsuspecting walker. Boats were moored just offshore, and these were used for sport fishing. This was one of the best-kept secrets in the fishing world. When they arrived there was a huge blue marlin hanging up on the derrick in front of the hotel bar area with a group of fisherman tourists who were posing for photos. It might even end up with the taxidermist for display, like many other specimens in the main bar and reception.

After introductory drinks Steven and Sophia had to make the return trip home to Mombasa for the children. They would come back in four days to collect them for a two-day stay in and around Mombasa but in the meantime, they were there as family guests and should treat the place as their home. Steven had arranged a fishing trip for the following day.

The next day, Ash and Boynton had readied themselves for the fishing trip and boarded a powerful thirty-foot cabin cruiser that was moored a few yards out. Helen and Aggie were going to enjoy the pool and the sun and take a walk up to the village to look at the school. Ash and Boynton intimated that they were not looking to catch a monster and if they did, they would rather take a photo and release such a beautiful fish back into the sea. They would rather catch some good-sized tuna that they could eat.

The boat took off, and a mile from the shore they passed through a gap in the fringing reef where the big ocean waves would break. They headed out, and the waves got larger and as they powered their way diagonally across, at times, the oncoming waves were higher than the boat. It was an uplifting experience to watch dolphins break the surface above them as they cruised on with gulls and frigate birds at the back of the boat, waiting for any morsels. These were big ocean waves that had come thousands of miles across the Indian Ocean, where there was nothing between them and Western Australia other than a few islands.

They started fishing by letting out lines with lures or baited with whole mackerel-type fish and travelling at about six knots –

a method called trolling. Every thirty minutes or so there was a bite, and they caught half a dozen good-sized tuna that weighed in at 20 pounds each. Two hours later, the large waves had gone, and the sea was a mass of small waves. This was the 'pot boiler' where two currents met. It brought up food from deep down that resulted in more plankton and small fish that the larger fish preyed on. The bites came more often, and the fish got larger. They took two large barracuda, four good-sized snappers and a couple of thirty-pound tuna. Then one line really took off. Ash knew there was something big on it, and he played it for the next hour and gradually hauled it closer. It was a sailfish, probably about 150 pounds in weight, and it leapt from the water in a spectacular display with iridescent blue from the dorsal fin. Eventually, it tired, and Ash hauled it in close to the side of the boat. Boynton put a gloved hand around the bill as Ash leaned over to release the hook while a boat boy held the tail. Suddenly a huge head appeared up from the depths and bit the centre of the fish, shaking it to rip out a massive chunk and virtually cut the fish in two. They let go, and the massive head reappeared to take another large chunk.

"Tiger Shark – big one at least fourteen feet!" said the boat's skipper at the helm. "It happens, and they always seem to know the best time to strike. Nothing we can do. We just let it go, and more will turn up for the crumbs."

And that is what happened. Another smaller tiger shark turned up, then a couple of oceanic white tip sharks, all thrashing around to take the remains. It was a good day, but not for the sailfish.

That evening, they dined on big tropical prawns in a salad, followed by massive tuna steaks that could not be fresher, as they told each other the tales of the day.

Helen and Aggie had walked for a couple of miles on the beach making sure they were devoid of any jewellery or watches. Local boys who came out to trade carvings and beads had their hopes dashed when Helen practised her Swahili and said, "Hapana Asante" (No thank you). They got the impression they were dealing with locals not tourists and whilst they remained friendly, they didn't push for a sale. Helen and Aggie went on to the school where they found the head teacher with a class of sixty children on his own. They had three other teachers and over 200 children. The children were very smart, well-disciplined and eager to learn. Desks were made from old pallets and packing cases. Their parents valued education, but there was a dire shortage of pens, pencils, exercise books, rulers, rubbers and simple textbooks. They were all learning English. They spent two hours there, helping with the teaching. Aggie took pictures and told them about her school. She promised to send a large parcel with some of what they needed along with photos of Spelthorpe School. It was the start of a long relationship.

Six days later, after spending a couple of days with Steven and his family, they caught the morning train back to Nairobi. Helen had not seen her brother since he was five years old. The fishery was doing well. They had six boats and were supplying the local market and Nairobi, as well as a canning factory that dealt mainly in tuna for export.

By the time they had returned, George had gone back to Malta, and after four more days it was time for fond farewells. Albert asked that they pass on his best regards to Amrik and his wife, and there were small presents to take back for them. Ash and the Boyntons could now understand Helen's passion, with the with pet names in Swahili as a permanent reminder and the carvings and paintings that blessed some of the walls at the Hall. They had purchased three zebra skin rugs for the Hall and the two cottages and a few more carvings, and they took back a load of coffee and tea from the estate. For them, Kenya was not a mere tourist destination. It had become an addiction that flowed through their bloodstream, and they would return.

16

The queen's peace

1951 -1953

The relationship that the Spelthorpe family had with the house of Windsor was a private one and not one to be aired at public events. Both parties wanted it that way because there was a need for true friends out of the limelight. This worked with their low-key visits to their respective estates over the years and the phone calls. It was both private and intimate, and what was said, was said with transparency and sincerity, and it remained that way. It was a relationship that had evolved through two generations.

In September, the king's smoking habit finally caught up with him, and he had a lung removed. The operation was performed at Buckingham Palace, and such was the affection in which he was held, that the crowds waited at the palace gates for news. Steadfastly, but knowing of his condition he carried on both publicly and privately and the annual shooting visits continued.

In December, it was at Spelthorpe, and he came with the queen, Elizabeth and Philip. On that occasion, he was a spectator rather than a shooter, but he was glad to be there and the same applied in early January 1952 at Sandringham. Windsor and

Buckingham Palace were his places of duty, but Sandringham was his heart and soul.

At the end of January, Philip and Elizabeth took off for a state visit to Kenya and Australia in the place of the king and queen and it was while they were at Treetops in Kenya that the sad news came in. The King died in his sleep at his beloved Sandringham on the sixth of February 1952 and the crown passed immediately to Elizabeth. Treetops became immortalised as the place where the princess climbed into a tree and came down as the queen. The couple flew home straight away.

The funeral on the fifteenth of February was attended by Helen, Ash, Victoria and Michael, and they carried a message of deep affection and condolence signed by the entire greater Spelthorpe Company, including Reverend Paddy and his wife Ruth.

For the rest of the year, the new queen was tied up by matters of state, but the couple did manage a two-day visit in June with strict instructions left with the Royal household that they were not to be disturbed. The shooting visits continued as before.

The estate continued to build on the success of previous years.

It was now dealing in the new Land Rover vehicles that were destined to replace the Jeep within areas of British influence. Contact with Kenya resulted in a dealership being established in Nairobi as part of the Armstrong Estate. Helen got a message to tell Boynton that the firearms had arrived and not before time, following the murder of a white woman near her home in Thika near Nyeri in October. Shortly afterwards, a tribal chief, who was supportive of the British was shot dead. A state of emergency was declared, and a robust response by the British authorities followed, and that would last for the next four years. Critics would later describe the response as brutal and indeed it was, but at the time hundreds of their own people were being murdered by the Mau Mau and surprisingly, only thirty-two white settlers lost their lives. The Mau Mau were poorly armed. The British detained thousands and executed large numbers, with suspects shot on sight at certain locations. The relative remoteness of the region allowed a far lesser degree of scrutiny over British tactics. Helen was relieved because when the emergency was declared, George still had several months to run in Malta and so for the time being, he was out of it. She and Ash had gone to Malta in October 1951 and had spent a week with George and his 'wives'. It took a bit of getting used to, but what came shining through was that there was a unique loving relationship between the three of them and the children were happy and thriving. Helen and Ash had determined that their full support would be forthcoming.

At the end of May 1953 Everest was finally conquered and four days later the Queen's coronation took place in an atmosphere of public euphoria. It was attended by Helen, Ash, Victoria and Michael although understandably, with so many attending, there was no opportunity for contact, but they had a duty to be there. Nothing affected the private relationship.

For the country, despite the great affection for King George and his queen, this represented the dawn of a new age, as rationing was coming to a gradual end, and economic optimism was present despite the huge burden that was still taking place in the transition of the empire. Nationally there had been a major change. In 1951 the voters, tired of rationing, had rejected the socialist administration, and Churchill was back in power. The queen respected him and valued his guidance, although on occasions his administration wavered. He was not in the best of health.

At Spelthorpe the farming and dealership profits were good, and this had enabled the December bonus to employees to continue, although it was always made clear that a bonus could only be paid if performance allowed it. Victoria would periodically publish a bulletin to keep staff aware of developments and why their efforts merited a bonus. This spread a feeling of ownership and responsibility throughout the estate and kept the malign aspects of trade unionism at bay.

After five years, the RAF pulled out of the pilot training facility, but the University Air Squadron remained. This provided a profit coupled with shared use of three de Havilland Chipmunk aircraft, which the RAF had supplied. The two Moths remained as they provided a popular link to the past. The Dragon Rapide and Harvard also remained. Both were well maintained and reliable so there was no immediate need to change them. The flying school, shooting school, conference facility and chalet business all made good profits.

By 1953, Boynton was planning on 12,000 pheasants and a similar number of partridges as commercial interest had doubled. Increasingly, Harry Boynton was getting involved in game keeping but his butchery skills would always provide a second string to his bow. Beverley Boynton had completed her nurse training and was now undergoing a year's midwifery course. She was in a relationship with a young doctor who was training as a surgeon, and they were living in a rented flat in Norwich. They would come home to Spelthorpe at least once a month.

Julian Johnson and Rufus de Lisle were now both in their 70's and had retired on a pension, but both would always help out in their respective roles if there was a need. Jeremy was now the head veterinary surgeon, ably assisted by Joanna. Their son, James, who was attending the private school, was now sixteen and hoped to follow in their footsteps.

Victoria was now running the estate from the office side, with Michael as the hands-on estate manager across the entire business. He was ably assisted by William who dealt with all things mechanical and the dealerships.

In July 1953, George returned from Malta with Emma, Caroline and the children. They took up residence at the Hall. Caroline was five months pregnant. After the three years overseas posting-George was entitled to an extended period of leave. George was recognised as one of the country's leading experts in dealing with unexploded munitions. In Palestine he had courageously proved himself in anti-terrorist operations. His work on the diving role of the Royal Engineers had been acclaimed alongside his preparatory work in Kenya. He had been accepted to attend the Army Staff College course at Camberley, Surrey. The course was for those earmarked for the higher leadership roles in the army. This was a year-long course and would start in September. On the domestic front he decided to regularise his affairs. With full agreement of the family Caroline changed her name to Caroline Spelthorpe, and young George took the same name. At a private family-only meeting in the church, Reverend Paddy blessed their relationship. As ever, Paddy took his guidance from the good book.

"If King Solomon who was noted for his wisdom, had 700 hundred wives how could it be wrong for George to have just two wives before God?"

Caroline and Emma remained inseparable.

Emma took up a role as the company accountant. Given her expertise and the expansion of the estate business, this role became essential. Within days of taking up the position, she was able to save over three thousand pounds in taxation that could be legitimately avoided. With immediate effect Victoria placed her on the management board. Caroline took a vacancy for a senior teacher at the primary school that had expanded considerably with the post-war explosion in births. There was a need for a further classroom, and while the education authority was procrastinating, the estate just built it and took what they could get from the authority, but it still covered its costs. The estate owned the land on which the school was built. Aggie was impressed by Caroline and swiftly lined her up for her to take over when she eventually retired. Linda was happy with her role as Deputy Headmistress and did not wish the extra responsibility of headship, at which Caroline was fully experienced.

By September when George started his course, Emma and Caroline had made it absolutely clear that they would be staying at Spelthorpe. George soon accepted that the disadvantage of his unique regime was that he could be out voted, but as a career minded officer, that presented few difficulties and for army social events, he found it amusing to turn up with Mrs Spelthorpe, but nobody could work out how Mrs Spelthorpe was able to change her appearance between functions.

Weekends and leave with his ladies suited him, even if Boynton referred to them in jest as Mrs Friday Night and Mrs Saturday Night.

In November to the delight of George and Emma, Caroline had a daughter, Olivia. Young George was not disappointed because at the Hall he had Lucy's Leo to play with. Compared to the 1930's, the Hall had come to life with a total of eight children and three Labradors. It was not just a Hall but a home.

Traditions continued with the November bonfire, Christmas, and Boxing Day polar bear dip, over which, near the cottage by the sea, Helen and Ash now presided as they lived in partial retirement with their dogs and two recently added Siamese cats, Jambo and Karibu. There was no greater symbol that the greater Spelthorpe family had endured than when they and many of the workers and their families walked through the gap in the dunes and the pines to charge into the sea under the watchful eye of the peregrines from the castle keep. Only the babes in arms were excused and that included young Aldous Spelthorpe, the son of the recently appointed Professor Edward Spelthorpe and his wife from Cambridge University. More polar bear badges were handed out than in any previous year.

The year 1953 had been a special year where the new generation had taken up the baton from the previous team both nationally and locally at Spelthorpe. At his end of year sermon Reverend Paddy reflected on their situation:

Spelthorpe from the creek at low tide – at peace.

"Between 1939 and 1945, we were at war and at the end, we thought that we had peace, even though we bore the scars of that conflict. But that peace resulted in new wars and matters are still to be resolved. Sadly, the normal state of our society is one of war. True peace is merely transient, but it remains a gift from God that we must treasure. We have three gifts to get us through the bad times. With courage and loyalty, you have used those gifts. Those same gifts are available to us now as we go forward in the new age under the queen's peace, as indeed, they were available in the years we have endured. We got through it with faith. We got through it with hope, and the greatest of those gifts is the love that we share today and every day. May God bless you all! Amen."

Historic note

This book, like the others remains a work of fiction. Accordingly, the reader must be aware that the Spelthorpe family, the estate and the relationship with persons alive or dead are entirely a product of the author's imagination.

That said, the historical events as described are essentially accurate although the opinions expressed by the characters remain as mere opinions.

Those who wish to delve further into the period covered will find several books that might be helpful: There is Anton and Nicola Rippon's *'Life in Post-war Britain:' Toils and Efforts Ahead'* and Andrew Marr's *A history of modern Britain*. Both are excellent.

The television series *Danger UXB* by Euston Films provides a superb introduction to the work of the Royal Engineers' bomb disposal. At the time of writing, it was still available on DVD.

Much of the other material has been gleaned from the author's professional background and extensive travels and research over many years.

About the author

Ashley Clark spent some thirty years with the Kent County Constabulary. In his early service at the age of twenty years he was probably the youngest village constable in England when he looked after several villages around Betteshanger near Deal, Kent. The bulk of his service was spent as a detective. For his last twelve years, for much of the time he was based in France, where he worked closely with French counterparts from the Police Nationale and the Gendarmerie.

On retiring from the police, he worked as a battlefield guide for some fifteen years taking both school and adult groups to the battlefields of France and Belgium. At the same time, he intermittently occupied himself on a Kent sheep farm and a large Exmoor shooting estate. He is widely travelled and lives in Whitstable, Kent, where for the last 20 years has led the group that manages and maintains an award-winning nature reserve – believed to be the largest village green in England.

In the warmer months he swims daily in the sea with his labradors.

The Spelthorpe Trilogy

The Tale of the Merdogs
Spelthorpe at War
Spelthorpe at Peace

A delightful tale of history, romance and mystery set on the stunning Norfolk Coast in three books spanning two decades between 1932 and 1953 in a rural community called Spelthorpe. The community fiercely protects its own.

Despite personal tragedy, the trauma of war and its aftermath Spelthorpe emerges with flying colours. The stories will take the reader on a roller coaster ride packed with robust action, human kindness, humour, determination and legacy with courageous, compassionate and unorthodox characters – both male and female, who will entertain and inspire you. It will take the reader back to a time that has been lost. Some events in the books take place further afield in France, Palestine, Malta and Kenya, but Spelthorpe is a place where you feel you should belong. You will want to go there and never leave.